I0667600

TILL THE
CLOCK STOPS

JOHN JOY BELL

Till the Clock Stops

John Joy Bell

© 1st World Library – Literary Society, 2005
PO Box 2211
Fairfield, IA 52556
www.1stworldlibrary.org
First Edition

LCCN: 2004195640

Softcover ISBN: 1-4218-0461-1
Hardcover ISBN: 1-4218-0361-5
eBook ISBN: 1-4218-0561-8

Purchase *"Till the Clock Stops"*
as a traditional bound book at:
www.1stWorldLibrary.org/purchase.asp?ISBN=1-4218-0461-1

1st World Library Literary Society is a nonprofit organization dedicated to promoting literacy by:

- Creating a free internet library accessible from any computer worldwide.
- Hosting writing competitions and offering book publishing scholarships.

Readers interested in supporting literacy through sponsorship, donations or membership please contact:
literacy@1stworldlibrary.org
Check us out at: www.1stworldlibrary.ORG
and start downloading free ebooks today.

Till the Clock Stops
contributed by Tim, Ed & Rodney
in support of
1st World Library Literary Society

THE PROLOGUE

On a certain brilliant Spring morning in London's City the seed of the Story was lightly sown. Within the directors' room of the Aasvogel Syndicate, Manchester House, New Broad Street, was done and hidden away a deed, simple and commonplace, which in due season was fated to yield a weighty crop of consequences complex and extraordinary.

At the table, pen in hand, sat a young man, slight of build, but of fresh complexion, and attractive, eager countenance, neither definitely fair nor definitely dark. He was silently reading over a document engrossed on bluish hand-made folio; not a lengthy document - nineteen lines, to be precise. And he was reading very slowly and carefully, chiefly to oblige the man standing behind his chair.

This man, whose age might have been anything between forty and fifty, and whose colouring was dark and a trifle florid, would probably have evoked the epithet of "handsome" on the operatic stage, and in any city but London that of "distinguished." In London, however, you could hardly fail to find his like in one or other of the west-end restaurants about 8 p.m.

Francis Bullard, standing erect in the sunshine, a shade over-fed looking, but perfectly groomed in his regulation city garb, an enigmatic smile under his neat black moustache as he watched the reader, suggested nothing ugly or mean, nothing worse, indeed, than worldly prosperity and a frank enjoyment thereof. His well-kept fingers toyed with a little gold nugget depending from his watch chain - his only ornament.

The third man was seated in a capacious leather-covered, easy chair by the hearth. Leaning forward, he held his palms to the fire, though not near enough for them to have derived much warmth. He was extremely tall and thin. The head was long and rather narrow, the oval countenance had singularly refined features. The hair, once reddish, now almost grey, was parted in the middle and very smoothly brushed; the beard was clipped close to the cheeks and trimmed to a point. Bluish-grey eyes, deepset, gave an impression of weariness and sadness; indeed the whole face hinted at melancholy. Its attractive kindliness was marred by a certain furtiveness. He was as stylishly dressed as his co-director, Bullard, but in light grey tweed; and he wore a pearl of price on his tie and a fine diamond on his little finger. His name was Robert Lancaster, and no man ever started life with loftier ideals and cleaner intentions.

At last the young man at the table, with a brisk motion, dipped his pen.

"One moment, Alan," said Bullard, and touched a bell-button.

A couple of clerks entered.

"Rose and Ferguson, you will witness Mr. Alan Craig's signature. All right now, Alan!"

The young man dashed down his name and got up smiling.

Never was last will and testament more eagerly, more cheerfully signed. The clerks performed their parts and retired.

Alan Craig seized Bullard's hand. "I'm more than obliged to you," he said heartily, "and to you, too, Mr. Lancaster." He darted over to the hearth.

The oldish man seemed to rouse himself for the handshake. "Of course, it's merely a matter of form, Alan," he said, and cleared his throat; "merely a matter of form. In ordinary times you would have been welcome to the money without - a - anything of the sort, but at present it so happens -"

"Alan quite understands," Bullard interrupted genially, "that in present circumstances it was not possible for us to advance even a trifle like three thousand without something in the way of security - merely as a matter of form, as you have put it. We might have asked him to sign a bill or bond; but that method would have been repugnant to you, Lancaster, as it was to me. As we have arranged it, Alan can start for the Arctic without feeling a penny in debt -"

"Hardly that," the young man quickly put in. "But I shall go without feeling I must meet grasping creditors the moment I return. Upon my word, you have treated me magnificently. When the chance came, so unexpectedly, of taking over Garnet's share and place in the expedition, and when my Uncle Christopher flatly refused to advance the money, I felt hopelessly knocked out, for such a trip had been the ambition of my life. Why, I had studied for it, on the off-chance, for years! I didn't go into a geographical publisher's business just to deal in maps, you know. And then you both came to the rescue - why I can't think, unless it was just because you knew my poor father in South Africa. Well, I wish he and my mother were alive to add their thanks -"

"Don't say another word, old chap," said Bullard.

"I will say just this much: if I don't come back, I honestly hope that will of mine may some day bring you the fortune I've been told I shall inherit, though, candidly, I don't believe in it."

"But the will is only a matter of -" began Lancaster.

Bullard interposed. "You will repay us from the profits of the big book you are going to write. I must say your publisher mentioned pretty decent terms. However, let's finish the business and go to lunch. Here you are, Alan! - our cheques for £1500 each."

Alan took the slips of tinted paper with a gesture in place of uttered thanks. He was intensely grateful to these two men, who had made possible the desire of years. The expedition was no great national affair; simply the adventure of a few enthusiasts whose main object was to prove or disprove the existence of land which a famous explorer had believed his eyes had seen in the far distance. But the expedition would find much that it did not seek for, and its success would mean reputation for its members, and reputation would, sooner or later, mean money, which this young man was by no means above desiring, especially as the money would mean independence and - well, he was not yet absolutely sure of himself with respect to matrimony.

He regretfully declined Bullard's invitation to lunch. There were so many things to be done, for the expedition was to start only eight days later, and he had promised to take a bite with his friend Teddy France.

"Then you will dine with us to-night," Lancaster said, rising. "You must give us all the time you can possibly spare before you go. My wife and Doris bade me say so."

"I will come with pleasure," he replied, flushing slightly. Of late he had had passages bordering on the tender with Doris Lancaster, and but for the sudden filling of his mind with thoughts of this great adventure in the Arctic he might have slipped into the folly of a declaration. Folly, indeed! - for well he was aware that he was outside any plans which Mrs. Lancaster may have had for her charming and very loveable daughter. And yet the mention of her name, the prospect of seeing her, stirred him at the moment when the great adventure was looming its largest. Well, he was only four-and-twenty, and who can follow to their origins the tangling dreams of youth? One excitement begets another. Romance calls to romance. He was going to the Arctic in spite of all sorts of difficulties, therefore he would surely win through to other desires - however remote, however guarded. As a matter of fact, he wanted to be in love with Doris, if only to suffer all manner of pains for her sake, and gain her in the end.

He shook hands again with his benefactors.

"You'll be going to Scotland to see your uncle before you start, I suppose?" said Lancaster.

"Yes; I'll travel on Sunday night, and spend Monday at Grey House. You must not think that he and I have quarrelled," Alan said, with a smile. "It takes two to make a quarrel, you know, and I owe him far too much to be one of them. I'd have given in to his wishes had it been anything but an Arctic Expedition. But we shall part good friends, you may be sure."

"It's understood," Bullard remarked, "that he is not to be told of this little business of ours. As you know, Lancaster and I are his oldest friends, and he might not regard the business as we should like him to regard it."

"You may count on my discretion," returned the young man, "and I fancy Uncle Christopher will be too proud to ask questions. Well, I must really go."

When the door had closed, Bullard took up the document, folded it, and placed it in a long envelope.

"Lancaster!"

Lancaster did not seem to hear. He had dropped back into the easy-chair, his hands to the fire.

Bullard went over and tapped him on the shoulder, and he started.

"What's the matter, Lancaster?"

"Oh, nothing - nothing!" Lancaster sat up. "I feel a bit fagged to-day. I - I'm rather glad that bit of business is over. I didn't like it, though it was only a matter of -"

"Perhaps nothing; perhaps half a million -"

"'Sh, Bullard! We must not think of such a thing. Christopher may live for many years, and -"

"He won't do that! The attacks are becoming more frequent."

"- And with all my heart I hope the boy will return safely."

"And so say we all of us!" returned Bullard. "Only I like to be prepared for emergencies. After all, we can't be positive that Christopher will do the friendly to us when the time comes, and Alan being the only relative is certain to benefit, more or less. Our own prospects are not so bright as they were. Of course, you've run through a pile - at least, Mrs. Lancaster has done it for you -"

"If you please, Bullard -"

"Come in!"

A clerk entered, handed a telegram to Lancaster, and withdrew.

Bullard lounged over to one of the windows, and lit a cigarette. Presently a queer sound caused him to turn sharply. Lancaster was lying back, his face chalky.

"Fainted, good Lord!" muttered Bullard, and took a step towards a cabinet in the corner. He checked himself, came back and picked up the message. He read:

"Just arrived with valuable goods to sell. Shall I give first offer to Christopher or to you and Bullard? Reply c/o P.O., Tilbury. Edwin Marvel."

"Damnation!" said Bullard.

CHAPTER I

Despite its handsome and costly old furnishings, the room gave one a sense of space and comfort; its agreeable warmth was too equable to have been derived solely from the cheerful blaze in the veritable Adam's fireplace, which seemed to have provided the keynote to the general scheme of decoration. The great bay-window overlooked a long, gently sloping lawn, bounded on either side by shrubbery, trees, and hedges, terminated by shrubbery and hedges alone, the trees originally there having been long since removed to admit of a clear view of the loch, the Argyllshire hills, and the stretch of Firth of Clyde right down to Bute and the Lesser Cumbrae. Even in summer the garden, while scrupulously tidy, would have offered but little colour display; its few flower beds were as stiff in form and conventional in arrangement as a jobbing gardener on contract to an uninterested proprietor could make them. And on this autumn afternoon, when the sun seemed to rejoice coldly over the havoc of yesterday's gale and the passing of things spared to die a natural death, the eye was fain to look beyond to the beauty of the eternal waters and the glory of the everlasting hills.

Turning from the window, one noticed that the brown walls harboured but four pictures, a couple of Bone etchings and a couple by Laguilérmie after

Orchardson. There were three doors, that in the left wall being the entrance; the other two, in the right and back walls, near the angle, suggested presses, being without handles. In the middle of the back wall, a yard's distance from the floor, was a niche, four feet in height by one in breadth by the latter in depth, a plain oblong, at present unoccupied. Close inspection would have revealed signs of its recent construction.

Near the centre of the room a writing-table stood at such an angle that the man seated at it, in the invalid's wheeled chair, could look from the window to the fire with the least possible movement of the head. You would have called him an old man, though his age was barely sixty. Hair and short beard were white. He was thin to fragility, yet his hand, fingering some documents, was steady, and his eyes, while sunken, were astonishingly bright. His mobile pale lips hinted at a nature kindly, if not positively tender, yet they could smile grimly, bitterly, in secret. Such was Christopher Craig, a person of no importance publicly or socially, yet the man who, to the knowledge of those two individuals now sitting at his hearth, had left the Cape, five years ago, with a moderate fortune in cash and shares, and half a million pounds in diamonds. And he had just told those two, his favoured friends and trusted associates of the old South African days, that he was about to die.

Robert Lancaster and Francis Bullard, summoned by telegraph from London the previous afternoon, had not been unprepared for such an announcement. As a matter of fact, they had been anticipating the end itself for months - long, weary months, one may venture to say. Yet Lancaster, who had been unfortunate in getting the easy-chair which compelled its occupant to face the strong, clear light, suffered an emotion that constricted his throat and brought tears to his eyes. But Lancaster had ever been half-hearted, whether for good or evil. He looked less unhealthy than on that spring morning, eighteen months ago, but the furtiveness had increased so much that a stranger would have pitied him as a man with nerves. To his host's calmly delivered intimation he had no response ready.

Bullard, on the other hand, was at no loss for words, though he allowed a few seconds - a decent interval, as they say - to elapse ere he uttered them. He was not the sort of fool who tosses a light protest in the face of a grave statement. If his dark face showed no more feeling than usual, his voice was kind, sympathetic, sincere.

"My dear Christopher," he said, "you have hit us hard, for you never were a man to make idle assertions, and we know you have suffered much these last few years. Nevertheless, for our own sakes as well as your own, we must take leave to hope that your medical man is mistaken. For one thing, your eyes are not those of a man who is done with life."

Christopher Craig smiled faintly. "Unfortunately, Bullard, life is done - or nearly done - with me."

Said Lancaster, as if forced - "Have you seen a specialist?"

The host's hand made a slightly impatient movement. "Let us not discuss the point further. I did not bring you both from London to listen to medical details. By the way, I must thank you for coming so promptly."

"We could not have done otherwise," said Bullard, fingering his cigar. "It is nearly two years since we saw you - but, as you know, that has been hardly our fault."

"Indeed no," Lancaster murmured.

"Go on smoking," said the host. "Yes; I'm afraid I became a bit of a recluse latterly. I had to take such confounded care of myself. Well, I didn't want to go out of the world before I could help it, and I was enjoying the quiet here after the strenuous years in Africa - Africa South, East, West. What years they were!" He sighed. "Only the luck came too late to save my brother." He was gazing at the loch, and could hardly have noticed Lancaster's wince which called up Bullard's frown.

Bullard threw his cold cigar into the fire and lit a fresh one with care. With smoke coming from his lips he said softly, "Your brother was devilishly badly treated in that land deal, Christopher. Lancaster and I would have helped him out, had it been possible - wouldn't we, Lancaster?"

Lancaster cleared his throat. "Oh, surely!"

"Thanks," said Christopher. "Of course we've gone over all that before, and I'd thought I had spoken of it for the last time. Only now I feel I'd die a bit happier if I could bring to book the man or men who ruined him. But that cannot be, so let us change the subject with these words, 'They shall have their reward.'"

"Amen!" said Bullard, in clear tones.

Lancaster took out his handkerchief and wiped

John Joy Bell

his forehead.

Still gazing at the loch, Christopher continued -

"I will speak of the living - my nephew, Alan." He lifted his hand as though to check a contradiction. "I am well aware that you believe him dead, and I cannot get away from the fact that the wretched twopence-ha'penny expedition came home without him. But no member could assert that he was dead - only that he was lost, missing; and though I shall not live to see it, I will die in the firm belief of his return within a year."

For once Bullard seemed to have nothing to say, and doubtless he was surprised to hear his colleague's voice stammer -

"If you could give me any grounds for your belief, Christopher -"

"Men have been lost in the Arctic before now, and have not died."

"But Alan, poor fellow, was alone."

"He had his gun and some food. As you know, he was hunting with a man named Flitch when they got separated in a sudden fog."

"And all search proved vain," said Bullard.

"True. But there was an Eskimo encampment within a day's march," retorted Christopher, mildly.

"It had been broken up -"

"Yes; by the time the search party reached it. I may tell you that I have seen and questioned every member of the expedition excepting the man Flitch, who seems to have disappeared, and several admitted the possibility which is my belief." The pale cheeks had flushed, the calm voice had risen.

Bullard gave Lancaster a warning glance, and there was a pause.

"I must not excite myself," resumed Christopher, his pallor back again. "But the boy grew dear to me when, like other happenings in my life, it was too late. I was angry when he went, though I had done little enough to attach him to myself, and I cursed whomever it was that supplied him with the necessary funds. He had friends, I suppose, whom I did not know of. Served me right! But once he was gone my feelings changed. He had a right to make his own life. He had as much right to his ambitions as I" - a faint smile - "to my diamonds. Well, I'm always thankful for the few hours he spent here before his departure. The Arctic was not mentioned, but we parted in peace."

The speaker halted to measure five drops from a tiny phial into a wine-glass of water ready on his desk.

"You're overtaxing yourself," said Bullard compassionately.

"I'll rest presently."

With a grimace at the bitterness of the draught, Christopher Craig proceeded: "The day after he went I signed a deed of gift by which Alan became possessed of this house and all I possess" - he paused, turning towards his visitors - "in the way of cash and securities, less a small sum reserved for my own use. I wanted the boy to know my feeling towards him in a way that a mere will could not show them. However, it is no great fortune - a matter of fifty thousand pounds."

"Much may be done with fifty thousand pounds," remarked Bullard, as if rousing himself. "It is a generous gift, Christopher," he went on. "With the house, I presume you include all it contains." Bullard knew that his voice was growing eager in spite of him. "Naturally," he said, with a frank laugh, "we are curious to know what is going to become of the diamonds - eh, Lancaster?"

The man addressed smiled in sickly fashion.

"In what, I still trust, is the distant future," Bullard quickly added.

"Ah, the diamonds!" said Christopher tenderly. "I shall be sorry to leave them. A man who is not a brute must worship beauty in some form, and I have worshipped diamonds." He leaned over to the right, opened a deep drawer, and brought up an oval steel box enamelled olive green. It was fifteen inches long, twelve across, and nine deep. He laid it before him and opened it with an odd-looking key. It contained shallow trays, divided into compartments, each a blaze of light.

Bullard half rose and sat down again; Lancaster shivered slightly.

"In times of pain and depression I have found distraction in these vain things," said Christopher. "Give me a few sheets of wax and a handful of these, and time ceases while I evolve my jewel schemes. You may say the recreation costs me a good income. Well, I have preferred the recreation. At the same time, diamonds have risen in price since I collected mine." He shut the lid softly, locked it, and added impressively, "Six hundred thousand pounds would not purchase them to-day."

"Great Heavens!" escaped Lancaster; Bullard ran his tongue over dry lips.

"With one exception, you are the first to see them, to hear me mention them, since they left South Africa," said Christopher. "No, not even my nephew knows of their existence. My servant, Caw, is the exception, but he is ignorant of their value."

"Very handsome of you to trust us, I'm sure," Bullard said with well-feigned lightness. "I, for one, had never guessed the greatness of your fortune."

"I have trusted you with much in the past; why not now? And I grant that your interest in the ultimate destination of my diamonds is the most natural thing in the world. Incidentally, your friendship shall not go unrewarded." He waved aside Bullard's quick protest. "But I have grown whimsical in my old age, and you must bear with me." He smiled gently and became grave. "Ultimately my diamonds will be divided into three portions. But - and I emphasise this - nothing shall be done, nor will the diamonds be available for division, till the clock stops - in, I pray God, the presence of my nephew, Alan."

"Till the clock stops?" exclaimed Lancaster stupidly.

"The saying shall be made clear to you before long, Lancaster. And now I must make an end or I shall be giving my doctor more trouble."

With a sigh he pressed one of three white buttons under the ledge of the table. "You will forgive my handing you over to a servant. Caw will see you to your car. Farewell, Lancaster; my regards to your wife, my love to Doris. Farewell, Bullard; yet there are better things even than diamonds."

The door was opened. A middle-aged man in black, with clean shaven ascetic face, and hair the colour of rust, and of remarkably wiry bodily appearance stood at attention.

There was something in Christopher's sad smile that forbade further words, and the visitors departed. Lancaster's countenance working, Bullard's a mask.

The door was shut noiselessly. Christopher's hand fell clenched on the green box. His pallid lips moved.

"Traitors, hypocrites, money maniacs! Verily, they shall have their reward!" He reopened the box, took out all the five trays, and gazed awhile at the massed brilliance. And his smile was exceeding grim.

CHAPTER II

Within a few minutes the servant returned.

"The gentlemen have gone, sir, and Monsoor Guidet is ready," he said, then looked hard at his master.

The master appeared to rouse himself. "Tell Guidet to go ahead. He'll require your assistance, I expect. Stay!" He pointed to the diamonds. "Put them in the box, Caw."

The man restored the glittering trays to their places with as much emotion as if they had contained samples of bird-seed. When he had let down the lid -

"Your pardon, Mr. Craig, but won't you allow me to ring for Dr. Handyside now?"

"Confound you, Caw, do what you're told!"

"Very good, sir," said Caw sadly, moving off.

"And look here, Caw; if I'm crusty, you know why. And I shan't be bullying you for long. That's all."

Caw bowed his head and went out. On the landing he threw up his hands. "My God!" he said under his breath, "can nothing be done to save him?" For here was a man who loved his master better than himself. One wonders if Caw had ever forgot for an hour in all those twenty years that Christopher Craig had lifted him from the gutter and given him the chance which the world seemed to have denied him.

Shortly afterwards he entered the room with Monsieur Guidet. The two moved slowly, cautiously, for between them they carried a heavy and seemingly fragile object.

"Go ahead," said Christopher, "and let me know when it is finished." He closed his eyes.

Nearly an hour passed before he opened them in response to his servant's voice.

"Monsieur has now finished, sir."

He sat up at once. From a drawer he took a large stout envelope already addressed and sealed with wax.

"Caw, get on your cycle and take this to the post. Have it registered. And put a chair for Monsieur Guidet - there - no, nearer - that's right. Order a cab to take Monsieur to the steamer. He and I will have a chat till you return.... Monsieur, come and sit down."

As Caw left the room the Frenchman turned from his completed handiwork to accept his patron's invitation. He was a dapper, stout little man, merry of eye, despite the fact that a couple of months ago he and his family had been in bitter poverty. He smiled very happily as he took the chair beside the writing table. He was about to receive the balance of his account, amounting, according to agreement, to two hundred pounds.

The work done was embodied in the clock and case which now filled, fitting to a nicety, the niche in the back wall. Outwardly there was nothing very unusual about the clock itself. A gilt box enclosing the mechanism and carrying the plain white face, the hands at twelve, occupied the topmost third of the case, which was of thick plate-glass bound and backed with gilt metal. There was no apparent means of opening the case. From what one could see, however, the workmanship was perfect, exquisite. The compensating pendulum alone was ornamented - with a conventional sun in diamonds, and one could imagine the effect when it swung in brilliant light. At present it was at rest, held up to the right wall of the case by a loop of fine silk passed through a minute hole in the glass, brought round to the front, and secured to a tiny nail at the edge of the niche; a snip - the thread withdrawn - and the clock would start on the work it had been designed to perform. The only really odd things about the whole affair were that the lowest third of the case was filled with a liquid, thickish and emerald green and possessing a curious iridescence, and that just beneath the niche was fixed a strip of ebony tilted upwards and bearing in distinct opal lettering the word:

DANGEROUS

"Well, monsieur," said Christopher Craig, opening cheque-book, "I suppose I can trust your clock to perform all that we bargained for. You will give me your word for that?"

"Mr. Craik, I give you my word of honour that the clock will go for one year and one day; that he will stop on the day appointed, within two hours, on the one side or the other, of the hour he was to start at; that he will make alarum forty-eight precise hours before he stop; that he will strike only at noon and at midnight; and that, when the end arrive, he will -"

"Thank you, monsieur."

"But more! I give you more than my word; the credit of the work is so much to me. I beg to take only one-half of the money now - the other half when you have seen with your own eyes -"

"Enough. I am in your hands, Monsieur Guidet, for the clock shall not be started until I am gone."

"Gone?" The little man looked blank.

"Your clock is there to carry out the wishes of a dead man."

"Ah!" Guidet understood at last. All the happiness vanished from his face. He regarded this man, who had chosen him from a number of applicants responding to an advertisement, as his benefactor, his saviour. "But not soon, not soon!" he cried with emotion.

Christopher was touched. The little man seemed to care, though their acquaintance was not three months old. Still, they had met almost daily in the room assigned to Guidet for his work, and the patron had taken an interest in the man as well as his genius.

"I cannot tell how soon, my friend," he said, "but we need not talk of it. Now tell me, Guidet, how much do I owe you?"

Guidet wiped his eyes. "One hundred and thirty pounds," he murmured, "and I give you a thousand thanks, Mr. Craik."

"A hundred and thirty - that is the balance due on the clock itself?" inquired Christopher, filling in the date.

The other looked puzzled. "On everything, Mr. Craik."

"Don't you charge for your time?"

Guidet smiled and spread his hands. "Ah, you are not so unwell when you can make the jokes! Two hundred pounds was the price, and I have received seventy of it and the grandest, best holiday -"

"Your wife and children have had no holiday," said Christopher, continuing his writing.

"They have been happy that I am no longer a failure. They shall have a little holiday now, my best of friends, and then I take the small share in the business I told you about. Oh, it is all well with us, all rosy as a - a rose! But you!" His voice trailed off in a sigh.

"I am only sorry I shall not be your first customer, Guidet." Christopher blotted the cheque and handed it across the table. "So you must oblige me by accepting instead what I have written there."

The little man read the words - the figures - and gulped. Then his arms went out as if to embrace the man who sat smiling so very wearily. "It is too much - too much!" he cried, almost weeping. "You are rich, but why - why do you give me five hundred pounds?"

"Perhaps," said Christopher sadly, "that you may remember me kindly." His hand, now shaky, went up to check the other's flow of gratitude. "I'm afraid I must ask you to go now. I must rest - you understand?"

Guidet rose. "So long as we live," he said solemnly, "my family and I will not forget. And if it would give you longer life, Mr. Craik, I swear I would put this" - he held up the cheque - "into the fire."

"I thank you," said Christopher gravely, and just then Caw came in. "And now farewell."

CHAPTER III

It was dusky in the room when Caw brought tea to his master. Fitful gleams from the fire touched the latter's face, which had grown haggard. The Green Box was open again.

"Never mind the lights for the present," he said, as the servant's hand went to the switch. "Give me a cup of tea - nothing more - and sit down." He pointed to the chair recently occupied by the Frenchman. "I have something to say to you, Caw."

As he placed the tea on the table Caw winced slightly. "Mr. Craig," he said imploringly, "won't you have the doctor now?"

"Sit down," said Christopher a trifle irritably, "and pay attention to what I am about to say. Dr. Handyside," he proceeded, "cannot help me, and you can. In the first place, you have already given me your word to remain in my service for a year and a day after I am gone from here - in other words, until the clock stops."

"Yes, sir," said Caw in a low voice.

"And it is perfectly clear to you how and when you are to set the clock going?"

"By carefully cutting and removing the thread at the first hour of twelve following your - oh, sir, need you talk about it now?"

Christopher took a sip and set the cup down with a little clatter. "And in the event of my nephew, Mr. Alan Craig, returning within the year, you will serve him also as you would me, giving him all assistance and information in your power."

"Yes, sir."

"I have recommended you to him in a letter left with Mr. Harvie, the lawyer in Glasgow, to whom you registered the packet this afternoon. Mr. Harvie is acquainted with certain of my affairs, but not by any means all. It is not necessary that he should know all that you know or will know. I am leaving much to your discretion, Caw. You will find your instructions in this envelope.... Among other things, it is not my wish that you should live alone in this house, and until my nephew returns I have arranged that you shall have quarters in Dr. Handyside's house, and I do not doubt that you will make yourself useful there, helping him with his car and so on. If expedient, you may trust the doctor, but do not trouble him without grave cause. The passage will remain available, and you will make inspections of this house at intervals."

He paused for a moment, took another sip, and resumed. "Things may happen in this house, Caw; but you are not to think of that as more than a mere possibility, nor are you to consider yourself tied to the place. As a matter of fact, I would as soon have certain things happen as not, and, short of murder itself, I count on your avoiding or preventing any police interference. By the way, your own future is provided for."

Caw made an attempt to speak, but his master proceeded -

"There are two men whom it seems necessary to warn you against - the two who were here to-day."

"Sir," said Caw with sudden strength and warmth of voice, "I have long wished I might warn you against Mr. Bullard. Only a sort of instinct, sir, on my part, but I never could trust that man. As for Lancaster -"

"Your instinct was right. Lancaster is chiefly a fool, but Bullard is utterly rotten. You remember my younger brother, Caw?"

"Yes, sir" - rather awkwardly.

"Those two, particularly Bullard, brought him to ruin. They cheated him - legitimately of course! Mr. Alan is ignorant of the tragedy surrounding the end of his father - his mother, too - and I hope he may remain so."

Surprise as well as indignation was in the servant's expression. "But, sir, you were quite friendly -"

"You shall see! You remember Marvel coming here three months ago?"

"Yes, I do - and I wondered at his impudence, the dirty -"

"He brought me the truth, anyway. I suspect his silence

John Joy Bell

had already been bought by Bullard, but that would be nothing to Marvel's conscience. Well, he sold himself and certain papers to me. They proved that Bullard deliberately ruined my brother for his own profit, and Lancaster assisted, probably in ignorance."

"And - those two don't know that you know!" cried Caw. "Your pardon, sir, but it's a bit - exciting."

"They do not know. They do not suspect. While they were here to-day they could think of nothing but those diamonds. They are still thinking of diamonds - of that I am sure; and for the next year they will think of nothing else. And they were my trusted friends!"

"Do you mean the diamonds - there, in that box, sir?"

"Just so."

"They are of great value, no doubt."

"My diamonds are worth over half a million sterling."

Caw drew a long breath. "That box would be safer in the bank, sir," he said respectfully, at last.

"I daresay. But it is going to remain in this drawer." Christopher reached out, closed the lid, locked it, and handed the key to Caw. "Listen! Immediately you have set the clock going, you will go down to the shore and throw that key far into the loch. A duplicate key will be available when the clock stops. Now place the box in the drawer and shut the drawer, and then sit down again."

With a resigned expression Caw obeyed.

"Burglars," he muttered, as if to himself, resuming his seat.

"Yes; they may try it - after I am gone. But mark this, Caw, you are not responsible in this particular matter, and even should you be aware that the persons whom I have named are attempting burglary, you must not violently interfere in any way."

"Not interfere! Good God, sir, half a million and not interfere!" Caw peered at his master in the firelight "Why, Mr. Craig, you could not trust me to obey that order!"

"If I can trust you with the diamonds - and I tell you that no one knows of their existence here excepting those two men and yourself - I can surely trust you to obey - not a master's order, but a dying man's request. Later on you will understand everything. Give me your word that you will do nothing violent to secure what you may consider the safety of that Green Box. ... Come, Caw."

"Will the diamonds - excuse the question - belong to Mr. Alan?"

"That is a question that shall be answered when the clock stops. Your word?"

"I am bound to trust to your wisdom, sir," said Caw, slowly. "I promise, sir. But if Mr. Bullard gives me a chance apart from diamonds, I hope -"

"I hope nothing may happen to Mr. Bullard before the clock stops," said Christopher firmly. "And now I think that is all. Other details you will find in your written instructions. Give me some of that medicine - five drops - quickly!"

Caw sprang up, ran to the door and switched on the shaded light over the table, ran back and administered the dose. Then with something like a sob he cried: "Mr. Craig, oh, my dear master, I can't stand it any longer," and pressed one of the white buttons.

"All right, Caw, all right," said Christopher kindly - and the glass fell from his fingers. He did not appear to notice the mishap. "I'm afraid Handyside will be annoyed, but I had to get the whole business finished."

"Don't exhaust yourself, sir. Just try to think that everything will be done as you wish."

"One thing more - failing the doctor, you may trust Miss Marjorie Handyside in an emergency. And, Caw, don't forget -"

The door in the back wall opened noiselessly; and a tall bearded man in tweeds, with the complexion of an outdoor worker, entered. Closing the door he came quickly to the table.

"Sorry to trouble you, Handyside," said Christopher with a faltering smile, "but the interfering Caw insisted."

The newcomer glanced a question at the servant.

"No, sir," said Caw. "No attack, but -"

"Have his bed made ready," interrupted the doctor, softly, and Caw left the room.

"I've been overdoing it a little," the invalid said, apologetically, "but it was in doing things that had to be done. I'll be all right presently, my friend.... I say, Handyside, I want you and your daughter to come along and take supper with me to-night. I haven't seen Marjorie for more than a week."

"She has been away at her sister's for a few days. Only came home an hour ago." Handyside let go his patient's wrist and moved over to the hearth.

As he stared into the fire his face betrayed disappointment and grave concern, but when he turned it was cheerful enough.

"Yes, Craig, you've overdone it to-day. However, I'll try to forgive you. Only I'd like you to see Carslaw again - to-morrow."

"He can't do anything more for me - anything you can't do."

"Possibly not. Still, we must remember that I've been out of harness for five years."

"I remember only that you have virtually kept me alive for the last two."

"Your constitution did that," the doctor replied untruthfully. "And you've been a good patient, you know, except once in a while."

"You've been a good friend, Handyside, though we met for the first time only five years ago. Yes; I'll see Carslaw to please you. Now there are several things I want to say to you -"

"They must keep," Handyside said firmly. "You are going to bed now."

"But I've asked you to fetch Marjorie -"

"That pleasure for her must keep also."

"Bed?" muttered Christopher. Then he looked straight at his friend, a question at his lips.

At that moment Caw reappeared.

"I'm ready," said his master. "I say, Handyside, what do you think of my new clock?" he asked as he was being wheeled to the door.

"I'll have a look at it later, Craig. It's not going yet."

"No" - gently - "not yet. Stop, Caw! Take me over to the window and put out the lights."

Caw looked towards the doctor, who nodded as one who should say, "What after all, can it matter now?"

At the window, for the space of five minutes, Christopher sat silent. A full moon shone clear on the still waters and calm hills. From across the loch twinkled little yellow homely lights. The evening steamer exhibited what seemed a string of pale gems and a solitary emerald.

"Almost as beautiful," he murmured at last, "as diamonds." He chuckled softly, then sighed. "Bed, Caw."

Within the hour he had a bad heart attack, and it was

the forerunner of worse.

Precisely at midnight Caw stole into the sitting-room and released the pendulum. Thereafter he went down to the shore.

"Hard orders, dear master," he sighed, "but I'll carry them out to the letter."

John Joy Bell

CHAPTER IV

In his home at Earl's Gate, Kensington, Mr. Lancaster had made an indifferent meal of an excellently cooked and temptingly served breakfast. He was feeling dejected, limp, and generally "seedy" after the two nights in the train. He and Bullard had occupied a double sleeping berth, and Bullard had persisted in discussing many things, and thereafter slumber had proved no match against a host of assaulting thoughts. Perhaps he might have made a better meal had he been left to himself, but ever since the moment of his arrival - save in the brief seclusion of his bath - Mrs. Lancaster had harried his wearied mind with questions.

Mrs. Lancaster had learned several important things since wealth began to come to her husband, about ten years ago. She had learned to dress well, no less so than expensively; she had acquired the art of entertaining with an amount of display that just escaped vulgarity; and she had even learned to hold her tongue in company. (Possibly that was why Mr. Lancaster got so much of it.) She was a big, handsome creature, with a clear, dusky complexion and brown eyes that either shone with a hard eagerness or smouldered sullenly. And it may be well to state at once that she had no "past" worth mentioning, and no relatives, as far as one knows, to mention it. Lancaster had wooed her in a boarding-house in Durban, Natal. Always ambitious, though never so keenly so as when money began to become more abundant, she had never yet attained to the satisfaction of having as much money as she desired, or imagined she needed. As for social prominence, she spent recklessly on its purchase. But she was an unreasoning woman in other ways. She was proud of her daughter one day, jealous of her the next; it seemed as though she could not forgive Doris for growing up, and yet when Doris was barely eighteen she displayed the girl on all occasions and strove hard to force her into the arms of a horrible little middle-aged baronet. She still craved a title for Doris, no matter what moral and physical blemishes that title might decorate. More than once she had hinted to Bullard that he might purchase a "handle." And glancing sidelong at Doris, Bullard had more than once reflected that she would be worth the money - if only he had it to spare. For Bullard's wealth was not quite so unlimited as many supposed.

Mrs. Lancaster's eyes were now smouldering.

"Once more," she was saying, "you seem to have made a pretty mess of it."

With a slight gesture of weariness her husband replied: "Bullard was in charge, and I suppose he did his best."

"I am beginning to lose faith in Mr. Bullard. You and he had a great opportunity yesterday of learning definitely Christopher Craig's intentions regarding his diamonds, and now you come home with a rambling story about a crazy clock that's going to stop goodness knows when."

"Get Bullard to explain it to you, Carlotta. I'm dead

beat. Two nights running in the train -"

Cutting him short, she continued - "You tell me that old Christopher is in a weak state physically and, you suspect, mentally. In these circumstances you ought surely to have been able to do two things - convince him of his nephew's death and -"

"He is wholly convinced that Alan will yet turn up. I can't understand - "

"Alan Craig will never turn up! Can't you take Mr. Bullard's word for that?"

"Bullard was not with the Expedition -"

She made a movement of impatience. "Well you ought to have gained Christopher's confidence as to the other matter. Why on earth didn't you find out what your share is going to be?"

"As I have already told you, Carlotta, he mentioned that the diamonds would be divided into three portions."

"Equal?"

"I assumed so. And he said Bullard and I would not be forgotten - 'Reward' was the word he used."

"He may leave you a diamond to make a pin of! Aren't you sure of anything, Robert?"

"I felt sure at the time, but during the journey I began to have doubts. So had Bullard. I tell you I simply could not tackle the dying man about his affairs."

"He may live for a long time yet." She drew a breath of exasperation. "But the moment he dies you and Mr. Bullard must act on Alan's will. It simplifies matters, I should imagine, that the old man made a gift of that property instead of willing it. Unfortunately it may mean only £25,000 for us."

Lancaster sat up stiffly and looked at his wife.

"It means not a penny for us. That debt to the Syndicate must be paid with the first large sum I can lay hold of. You must clearly understand that, Carlotta. I have said the same thing before."

"You have! May I ask whether the Syndicate has asked you to pay the debt?"

He looked away, then downwards. "The Syndicate," he said slowly, "has not asked me to pay the debt, for the simple reason that the Syndicate does not know of it - yet." His breath caught, and he added huskily, "I have wanted to tell you this for some time, Carlotta."

"You mean -?" But she knew what he meant, had suspected it for months. Also, she knew why he had borrowed, or made free, with the money. Simply to give her what she asked for in cars, furs, and jewels. The thing had been done at a time when a certain mine was promising brilliantly. The mine was still promising, but not so brilliantly.

The incident, along with Lancaster's mental suffering and futile efforts to right himself, would make a story by itself.

" You are shocked , Carlotta ? " he murmured

shamefacedly, appealingly.

"Naturally!" But anger was the emotion she strove to suppress.

"I have paid bitterly in worry," he said, and there was a pause.

"You can hold on yet awhile?" she asked at last.

"Oh, yes, I think so. The danger is always there, but I'm not greatly pressed for money otherwise." Not "greatly" pressed, poor soul! "It's a case of conscience, you know," he stammered. "The thought of discovery is always with me, too."

"No thought, I presume, of your wife and daughter!"

"Carlotta!"

"Oh, Robert, what a blind fool you are! Why not have asked Christopher for the money, even if it had involved a confession? He would not see us ruined - Doris, at all events."

"No; I don't think he would. He sent his love to Doris. But Bullard was there yesterday, all the time, and I would not have *him* guess -"

"You may be sure Mr. Bullard has guessed long ago."

"My God! do you think so?"

"Well, it doesn't much matter, does it? But I am certain if you had told Christopher and made the debt a hundred thousand you would have got the money."

"I don't know," he sighed, shaking his head. "Christopher was different yesterday, kind enough but different from the man I used to know -"

"Of course he was different. He's dying, isn't he?"

"Don't be so heartless."

"Don't be silly, my dear man!" Mrs. Lancaster said sharply. "Now, look here, Robert," she went on, "there is only one thing to be done. Say nothing to Mr. Bullard, but take the Scotch express to-night and go and see Christopher privately. I don't care what you tell him, but a public scandal - public disgrace - I will not have! Get the horrid thing settled, and let us go on as if nothing had happened until some of your shares go up and put you safely on your feet again."

He sat up as if trying to shake off the horror. "Carlotta," he said, "can't we contrive to - to live on less?" It was no new question.

"No, we can't," she answered in a tone of finality. "You will go to-night? Fortunately the people coming to dinner are a set of crocks. No bridge, and leave early. You can easily catch the midnight train."

"I will go," he said at last, "for your sake and Doris's."

"Good man!" she returned with sudden good humour, her eyes bright. "It will all come right - you'll see! Tell old Christopher that his little sweetheart of the old days - Doris, I mean; he never loved *me!* - is in danger of the workhouse and so forth, and ask for fifty thousand at least."

"It will end any chance we have of a share in the di -"

"'Sh!"

Doris came in. She was a tall girl with something of her mother's darkness, but she had the blue-grey eyes of her father and his finely-cut features. Of late a sadness foreign to youth had dwelt in her eyes, and her smile had seemed dutiful rather than voluntary. Otherwise she had not betrayed her sorry heart and uneasy mind. She carried herself splendidly, and she had good right to be called lovely.

"Mother," she exclaimed, and kissed her father, "why didn't you tell me he was to be home for breakfast?"

"Because I did not know, my dear" - which was un-true - "and, besides, you were very late last night. Better to have your rest out." Mrs. Lancaster rose. "Persuade your father to have a fresh cup of coffee while you take your own breakfast, I must 'phone Wilders about the flowers for to-night." She left the room.

Doris poured the coffee and milk and placed the cup at his hand, saying -

"You must be tired, dear, after two nights in the train."

"A little, Doris," he answered, endeavouring to make his voice sound cheerful.

"And worried, I'm afraid," she added tenderly.

"A little that way, too, perhaps. But one must hope that there's a good time coming, my dear."

The girl hesitated before she returned: "I want to say something, and it's difficult. I've wanted to say it for a long time." She paused.

"Say on," he said. "A horrid bill - eh?" He knew it was not. Doris had never asked him for money beyond her big allowance.

"Don't! It's just this: Is there anything in the world I could do, father, just to make it a little easier for you?"

It was unexpected, and yet it was like Doris. Tears came into his eyes.

"Forgive me," she went on quickly, "but sometimes I can't bear to see you suffering. I'd give up anything -"

Mrs. Lancaster entered quickly.

"Robert, Mr. Bullard is in the library -"

"Bullard! - now?"

"He must see you at once. He has been to the office, and there was a wire -"

Lancaster, who had risen, caught at the back of his chair. "Alan Craig - safe?" he said in a husky whisper.

Neither noticed the girl's sudden pallor, the light in her eyes.

"Nonsense!" the woman rapped out. "Christopher Craig - died last night!"

CHAPTER V

Mrs. Lancaster would have accompanied her husband to the library, but for once, and despite the shock he had just suffered, he showed some firmness.

"I will see Bullard alone," he said, and left her in the hall.

He entered the library, closed and locked the door, and drew the heavy curtain across it. But there his spirit failed him, and he seemed to grope his way to his familiar chair.

Without a word Bullard put the telegram into his hands. It had been sent off at 8 a.m., the hour of opening for the local post office. It was addressed to both men, and was brief:

Mr. Craig died nine last night. Funeral private. - Caw.

"Caw must have had instructions," remarked Bullard presently. "One wonders how much Caw knows about his master's affairs."

Possibly Lancaster did not hear. He kept on staring at the message that had closed the door on his last hope. Carlotta's suggestion, or rather command, had been far from grateful to his inclinations, yet it had forced him towards the less of two evils, and for a few minutes he had imagined himself with Christopher's cheque in his pocket, immediate salvation and peace assured whatever it might cost him eventually. And now this telegram!

Impatiently Bullard touched him on the arm.

"Look here, Lancaster! - there is a train from St. Pancras at eleven, and it's now past ten. Pull yourself together."

"St. Pancras - eleven? To-night?" Lancaster checked himself.

"No, this morning! We shall be in Glasgow at eight, and a good car will run us down under a couple of hours.... Lancaster, for Heaven's sake, wake up! Can't you take in the situation? Listen! Point one: We saw the diamonds yesterday. Point two: Christopher died suddenly, sooner than even he expected, and the diamonds, in all probability, have not left the house - if he ever intended to send them elsewhere. They may even be still on the table or in the drawer! Point three: The sooner we discover their whereabouts the better, for if they are in the house we must act on Alan's will at once, though I'd have avoided that if possible. Alan knew nothing about the diamonds. Christopher distinctly stated that no one knows about them excepting ourselves and his servant. Well, if necessary, we must manage Caw, somehow. Now -"

"But - the clock -"

"Oh, damn the clock - mere tomfoolery! As for Alan's return, if you persist in doubting what I have already told you" - Bullard lowered his voice - "I shall be forced to introduce to you the man who - who saw Alan Craig die."

"Die!"

"Don't get hysterical. At this moment the one thing that matters is that we locate or lay hands on that green box."

"But I - I can't think to go prowling into Christopher's house, and he -"

"Don't think; I'll do all that's necessary in that way, and we shall have plenty of time for talk in the train. Now I want your cheque - open - for five hundred pounds. I'm going to draw the same amount on my own. We may have to buy things - Caw, for instance. Don't argue. We've got to catch that train, and I've got to go to the bank first."

Lancaster sat up. "Bullard," he said hoarsely, "I won't have anything to do with this beastly business."

Bullard smiled. "Very well, Lancaster," he said pleasantly; "I'll take your cheque for twenty-four thousand and seventy-five pounds."

"My God!" It was the sum he owed the Syndicate.

Moments passed, and then with a white face he got up and went feebly to the writing table.

* * * * *

In the last hour of the journey they dined. Bullard

ordered champagne, and saw to it that his companion's glass was kept charged. He was not a little afraid of a general collapse on Lancaster's part, but if such were imminent, the wine averted it. The physician, however, took little of his prescribed medicine.

A car, ordered by telegraph, awaited them at the Glasgow terminus. Bullard, who was known to the hirers, dismissed the chauffeur and took the driving seat. He glanced up at the big clock, and remarked to Lancaster, clambering in beside him, that they ought to reach their destination by ten.

The car rolled out of the station down the declivity into the Square, thence into Glasgow's longest street, then swarming with pedestrians and traffic.

"Damn it!" exclaimed Bullard, "the air's frosty. We'll meet with fog presently."

He was right. They met it before they were clear of the city, and over the twenty miles that followed it lay thick, blanketing the river and countryside. Bullard was a seasoned but not a reckless driver; besides he was no more than acquainted with the road. He drove cautiously, his impatience escaping now and then in curses. They were nearing Helensburgh when they came almost abruptly into clear weather. The sky was cloudless, starry.

"This is better," said Bullard, "but I'm afraid it'll be a case of routing the estimable Caw from his virtuous couch."

Lancaster struggled out of his stupor of weariness. "Are we nearly there?"

"Hardly, but we can let her go now. I say, don't sleep; or you'll be too stiff for anything. Think over what I told you in the train; don't talk."

Five minutes later they were speeding up the Gareloch; still later, down the west side; then through the village of Roseneath, over the hill into Kilcreggan; then round the point and up Loch Long side....

At the last, as it seemed, of the houses Bullard slowed down.

"Aren't we going too far?" Lancaster inquired in a voice unnecessarily low.

"You are no observer," the other returned pleasantly, "or you would have remembered that there are here first a small wood and then a biggish field, after which we come to a couple of solitary houses, the further and larger being Christopher's. The other belongs to a doctor - retired, though I believe he has attended our old friend. As it may not be advisable to advertise our call more than we can help, we are going to run the car into the wood - there's a sort of track - and make our approach on foot. We can do with the exercise."

Within five minutes they started briskly along the deserted road.

"No need to walk on tiptoe," said Bullard with a laugh. "Hardly any one living here at this time of year. Don't let your nerves get the upper hand. We're not going to do anything sensational, you know. Cold, isn't it? We shall begin by requesting the amiable Caw to serve drinks."

"Don't jest, Bullard. I'm honestly hoping that the Green Box was somehow put away into safety."

"If not, we must rectify the error."

Lancaster sighed. "If the box is there, do you mean to - to -"

"'Pinch' is possibly the word you are hunting for. Expressive if not pretty. Well, it will all depend on circumstances."

"Bullard, I wish to say that I refuse to take more of the diamonds than will just pay my debts."

"A thousand thanks, old chap, but I really cannot accept such generosity." Bullard threw out his hand. "Yonder are the houses, and you will perceive that the doctor has not yet retired - to bed. Christopher's, however, looks less hospitable. Never mind! We can take turns at pushing the button."

"Bullard, for Heaven's sake, let us respect the - the dead."

"And let us refrain from hypocrisies. Come along, man!"

In silence they came to the gates, where Bullard spoke -

"Now remember, all you've got to do is to follow my lead, and not take fright at anything. Caw may not be alone in the house. It is even possible that he may have the company of some wretched lawyer fellow who has been nosing around all day. Come, buck up! You'll feel

John Joy Bell

fitter after a drink. Allons!"

Taking Lancaster by the elbow, he led him up the gravel path, leaves rustling about their feet. They mounted the three broad steps to the closed outer door, and, with a muttered "Here's luck!" Bullard rung the electric bell.

"Good!" he exclaimed a few seconds later, as a flood of light poured from the fan-light.

They heard the inner door being opened; then with the minimum of noise, a large key was turned, and half of the outer door swung inwards. The late Mr. Craig's servant, in his customary black lounge suit, stood there regarding them quite calmly.

Bullard had expected at least a word of astonishment, so that there was a little pause until his own words arrived.

"Good evening, Caw," he said gravely. "We very much regret to disturb you at this hour, and at this tragic time, but our business is of the utmost importance. May we have a word with you?"

Still silent, the servant stood aside, and they entered.

Said Bullard - "I need not say that we were both greatly shocked by your wire this morning. I trust our old friend did not suffer much."

"Too much, sir," answered Caw quietly, turning from closing the door. His countenance had a bleak look; his eyes were heavy. He stepped past them and opened a door on the right, switching on the lights inside. "This way, if you please, gentlemen."

Lancaster showed a momentary hesitation, or confusion, but Bullard touched his arm and he accepted the invitation.

Caw followed them a couple of paces into the room and stood &t attention. The two visitors remained standing, their hats in their hands.

Bullard had foreseen a hundred difficulties, but strangely enough, he had never thought of not being admitted to the right room. Nevertheless, his chagrin was not apparent.

"A few words will explain our unseasonable call," he said pleasantly. "Our visit yesterday afternoon was partly of a business nature, and we brought for Mr. Craig's inspection a number of documents which, after perusal, he returned to us - as it seemed at the time. But in the train, late at night, we discovered we were one short. And that document is of such vital importance that we left London again this morning, and have regretfully disturbed you now. As a matter of fact, it was a pale green share certificate in our joint names - Mr. Lancaster's and mine - and as we have sold the shares and have to deliver them two days hence, you will probably understand the necessity of recovering it immediately. Possibly you have come across such a document in the room upstairs?"

"No, sir."

"Ah! I suppose Mr. Craig's legal man was here today?"

"No, sir."

"Then nothing has been disturbed?"

"No, sir."

"You will, I hope, excuse these questions, Caw? We are considerably harassed about the matter. Will you tell us whether there were many loose papers on Mr. Craig's table last night?"

"None, sir."

"Then he must have tidied up after we left?"

"Yes, sir."

Bullard gave a tiny cough and glanced at Lancaster, who immediately said in a somewhat recitative fashion:

"I stick to my theory, Bullard, that Mr. Craig, in placing some of his own papers in a green metal box, placed ours along with them."

Bullard turned to the servant with a frank look of appeal. "A green metal box. Can you help us, Caw?"

It was on Caw's tongue to reply "No, sir." But in that moment, as it does with most of us at times, vanity pushed aside discretion. "Yes, sir," he answered. "I was the last to see inside that box, closing it at Mr. Craig's request, and I can assure you there were no papers in it."

"Wrong again, Lancaster!" Bullard lightly remarked. Then gravely - "The matter is so serious, Caw, that I must ask you who has charge of the papers and so on upstairs?"

"I, sir."

"And to whom are you responsible?"

"My master and Mr. Alan Craig - till the clock stops, sir."

After a moment's pause Bullard said - "Yes, of course, we are aware that all here was gifted to Mr. Alan; also Mr. Craig mentioned the clock. But now, would you have any objections to taking us upstairs, on the chance that our document is lying about where we were sitting?"

Caw considered quickly. To his mind, their story had been damned by the mention of the Green Box; at the same time, he was quite aware that they had only to persist in their story to obtain legal authority to search the room upstairs, and his master had commanded "no police interference." He felt pretty confident, too, that they would hardly attempt to play the burglar game in his presence, but he was curious to see how far they would go, and he was not unarmed.

"Be so good as to follow me, gentlemen," he said in his stiff way, and led them in the desired direction.

The master's room, though fireless, was warm. In silence they entered, their footfalls soundless on the heavy carpet.

Bullard halted in front of the clock with its flashing pendulum. "Is this what he spoke of," he enquired softly, "and when does it stop?"

The servant cleared his throat. "A year to-night, sir."

"Ah! ... And why this - and this?" He pointed first to the ebony slip, then to the green fluid.

"To prevent its being interfered with; also, no doubt to protect the jewels in the pendulum."

"Is it the liquid that is dangerous?"

"So I understand, sir."

"Poison? - explosive?"

"I could not say, sir."

Bullard turned to Lancaster, who had sunk into a chair, then back to the servant.

"I say, Caw," he said, "could you possibly get Mr. Lancaster something to drink? He's knocked up with the travelling, and it's a bitter night outside. I could do with something myself."

"Very good, sir," came the reply, without hesitation, and Caw went out, closing the door behind him.

"Now," whispered Bullard, and made straight for the writing table, taking from his pocket an instrument of shining steel.

But it was not needed. The deep drawer opened obediently, sweetly.

"Lancaster, we've got it first time!" He lifted out and placed the Green Box on the table. "The diamonds!"

Lancaster got up with a jerk and shudder. "Quick! Look in the other drawers for the keys."

All the other drawers were locked.

"Then we must take the whole thing."

"Good Heavens! We can't do that! How can -"

Bullard darted to the door and listened. After a moment he turned the handle gingerly. Then he grinned.

"I'm hanged," said he, "but the artful Caw has locked us in!"

"He suspects us!"

"Can't help it." Bullard sped to the bay window and drew aside one of the heavy curtains.

"I've got it!" he exclaimed.

Christopher Craig had had a craze for things that worked silently and easily. Bullard lifted the heavy sash with scarce a sound.

"Switch off the lights and come here!" he ordered. "Don't fall over things and make a row."

When Lancaster joined him Bullard was leaning half out of the window, directing the ray from an electric torch on the ground below. An incessant murmuring came from the loch, filling their ears.

"Lancaster, could you drop that height?"

"Oh, God, no!"

"There's a great heap of gathered leaves there - see! Think! Six hundred thousand pounds!"

"No, no! If one of us got hurt -"

"Perhaps you're right. There nothing for it but to drop the box and collect it when we get out. 'Sh! did you hear something just now?"

Lancaster started and caught his head a stunning blow on the sash. At the same time he inadvertently knocked the torch from the fingers of Bullard, who was going to flash it into the darkness behind them.

"Idiot!" muttered Billiard. "Don't move till I fetch the box." He stole across the floor, feeling his way.

Lancaster, nursing his head, waited - waited until a gasped expletive reached his ears -

"Damnation!" Then - "Quick! Close the window, draw the curtain!" The speaker blundered to the electric switch.

Fumblingly, Lancaster obeyed, then turned to face a blaze of light, Bullard, white with fury and dismay, and the writing table with nothing on it.

CHAPTER VI

Next moment, his wits in action again, Bullard made for the table, closed the deep drawer, and threw himself on an easy chair, hissing at the gaping Lancaster, "Sit down, you fool!"

Lancaster collapsed on the couch as Caw, bearing a salver with decanters, a syphon, and glasses, entered the room.

"Your doors open quietly enough," remarked Bullard.

"Yes, sir. Mr. Craig disliked unnecessary noise." He presented the salver to Lancaster, who mixed himself a brandy and soda with considerable splutter.

While he was doing so, Bullard produced from his breast pocket a pale-green folded paper - a hotel bill, as a matter of fact - and gaily waved it, crying - "You see, we have found it, Caw, without much trouble!"

"In your pocket, sir?"

"On this chair, which I was sitting on yesterday."

"Indeed, sir! Then you are quite satisfied, sir?"

" Perfectly. By the way, Caw - no , I'll take

whiskey - are you aware that the stones in that pendulum over there are worth a couple of thousand pounds?"

"If you say so, sir."

"Are you interested in diamonds, Caw?"

"Very much, sir - from an artistic point of view, sir."

"Their value does not interest you?"

"It does not excite me, sir."

"A capital answer! You have seen Mr. Craig's collection?"

"Frequently, sir."

Bullard took a bundle of notes from his pocket. "I offer you ten pounds to guess correctly the value of the collection."

"Six hundred thousand pounds, sir.... Thank you, sir." With supreme stolidity Caw presented the salver as a waiter might do for his tip.

Though taken aback, the loser laughed. He took a long drink, and laughed again.

"Excuse me, sir," said Caw, "but my master is still in the house."

Lancaster started, and took a hasty gulp, spilling a little.

"I beg your pardon - and his," said Bullard gravely. "But I am not often 'had.' Now, look here, Caw; I have still nine hundred and ninety pounds here. They are yours, if you can tell me where the collection is at the present moment."

The topmost thought in Caw's mind then was that the brutes might have had the decency to have waited until his master was laid in the grave. He felt helpless, powerless. He could not doubt that Bullard was playing with him. And in view of the promise to his master he could do nothing to prevent the crime, the desecration as he felt it to be. He could do nothing but look on in silence while they searched, until they found - But stay! he might as well despoil the spoilers when he had the chance.

"I will take your money, sir," he said, in an odd voice. "Look in the bottom right-hand drawer in the writing table."

Bullard's eyebrows rose. Then he got up and, with his eyes on the servant, opened the empty drawer.

Caw was within an ace of dropping the salver. After a moment he carried it to a side table and set it down with a small crash. Turning, he looked searchingly round the room. His gaze stopped at the curtain; he thought he understood. They had had an accomplice outside! ... He seemed to glide across to Bullard, and Bullard found himself looking into the barrel of a stout revolver.

"Out o' the house, the pair o' ye," he ordered hoarsely, "or, by God, I'll forget the holy dead!"

"But look here -"

"Not a word! Take your hats and go! You've got what you came for -"

"Listen, you madman!" Bullard held up a hand, the one with the notes in it.

"Thanks!" With a flash-like movement Caw nipped away the notes. "You've got to pay something!"

Springing round behind Bullard, he shoved the cold steel into the nape of his neck. "March! and you, too, Mr. Lancaster. Take your friend's hat!"

Ignoring his colleague's gaze, which had moved suggestively from himself to the fire-irons, Lancaster obeyed and made for the door.

"You'll be devilish sorry," began Bullard, beside himself -

"Another word, and you'll lose one ear - to begin with. March!"

Sullenly Bullard moved forward. Not until he was in the garden did he attempt speech, and then his voice was thick, though fairly under control.

"Well, my man," he said, "you've got yourself into a nasty hole. Robbery, with a revolver in your hand, is rather seriously regarded by the law. But as you have acted on impulse and misapprehension, I am disposed to give you a chance. Restore those notes -"

"Looks like being a wet night," said Caw, and shut the

outer door.

When he had made it fast he switched off the lights in the hall and went upstairs. In his master's room he wavered, and his eyes rested longingly on the decanters, for he was feeling the reaction. But he was a good servant still, and it would be "hardly the thing" to take a dram there and then. Yet he forgot the conventions of service when, a moment later, he sank upon a chair and bowed his head on his master's table, sick at heart, sore in pride. He had been so easily tricked! And yet what difference would it have made if they had walked out of the room with the Green Box in their possession? But he was very sure they would not have dared so greatly, unless, perhaps, with force of arms - in which case, despite all promises, he knew he would have resisted. It never occurred to Caw to doubt his master's sanity, but now he began to wonder what had possessed Mr. Craig in regard to the Green Box. Six hundred thousand pounds! He seemed to see his master seated at the table, calmly naming the stupendous sum - and in the same instant he realised that he himself was sitting in his master's place. He sprang up, and almost fell over the open drawer. He stooped to close it, straightened up with an exclamation, only to drop to his knees, staring, staring at - the Green Box! Suddenly he gave a short chuckle, rose, and made for the door in the back wall.

Ere he reached it, it opened. A girl came in.

He was taken aback, and she was first to speak.

"Would you mind shaking hands?" said she.

" Miss Handyside, was it you?" he cried, taking her

hand with diffidence.

She nodded. "At least, I suppose so, for it all happened so quickly that I'm still in a state of wonder."

"It was splendid, miss! I shall never be able to thank you."

"I couldn't help doing it, though I'm not used to adventures. It was all done on an impulse."

"Woman's wit, miss, if you'll excuse my saying so."

"Well, I was in the dark in more senses than one, but the proceedings of those two gentlemen were so peculiar, to say the least of it, that I felt justified in playing the spy."

"When did you arrive on the scene, miss?" Caw enquired, removing his admiring glance. For several years he had adored the doctor's daughter - from a strictly artistic point of view, as he would have explained it - and undoubtedly Marjorie had her attractions, though it would be difficult to analyse and tabulate them. A Scot with more perception than descriptive powers would have called her bonny. To go into brief detail, she had nut-brown hair, eyes of unqualified grey, a complexion suggesting sea-air, splendid teeth in a humorously inclined mouth, and a nicely rounded chin. Very few people have beautiful noses; on the other hand, not the most beautiful nose will redeem an otherwise unattractive countenance, whereas an ordinary nondescript nose in a charming face simply becomes part of it. Marjorie's was nondescript, but did not turn up or droop excessively. Without being guilty of stoutness, she lacked the poorly nourished look of so many young women of the day.

"I must explain why I arrived at all," she said, in answer to Caw's question. "I came with a message from the doctor - he twisted his ankle in the dark - not seriously, but quite badly enough to prevent his coming along himself. Well, when I reached the door I noticed from a thread of light that it was not absolutely shut -"

"My fault, miss. I was just about to come along for the night when the ring came."

"Then I heard voices - faintly - but clearly enough for me to judge they were those of strangers, and I was going to go back when I heard a voice say 'Lancaster, we've got it first time!' I'm ashamed to say my curiosity was too much for me -"

"Thank God for female curiosity, miss, if you'll excuse my saying so."

She checked a laugh. "You know how quietly the door works, I switched off the light behind me and opened it slightly - all trembles, I assure you - and looked in. The younger man was lifting a greenish box from a drawer to the writing-table, and the other man seemed half-paralysed with nervousness." She proceeded to relate what the reader already knows up to the episode of the window. "Then, with my heart in my mouth, I opened the door wide and stole in. The faint light from the water guided me to the table, but I almost lost my way going back with the box. I think they did hear something, but I was in safety by the time they could have turned their light into the room. But now I had closed the door tight, and could hear no more except indistinct voices, among which I fancied I heard yours. You were talking angrily, I think. And after a while there was a silence, and I waited and waited until I could wait no longer. Is it true," she asked abruptly, "that there are sixty thousand pounds' worth -"

"Six hundred thousand pounds, miss."

"Oh! ... But why was it not in a safe place? And who were those men? And what -"

"It will be necessary," said Caw, as one coming to a decision, "to tell you all about it, Miss Handyside. My master said I might trust you. It's too much," he added, "for me to carry alone. And if you think the doctor -"

"Goodness!" she exclaimed; "he'll be wondering what has come over me - and I've forgotten to give you his message! It was just to tell that he thought it was time you were leaving here for your new quarters."

"Very good, miss. I'll come now."

"But are you going to leave the box there?"

"Got to - master's orders."

"Extraordinary! It's locked, I suppose?"

"Yes, miss; and last night, or, rather, this morning, at 12:15 by the clock, I threw the key into the loch - master's orders."

"You are sure the diamonds are in it now?"

"I was the last to see them and shut them in - master's orders."

"Oh, I can't take in any more! Let us consult the doctor at once."

Presently they passed out by the way the girl had entered, closing the door behind them. They were at the top of a narrow and rather steep staircase of many steps covered with rubber. Descending they were in a tunnel seven feet high and four in width, so long that in the distance the sides seemed to come together. Roof and walls were white; light was supplied from bulbs overhead. The atmosphere was fresh, though the means of ventilation were not visible. Here again they trod on rubber. Christopher Craig had caused the tunnel to be constructed as soon as he realised the truth about his malady; but it was primarily the outcome of a joking remark by Handyside after a midnight summons in mid-winter. It should be said here that at first Handyside had demurred becoming his neighbour's physician, but growing friendship with the lonely man had gradually eliminated his scruples. The tunnel had been a costly undertaking, the more so owing to the hurrying of its construction, but Christopher would have told you that its existence had saved his life on more than one occasion. The secret of the doors, by the way, was known only to himself and Caw, Dr. Handyside and Marjorie.

CHAPTER VII

A week later Doris Lancaster was sitting alone by the drawing-room fire, a book on her lap. It was not so often that she had an evening to spend in quietness; one of her mother's great aims in life was to have "something on" at least six nights out of the seven. At the present moment Mrs. Lancaster was in her boudoir, accepting and sending out invitations for comparatively distant dates.

Sweetly the clock on the mantel struck nine, and Doris told herself that now no one was likely to call. She lay back in the chair, a graceful figure in pale green, stretched her pretty ankles to the glow, and sought to escape certain gnawing thoughts in the pages of a novel which had won from the reviewers such adjectives as "entrancing," "compelling," "intensely interesting."

And just then a servant announced "Mr. France."

Well, after all, she was not sorry to see Mr. France - or Teddy, as she had called him for a good many years. He was a frequent visitor, despite the fact that Mrs. Lancaster suffered him only because everybody else seemed to like him. He was fair, tall, and lanky, and so pleasant of countenance that it would not be worth while enumerating his defective features.

Mrs. Lancaster disapproved of him for three reasons: first, he had only two hundred a year plus a pittance from the insurance company that put up, as he expressed it, with his services; second, he had been Alan Craig's close friend; third, she suspected that he saw through her affectations. That he had been openly in love with Doris since the days of pigtails and short frocks troubled her not at all: he was too hopelessly ineligible. And it had not troubled Doris for a long time - not since Alan Craig had gone away. Since then Teddy had seemed to become more of a friend and less of an admirer than ever.

"This is great luck," he remarked, seating himself in the opposite easy chair with an enforced extension of immaculate pumps and silken sox. (People often wondered how Teddy "did it" on the money.) "It's so seldom one can find you alone nowadays. Well, how's things generally?"

"Pretty much the same, Teddy," she answered, with the smile that hurt him. "Mother's busy as usual -"

"Out?"

"No; writing, I think."

"How's your father? I haven't seen him for an age."

"I wish he were fitter. He has had to stay in bed for a few days - he came down for dinner to-night for the first time. Last week he had three nights and a day in the train - with Mr. Bullard."

"Oh, I say! Bad enough without Bullard, but -"

"Oh, I'm so glad," she cried softly. "You don't like Mr. Bullard, Teddy. I'm beginning to abhor the man."

"Keep on abhorring!"

Swiftly she looked at him. "You know something?"

He shook his head. "Not a thing, Doris. Merely my instinctive dislike. I'm a sort of bow-wow, you know. Still, your mother approves of him, and he is your father's friend."

"I sometimes feel it has been an unlucky friendship for father," she said in a low voice, "and yet I have nothing to go on. I suppose I'm horribly unjust, but I'd give anything to learn something positive against the man."

"And yet," said the young man slowly and heavily, "sooner or later Mr. Francis Bullard will ask you to marry him."

Doris threw up her head. "I'd sooner marry - " She paused.

"Me, for instance?"

"Don't be absurd, Teddy." She flushed slightly.

"Absurd, but serious," he quietly returned. "Doris, I came to-night to ask you. It wouldn't keep any longer. One moment, please. Two things happened yesterday. My father won the big law suit that has been our nightmare for years; and I got a move-up in the office. Never was more shocked in all my life. Mighty little to offer you, Doris -"

"Oh, don't speak about it."

"Well, I'll cut that bit out; but please let me finish. You know I've been in love with you for ages, though I did my best to get it under when a better man appeared; and I think you'll admit I haven't worried you much since. And I'm perfectly aware that you can't give me what you gave him.... Still, Doris, I'm not a bad fellow, and you could make me a finer one, and - well, I'd hope not to bore you with my devotion and all that, but, of course, you'd have to take that risk as well as your parents' disapproval. Perhaps I ought to have waited longer, dear, but I didn't imagine my chances would be any greater a year hence, and it has seemed to me lately that - that you needed some one who would care for you before and above everything else.... Doris, remembering how long I've loved you, can't you trust me and take me for - for want of a better?"

His words had moved her, and moments passed before she could answer. "Dear Teddy, it is true that I want to be cared for - no need to deny it to you - but it wouldn't be right to take all you could give and give nothing."

"You would give much without knowing it," he pleaded. "And you were not made to be sorry all your life."

"I'm not going to make you sorry, Teddy."

"You're doing it as hard as you can!"

She smiled in spite of herself. "No," she said presently, "I've no intention of shunning all joys and abandoning all hopes, but I can't do what you ask, Teddy. I will tell you just one thing that you may not know. Almost at the last moment before Alan went away I promised him I would wait."

Teddy cleared his throat. "I didn't know, though I may have guessed.... But I do know, Doris - I felt it on my way here to-night - that Alan, if he could look into my heart now, would give me his blessing. I'm not asking to fill his place, you know."

"Oh, you make it very hard for me! You - you've been such a faithful friend."

"Give in, Doris, give in to me!" He rose and stood looking down on her bowed head. "Dear, I'd bring Alan back to you if I could. Don't you believe that?"

"Oh, yes!"

"With all your heart?"

"With all my heart, Teddy."

"Then - " He stopped and took her hand. "Doris!" ...

He straightened up sharply. The door was opening. The servant announced -

"Mr. Bullard."

It was an awkward enough situation, but neither the girl nor the young man was heavy-witted. Doris rose slowly, languidly, it seemed, and though aware that her eyes must betray her, turned and greeted Billiard in cool, even tones. The two men exchanged perfunctory nods.

"Thanks, but I won't sit down," said Bullard. "I called to enquire for your father, and to see him, if at all possible. Is he feeling better to-night?"

"I think he is in the library at present," she replied, "but he has not yet got over his fatigue."

"Yes," he replied sympathetically, "he and I had too much trailing last week, but business must not be shirked, Miss Doris."

She was a little startled by hearing her name from his lips; until now he had addressed her with full formality. She was not to know that the sight of her eyes when she had turned to meet him had informed him of something unlooked for, and had put a period to his long-lived irresolution regarding her. Francis Bullard, in fact, had suddenly realised that if he wished to secure a wife in the only woman of whom he had ever thought twice in that respect, he would have to act promptly, not to say firmly. Accordingly, as though forgetting the stated purpose of his visit, he dropped into a chair and chatted entertainingly enough until Mrs. Lancaster made her appearance.

She offered to conduct him to her husband, and he allowed her to do so as far as the hall. There he halted and said -

"You will do me a great favour by getting rid of Mr. France and remaining with Miss Doris in the drawing-room until I return." In response to her look of enquiry he added - "Then you will do me a further favour by retiring."

"Really, Mr. Bullard, I must ask you to explain!"

"Your daughter is not going to marry a title - to begin with, at any rate." He smiled and passed on.

She overtook him. "Have you something unpleasant to say to my husband?" she demanded.

"I am going to return him some money he thought lost."

"How much?"

"Five hundred pounds."

"Is that all?"

"Patience!" he answered, and made his escape.

Lancaster, pencil in hand, was seated at his writing-table. On his retiral from his business in South Africa he had indulged dreams of a quiet room at home and the peaceful companionship of books, and he had got the length of providing the nucleus of a library. But his income, though large, had never been equal to the varied demands upon it, and the room had become simply a chamber wherein he escaped the irritations of society only to suffer the torments of secret anxieties, building up futile schemes for his salvation, striving to extract hope from vain calculations.

At the entrance of Bullard he lifted his head with a start, and into his eyes came the question - "What new terror are you going to spring upon me now?"

"Glad to see you are better," Bullard remarked, drawing a chair to the table and seating himself. "I didn't intend to trouble you to-night, but something arrived by the late afternoon delivery which I thought would interest you. No need to be nervy. It's nothing to upset you." He threw a bundle of notes and a registered envelope on the table. "Your five hundred comes back to you, after all."

Lancaster eyed the notes, then took up the envelope and drew out a sheet of paper of poor quality, bearing a few lines in a school-boyish hand.

"GREY HOUSE, LOCH LONG.

"3/11/13.

"*Sir,* - Herewith the sum of £990 which I accepted from you the other night owing to a misunderstanding. Without apologies for doubting your honesty - Yours truly,

"J. CAW."

Lancaster drew a long breath. "So he was fooling us, Bullard."

"Not at all! Some one was fooling him! - only he has managed - I'm convinced of that - to regain possession of the green box. As I impressed on you just after the fiasco, there was some one in one of the presses, and now it is evident that Caw captured that person after we had left. Unfortunately, it means that a fourth person has knowledge of the diamonds. Still, my friend, we have another chance."

"What? You don't mean to say -"

"Certainly , we shall try again, - we must ! And the

sooner the better! That is, unless we find we can settle amicably with the invaluable Caw. His note suggests that possibility, doesn't it? His impertinence gives me encouragement."

"It is the letter," said Lancaster heavily, "of an honest man -"

"Up to the tune of a thousand pounds. A wise man, if you like, who foresaw the possibility of the notes being stopped."

"You would not have dared do that."

"I had already written off my share as a bad debt," said Bullard, with a smile, "but Caw was not to know that."

The older man rested his head upon his hand. "You cannot be certain," he said slowly, "that the green box is still in the house."

"True. Otherwise I'd be tempted to produce Alan Craig's will and finish the business. All the nonsense about the clock and the postponed division could not prevent our taking possession of the house and every-thing in it. Why, even that absurdly costly clock would be ours.... And yet there's always the risk of -"

"Bullard, let us produce the will and dare the risk of losing the diamonds. From the bottom of my heart I tell you, I will be content with £25,000."

"So you think at the moment. But apart from your own feelings - not to mention mine - what about Mrs. Lancaster's?"

"I - I have already told her we cannot go on living as we are doing."

"Yes? And her reply?"

Lancaster was mute.

"Have you, by any chance, mentioned to her the matter of the! - a - debt to the -"

"For God's sake, don't torture!"

"I have no wish to do that," said Bullard quietly. "Let us change the subject, which is not really urgent at present, for one which, I trust, may be less disagreeable to you."

The host wiped his forehead. "What is it about?" he asked wearily.

"Your daughter."

CHAPTER VIII

Teddy was not afraid of Mrs. Lancaster, but he soon gathered that she had come to stay, and as the situation seemed to him difficult for Doris, he took his leave with assumed cheerfulness. In bidding the girl good-night he dropped in a whispered "to-morrow," which was, perhaps, more of a comfort to Doris than she would have admitted to herself. Immediately after his departure she expressed her intention of going to bed.

"Just for a moment, Doris. Do sit down again. We must settle what you are going to wear at the Thurstans' on the seventeenth." And Mrs. Lancaster plunged into a long discussion on frocks with numerous side issues.

A few weeks ago she would certainly have hesitated over Bullard as a son-in-law. Now she was prepared to accept him as such, not, it should be said, with joy and thanksgiving, yet not, on the other hand, with hopeless resignation. After all, he was richer than any of the men she knew, and in view of her husband's deplorable confession it would be well, if not vital, to have him on her side. Far better to abandon the idea of a title than to risk all continuing its pursuit. She would see to it that she did not have to abandon her other ambitions.

When Bullard made his appearance , however , she

betrayed no unusual interest in the man.

"Was Robert not thinking of going to bed?" she casually enquired.

"He ought to be there now, Mrs. Lancaster. If I were you -"

"I shan't be a minute," she said, rising, "but I really must look after him."

Bullard closed the door, and came back to the hearth.

"I am glad of this opportunity, Miss Doris," he said, "to tell you something that has been in my mind to say for a very long time. Don't be alarmed."

She rose, but made no attempt to go from him. Perhaps instinct told her that there could be no ultimate escape.

"I don't wear my heart on my sleeve," he went on evenly, "but I dare say you have at least suspected my feelings for you. I have never flattered myself that you have regarded me as more than a friend of the house - a good friend, I hope - and you have known me so long that you may have come to consider me an old friend in more senses than one. Yet here I am, Doris, asking you to marry me -"

"Please, Mr. Bullard -" The whisper came from pale lips.

He proceeded gently, steadily - "At present you would say that you cannot give me the affection I desire, yet I would ask to be allowed to try to earn it. I can give you many things besides a whole-hearted admiration,

Doris. You are the only woman I have ever thought of as wife. With me you would be secure from worldly hardships, and I venture to believe that you would never regret marrying me. One word more. You have been sad of late. No business of mine, perhaps, but if there is anything I can do, you may command me. Doris, will you marry me?"

Perhaps she liked him better at that moment than ever she had done; certainly better than ever she would like him again. For he broke the long silence with these words -

"I have your father's permission, your mother's approval."

"My father's permission!" she said faintly. For support she laid her arm on the mantel. Her mind was in a turmoil. At last - "I cannot marry you, Mr. Bullard."

"With all respect," he quietly answered, "I cannot take your words as final."

She was not indignant, only afraid. "You speak of my father's 'permission,'" she managed to say. "Does that include his 'approval'? You will forgive me, but -"

"I will forgive you anything but a refusal."

"Then please excuse my leaving you. I will come back."

She went quickly to the library. From the table Mr. Lancaster raised a face whose haggard aspect almost made her cry out - so aged it was, so stricken with trouble. She closed the door, went over to the table, and halted opposite him.

"Father, do you really wish me to marry Mr. Bullard?"

"My child, life - everything - is uncertain, and so - and so I would see you provided for."

"I am not afraid of poverty - compared with some things." She nerved herself. "Father, you and I used to be frank with each other. Will it - help you if I marry Mr. Billiard?"

The man writhed. "Yes, Doris," he whispered at last.

"In what way?" Again she had to wait for his reply.

"It - it would save me..."

"Save you?"

"...from a grave difficulty..."

"Difficulty?"

"...disgrace." His head drooped. And suddenly all that mattered to heart was swamped by a wave of loving pity. She ran round to him and clasped him, and kissed him. "Oh, my dear," she sighed, "it was never, never your fault."

Then she went back to the drawing-room. She looked straight at Bullard as he stood by the fire, well-dressed, well-groomed, and just rather well-fed. And there and then she made up her mind.

" Mr. Bullard , " she said calmly, "I promise to marry

you, if you still wish it, a year hence; but I will not be engaged to you formally or openly. That is all I can say - all I can offer you."

He frowned slightly at her tone rather than her words. The least trustworthy people are not the least trusting, and he did not doubt, knowing her as he did, that she would redeem any promise she made, nor was he particularly anxious for marriage within a year. But he had his vanity.

"Do you mean," he asked with increased suavity, "that you would wish to ignore my existence until the year is up?"

"Not your existence, Mr. Bullard - we should meet as before, I suppose - but - well, I think you must see what I mean."

He bowed. "It shall be as you will, Doris. Enough that I have your word for a year hence. Or" - he smiled - "let us say, when the clock stops, which your father will tell you is practically the same thing. Don't look so puzzled! Will you give me your hand on it?" The man was not without dignity; he made no attempt to detain her hand.

"Thank you and good-night," he said. "I will pay my respects to Mrs. Lancaster to-morrow afternoon."

He went out with the step of success. He had not only secured a wife to be proud of, but had, he believed, disarmed a possible enemy. For some time he had had vaguely uneasy moments with regard to Teddy France.

When the door had closed Doris dropped her face in

her hands, but her eyes remained dry. Five minutes later, Mrs. Lancaster, coming in, received the calm and brief announcement that her daughter had promised to marry Mr. Bullard a year hence; that until then he was to be regarded as an ordinary acquaintance, and that he would call upon Mrs. Lancaster on the following afternoon.

The mother was not heartless. "You are doing this to help your father, Doris. I know all about it. It is - it is noble of you!"

The girl looked at her, and the question rushed to her lips - "Oh, why have *you*, his wife, never done anything to help him?" But it remained unuttered. "Good-night, mother," she said, and hastened to the refuge of her room.

She wrote a few lines to Teddy, stating simply what she had done. After that she gave way.

* * * * *

About the same hour, in Dr. Handyside's study, four hundred miles away, a conference of three people was drawing to a close. Earlier in the day Caw had received a belated visit from Mr. Harvie, the Glasgow lawyer, who, owing to illness, had been unable to attend to business since his client's death. Beyond the information that Caw had been left the sum of £5,000 free of duty, the old housekeeper an annuity, and the doctor £1,000, Mr. Harvie had little to say. The rest of his late client's fortune, the house and its contents, were already Alan's - if the young man were still alive, and Mr. Harvie, whatever his own ideas might be, was under an obligation to assume as much until - a slight grimace of disapproval - "the clock stopped." "I have other instructions," he added, "but they are not to be acted on at present." He had returned to town by the last steamer.

"So we have come back to where we started," Dr. Handyside was saying. "The sum total of our discoveries is that we can do next to nothing. If I hadn't become so intimate with your master's character - not his affairs, you understand, Caw - I should have had very little respect for his methods. As for his motives, they are no business of ours."

"If I may say so," returned Caw, who would have been happier standing at attention than sitting in Miss Handyside's company, "you take a lofty view of the matter, sir, and you put it in a nutshell when you say that his motives are none of our business. I am sorry to have brought you and Miss Handyside into the trouble -"

"I rather think I came in," observed Miss Handyside with a smile.

"Which is a fact, miss. And very welcome, too, if I may say so. Also, Mr. Craig trusted you both."

"Wherefore it is up to us to trust his wisdom and respect his wishes," said Handyside. "The green box must remain where it is and take its chance."

"If you hadn't told us," said Marjorie to Caw, "that you were the last to see inside the box, I should be imagining all sorts of things. And those two men were his friends!"

Caw's expression resumed its usual stolidity. To have replied that they had ceased to be his master's friends would have involved explanations which he did not feel at liberty to impart even to those trustworthy people.

"Do you think they will try again, Caw?" the girl pursued. "I wish you had not sent back the money -"

"Don't be absurd, Marjorie!" said her father. "Caw had no choice."

"Well, sir, I was sorely tempted to stick to it as a bit of revenge, but I asked myself what my master would have done - and then, as you say, sir, there was no choice. As to your question, miss, I answer 'Yes.' A man like Mr. Bullard - I'm not so sure of the other - would not give up trying for such a prize. You see, I learned his ways out there in the old days. All his successes were made by bold methods. He feared nothing, cared for nobody. Oh, yes, he is bound to have another try, though I don't fancy it will be to-morrow or the next day."

"One would almost imagine," remarked the doctor, easing his injured foot on the supporting chair, "that the beggars guessed you were powerless in the matter."

Caw shook his head. "Hardly that, sir. They had a sight of my revolver - though, of course, that was after I had made sure they had got the box, and was only a miserable attempt to give them a shake-up. But they were not to know that. Their strong point is this, sir. They have the knowledge that the existence of the diamonds is practically a secret. Even Mr. Alan, even the lawyer has never heard of them. Only Bullard,

Lancaster, and Caw knew of them; and Caw is in the minority. And they say to themselves - 'Once we get the box, we have only to swear that it contained papers belonging to us, that Mr. Craig had the loan of it, and so forth.' Then how is Caw going to disprove their words? they ask themselves. 'Can't be done! If Caw begins to talk of half-a-million in diamonds left in a writing-table drawer, he'll only get laughed at, and if we've nothing better to do, we can get up an action for slander.' There you are, sir! That's what I fancy I see at the back of their heads, and I'm sure I'm right."

"I believe you are, Caw!" cried Marjorie. "What do you say, father?"

"I am inclined to accept the diagnosis," replied the doctor, smiling at her eagerness. "Well, Caw, just one question more. What is your position, supposing those two gentlemen made an attempt by deputy?"

At that Caw smiled for the first time. "If I may say so, sir, I think your services would be required for the deputy!" Becoming grave, he added - "I have taken the liberty of running a new wire along the passage, sir. The opening of the door of my master's room will cause a bell to ring - not too loudly - in the quarters you have kindly provided for me in this house."

"Capital!" said the doctor.

"And if you, sir, would be good enough to give your housekeeper some explanation that would satisfy her without giving away things -"

"That will be all right, Caw," Miss Handyside assured him. "When you get to know Mrs. Butters, you will realise that she is not as others are, being a woman absolutely without curiosity."

"Thank you, miss." Caw smiled faintly and got up. "Unless there is anything more, sir -" he began.

"Nothing at all," said the doctor kindly.

"Thank you, sir. Good-night, sir. Good-night, miss."

"Trustworthy chap," Handyside remarked when the door had closed. "The legacy seems to have made no difference, though it upset him for the moment. And he knows all that's worth knowing about cars and electric lighting," he added rather irrelevantly. "I believe we'll be able to give him enough to do, after all."

"Between ourselves, father," said Marjorie suddenly, "have you the slightest hope of Alan Craig's return?"

"Not the slightest, my dear. He was a fine lad. I wish you had met him, but you were always gadding somewhere when he visited his uncle."

"I shan't be doing much gadding in the near future," she remarked thoughtfully.

"Why this sudden change from years of neglecting your only father?"

"I'm going to be on the spot in case anything happens next door."

"Indeed!" said the doctor drily.

John Joy Bell

CHAPTER IX

When Teddy France, bidding Doris a formal good-night, whispered "to-morrow" he had in mind a certain reception at the house of a mutual acquaintance, and he went home looking forward to meeting her there with hopes irrepressible. He felt that the girl he had loved for years was - if not with her whole heart - on the verge of surrender; would have been his by now but for the untimely entrance of Bullard and the succeeding intervention of Mrs. Lancaster; and he lived most of the night and the following day in a state of exaltation.

Thus Doris's note, received in the evening, was a blow that seemed to crash to the centre of his soul. At first he imagined wicked, unreasonable things. Then, his wrath failing, he realised that only one thing could have made Doris act as she had done. She had been driven by a sudden overpowering pressure. Who had exerted it? Teddy did not doubt the mother's ability for coercion any more than her vaunting ambition, and he shrunk from blaming the father; yet he feared that Mr. Lancaster, beset by financial troubles of which he had long had an inkling, had sought a way out through the sacrifice of his daughter. Well, there was nothing to be done, he decided in his misery; interference on his part would be worse than vain, and would only cause Doris to suffer a little more.

At rather a late hour the craving for a glimpse of her drew him, after all, to the reception.

She was dancing when he entered the room, and, with a pang of angry pain, he discovered that she was lovelier than ever. Her face gave no hint of the heart-sickness she endured; she nodded to him in the old friendly way, and the easy recognition brought home to him the cool truth that, after all, the wild hopes of the previous night had been of his own making, not hers. Yet why had she written and so quickly, to inform him of her bargain with Bullard? Was her note just an uncontrollable cry for pity, sympathy?

It was after midnight when he led her to a corner in the deserted supper-room.

"Shall I congratulate you, Doris?" he asked gently.

"Why, yes, I think you had better," she answered with a bitter little smile, "on having done my duty. Don't look so shocked, Teddy," she went on, "I had to say it, and you are the only person besides father and mother who knows what I have done. And now I'm going to ask a great favour."

"Yes, Doris?"

"It is that you will prove your friendship to me - prove it once more, Teddy - by never, after to-night, referring to the matter. I'm going to try hard not to let it poison my life - for a year, at any rate."

"Very well.... But I must ask at least one question."

"Ask."

"Could *I* have done anything to prevent this?"

"No one," she answered sadly, "could have done anything, excepting one man, and he died last week - Christopher Craig."

"Christopher Craig - dead? No wonder your father has been upset. Of course I know of their long friendship in South Africa, and once I was Mr. Craig's guest in Scotland along with Alan. The old man had a tremendous admiration for you, Doris."

"I loved him, though I did not see him for several years before the end. Well, I have answered your question. Have I your promise?"

He put his hand tenderly over hers. "I will give you two promises, Doris," he said deliberately; "the one you ask for and another. I promise you that Bullard shall never call you his wife!"

"Oh!" she cried, pale. "Why do you say that?"

"Because I mean it - and it is all I have to say." He laughed shortly. "But I am going to lay myself out to confound Mr. Bullard within the year, and I will do it. Now tell me this, Doris; are you and I to continue being friends - openly, I mean?"

"Why not? I must have one friend."

He bent and kissed her hand, and rose abruptly. "Let us go back to the dancing before I lose my head," he said, with a twisted smile. "And I must not do that when at last I've got something to do that's worth doing!"

Teddy was a creature of impulses and instincts not by any means infallible. They had led him into blunders and scrapes before now. On the other hand, they had protected him from mistakes no less serious. Had he been a matter-of-fact person he would have said to himself: "What can I do? I know of nothing positive against Bullard. Being a poor man, I cannot, by a stroke of the pen, make Lancaster independent of him, and I need not waste my wits in plotting to confound him by some great financial operation such as I've read of in novels," But what Teddy said to himself was something to this effect: "I suspect that Bullard is not quite straight, and if one watches such a man for twelve months as though one's life depended on the watching, one is likely to learn something. The only question at present is where to begin."

It is not to be assumed that Teddy went home from the reception in a light-hearted, hopeful condition. On the contrary he was extremely harassed, and wished he had kept to himself the brave prophecy made to Doris. Nevertheless, dawn found him unshaken in his determination to make good that prophecy. If, instead of spending the whole morning in doing his duty to the insurance company, he had been able to spend an early part of it in a state of invisibility within Bullard's private office, he would have justified himself beyond his highest expectations.

Bullard on entering the outer office, about nine-thirty, received from the chief clerk a curious signal which was equivalent to the words "Undesirable waiting to see you. Bolt for private room." But either Bullard was slower than usual this morning, or the "Undesirable" too alert. Ere the former's hand left the open door the latter stepped round it, saying -

John Joy Bell

"How are you, Mr. Bullard? Been waiting -"

"Get out of this," said Bullard crisply, and stood away from the door.

"Really," said the visitor with an absurdly pained look, "this is a very unkind reception." He was a small individual of dark complexion, leering eyes and vulgar mouth. His clothing was respectable, if not fashionable; he displayed a considerable amount of starched linen of indifferent lustre.

"Get out!"

"Give me five minutes." The tone was servile, yet not wholly so. "Worth your while, Mr. Bullard."

Bullard looked him up and down. "Very well," he said abruptly. "Close that door and follow me." He said no more until they were in his room, himself seated at his desk, the other standing a little way off and turning his bowler hat between his hands.

"Now, Marvel, what the devil do you want?"

The visitor smiled deprecatingly into his revolving hat. "What do most of us want, Mr. Bullard?"

"I'll tell you what most of us do not want - the attentions of the police."

"Tut, tut, Mr. Bullard. Of course *we* don't want that, nor do *we* need it - do *we*?" The impudence of the fellow's manner was exquisite.

Bullard, toying with the nugget on his chain, affected

not to notice it. Harshly he said: "Eighteen months ago -"

"In this very room, Mr. Bullard -"

"- I handed you five hundred pounds on the express condition that you used the ticket for Montreal, which I supplied, and never approached me again."

"I am sorry to say," the other said after a moment, "that Canada did not agree with my health, and I assure you that I made the five hundred go as far as possible."

"All that may be very interesting to yourself and friends - if you have any."

"You, Mr. Bullard, are my sole friend."

Bullard grinned. "If you imagine I'm going to be a friend in need, you are mightily mistaken!"

"Please don't be nasty, Mr. Bullard -"

"Leave my name alone, and clear out. Time's up." Bullard turned to a pile of letters.

"This is a blow," murmured Marvel, "a sad blow. But I would remind you that the five hundred was not a gift, but a payment for certain documents."

"Quite so. And it closed our acquaintance. Go!"

"I wonder if it did. One moment. I desire to return once more to South Africa. Things are looking up there again. With five hundred pounds -"

"That's enough. I'm busy."

"Just another moment. Touching those documents relating to the affair of Christopher Craig's brother -"

"Shut up!"

"- it is one of the strangest inadvertencies you ever heard of, Mr. Bullard, but the fact remains that, eighteen months ago, I delivered to you - not the originals but copies -"

Bullard wheeled round. "Don't try that game, Marvel. You are quite capable of forgery, but I made certain that they were originals before I burned them."

"Ah, you burned them! What a pity! So you can't compare them with the documents I hold - in a very safe place, Mr. Bullard."

"I should not take the trouble in any case. Now will you clear out or be thrown?"

"You make it very hard for me. Do you wish me to take the originals to Mr. Christopher Craig?"

"Pray do. He's dead."

"Dead!" Mr. Marvel took a step backward. "Dear, dear!" He raised his hat to his face as though to screen his emotion and smiled into it. "When did it happen?"

"A few days ago. Now, once and for all -"

"Then nothing remains to me but to offer the papers to his brother's son, an undoubtedly interested party,

Mr. Alan -"

"Alan Craig is also dead."

Mr. Marvel's hat fell to the floor, and lay neglected. Mr. Marvel began to laugh softly while Bullard wondered whether the man's sanity, always suspect, had given way.

"Come, come, Mr. Bullard," Marvel coughed at last; "come, come!"

"Young Craig," said Bullard, restraining himself, "was lost on an Arctic expedition, a year ago."

"Then he must have been found again."

"... What do you say?"

"Why, I saw him - let me see - just fourteen days ago."

"Rot!"

"I'd know Frank Craig's son anywhere, Mr. Bullard; and there he was on the quay at Montreal, the day I left. What's the matter?"

With a supreme effort Bullard controlled himself.

"Marvel," he said, "what do you expect to gain by bringing me a lie like that?"

"It is no lie," the other returned with a fairly straight glance. "I was as near to him as I am to you at this moment. He was in a labourer's clothes -"

John Joy Bell

"Nonsense!"

"- working with a gang on the quay."

"You were mistaken. The search party gave up in despair."

"I know nothing of that, Mr. Bullard, but I'm prepared to take oath -"

"There is no need for Alan Craig, if it were he, to be working as a quay labourer. I tell you -"

"I am so sure of what I say, Mr. Bullard, that failing to get my price from you, I will cross the Atlantic again, working my passage if need be, to place the documents in the hands of that quay labourer. Since his uncle old Christopher is dead, there must be something pretty solid awaiting him." Marvel, stooping leisurely, picked up his hat and carefully eliminated the dent.

"Look here," said Bullard, breaking a silence. "Did you or did you not swindle me with those papers?"

"An inadvertence on my part, if you please, Mr. Bullard."

"Oh, go to the devil! You can't blackmail me. Go and work your passage, if you like."

The other took a step forward. "Do you think I had better see Mr. Lancaster? I could explain to him that he is less guilty in the matter of Christopher's brother than he imagines himself to be. I could even prove -"

"Lancaster is unwell -"

"My disclosures might make him feel better - eh?"

Bullard felt himself being cornered. He reflected for a moment; then - "How are you going to satisfy me that the papers you say you hold are the originals?"

"I'm afraid you must take my word for it."

"Your word - ugh! Will you bring them here at nine o'clock to-night?"

"Will you bring £500 in five-pound notes?"

It seemed that they had reached a deadlock. Bullard was thinking furiously.

At last he spoke. "No; I will bring one hundred pounds, and I will tell you how you may earn - earn mind - the remaining four. If you accept the job - not a difficult one - you will give me the papers in exchange for the hundred."

"But -"

"Not another word. Take my offer or leave it." Bullard turned to his desk. "And don't dare to lie to me again. Also, ask yourself what chance your word would have against mine in a court of law?"

At the end of twenty seconds the other said quickly: "I will be here at nine," and turned towards the door.

"By the way," Bullard called over his shoulder, "you had better come prepared for a night journey. And, I say! as you go out now try to look as if you had been damned badly treated. Further, before you come back, do what you can to alter that face of yours."

The door closed; Bullard's expression relaxed. For the first time in his life he had been within an ace of admitting - to himself - defeat. But all was not lost, even if he accepted Marvel's story, which he was very far from doing, his intelligence revolting no less at the bare idea of Alan Craig's existence than at that of the young man's supporting it as a quay labourer. Furthermore, were it proved to him that Alan had actually come from the Arctic, he would still not despair. He would have to act at high speed, but he was used to crises. As to Mr. Marvel, well, that clever person was going to be made useful to begin with; afterwards....

Bullard broke away from the clutches of thought to attend to the more urgent letters. He had just finished when his colleague came in.

"Hullo, Lancaster," he cried cheerfully, "I fancied your doctor had commanded rest. Glad to see you all the same. As a matter of fact, I was coming to look you up shortly."

"Couldn't rest at home," returned Lancaster, seating himself at the fire. "I say, Bullard," he said abruptly, "you'll be good to my girl - won't you?"

Bullard's eyebrows went up, but his voice was kindly. "Do you doubt it, Lancaster?"

"N-no. But you can surely understand my feelings - my anxiety. She - she has been a good daughter."

Bullard nodded. "It won't be my fault," he said quietly,

"if Doris regrets marrying me."

"Thank you, Bullard." As though ashamed of his emotion the older man immediately changed the subject. "Anything fresh this morning?"

The other smiled. "One moment." He got up, went to a cabinet and came back with a glass containing a little brandy. "The journey to the City has tired you. Drink up!"

"Thanks; you are thoughtful." Lancaster took a few sips, and went white. "Bullard, have you something bad to tell me?"

"Finish your brandy. ... Well, it might have been worse. Steady! Don't get excited, or I shan't tell you."

After a moment - "Go on," said Lancaster.

"Marvel has come back from Canada."

"Ah! ... But I always feared he would. More money, I suppose?"

"Precisely. Only he brought a piece of news which I have so far refused to credit, though doubtless stranger things have happened. Pull yourself together. Marvel declares that, a fortnight ago, he saw Alan Craig in the flesh."

"Alan Craig!" Lancaster fell back in the big chair. "Thank God," he murmured, "thank God!" Tears rushed to his eyes.

" Better let me give you details, few as they are, before

you give further thanks," Bullard said. "Bear in mind what manner of man Marvel is; also, that his story was part of a threat to extort money."

A minute later Lancaster was eagerly asking: "But don't you think it may be true, Bullard?"

"For the present," was the cool reply, "we are going to act as though it were true, as though the will were waste paper - not that I ever considered it as anything but a last resource, for its production would involve sundry unattractive formalities."

"And yet," said Lancaster uneasily, "you told me once of a man who had seen Alan die."

"Leave that out for the present. I shall deal with Flitch presently, and God help him if he has played a game of his own! Meantime, the one object in view must be the Green Box at Grey House."

"For Heaven's sake be cautious! You spoke of bribing the man Caw, but the more I have thought of it -"

"That's past. There is no time for delicate negotiations. If the box is still in the house, we must find and take it; if elsewhere, we must make other plans. But I'm pretty sure it has not gone to a bank or safe deposit. Christopher meant it to remain in the house, so that it should be part of his gift to Alan."

"Caw will be on the alert."

"He will not expect a second attempt all at once. Hang it, man, we must take risks! £600,000! I'm not going to let any chance slip." Bullard went over to his desk and picked up a cablegram. "The Iris mine is flooded again. That means at least a couple of thousand less for each of us this year."

Lancaster groaned helplessly. "Trouble upon trouble! But I cannot face another visit to Christopher's house -"

"Be easy. You shall be spared that. I think I had better tell you nothing for the present - except that I may take a run over to Paris within the next few days."

"Paris!"

"You can say I'm there if any one asks."

Lancaster drew his hand across his brow. "Sometimes," he said slowly, "I wish I were at peace - in jail."

"Don't be a fool! You'll feel differently when we open the Green Box."

The other shook his head. "There's another point that has worried me horribly. We have thought we were the only persons outside of Grey House who knew of the diamonds; but who was the person who took the box that night? Whoever he was he must have seen us and heard something of our talk."

"Yes," said Bullard, with a short laugh, "it seems very dreadful and mysterious, doesn't it? - especially as Caw recovered the diamonds so speedily. I've thought it out, Lancaster, and I've struck only one reasonable conclusion. There was no fourth person present that night. Caw was fooling us all the time. The cupboard is

John Joy Bell

really a passage to another room, made for old Christopher's convenience, no doubt. How's that?"

"Caw acted well, if he were acting. And why should he have suspected us at all?"

"Simply because he happened to know what was in the box. Who would trust a fellow creature alone with £600,000 in a portable form? And Caw was probably in the position of guardian. Have you a better theory?"

Lancaster leaned forward, staring at the carpet. "It came into my mind last night," he said in a queerly hushed voice, "that it might have been ... Christopher himself."

"Good God, man, positively you must have a change of air! Do you doubt that Christopher is dead?"

A pause.

"Bullard, what you and I, his friends, were doing that night was enough to - to make him rise - oh, no, I don't mean that - though the diamonds were so much to him. It was a crazy thought. I must get rid of it."

"I should say so." Bullard forced a laugh. "Meantime, you may comfort your soul with the assurance that you'll have nothing to do with this fresh attempt, except to share in the spoil. If I were you, I'd go home now and get Doris to join you in a long run into the country. Let the wind blow away those absurd fears and fancies. I'm calling on your wife this afternoon, you know."

The other rose obediently. "Your news has upset me. I

don't know what to think. Marvel was always such a liar. I - I suppose nothing I can say or do will move you from your present course?"

"Nothing, Lancaster."

Lancaster sighed and with shoulders bowed went out.

CHAPTER X

The same night Teddy France started on his quest, wishing with all his heart that it were cleaner work. Still a beginning had to be made. He had not the flimsiest clue to direct him, but the thought occurred to him that it might be worth while to attempt to learn in what manner Bullard spent some of his evenings. Bullard, he was aware, had of late been living at Bright's Hotel, a select and expensive establishment situated within hail of Bond Street.

About eight o'clock Teddy sauntered across the lounge of Bright's, as though looking for a friend, and glanced through the glass doors of the dining-room. To his satisfaction, he saw the man he wanted, seated at a table, alone, and not in his customary evening dress. Teddy retired, left the hotel, and at the opposite pavement engaged a taxicab. He got inside, after instructing the man to be on the alert. He lit a cigarette, telling himself that, by a thousand to one, he had embarked on a futile, idiotic errand. However, within half-an-hour, Bullard appeared in the hotel doorway, and spoke to a braided personage who promptly whistled for a cab. By the time he was on board, the motor of Teddy's cab was running, the chauffeur in his seat. Presently the two cabs rolled away from their respective pavements.

Five minutes later Teddy let out a grunt of disgust. Bullard was evidently making for the City, presumably for his office. "Drop it!" said common sense; "go on!" said instinct ... and Teddy went on.

It was nearing nine o'clock when Bullard's cab drew up at the magnificent entrance to Manchester House in New Broad Street, at that hour a well-nigh deserted thoroughfare. As Teddy was driven past he saw Bullard run up the steps. Twenty yards further on he got out, settled with his man, and strolled back. Entering the huge headquarters of several hundred mining and finance companies, and noting that the lift was closed for the night, he proceeded to search the oaken boards which formed a sort of directory of the tenants inscribed in gilt lettering. He learned that Bullard's office was on the fourth of the nine floors; at the same time he memorised the name of a firm on the fifth floor. Then he ascended leisurely. Care-takers and cleaners were about, but apparently they had finished their tasks above the fourth floor. He spoke to one of them, an elderly man.

"Can you tell me if Mr. Stern of Stern & Lynoch has returned?"

"No, sir. I've just left their office on the fifth floor. Nobody there."

Teddy consulted his watch. "I'm a little before my time; guess I'd better go up and wait."

The man nodded as one who didn't care whether the enquirer died or lived, and went about his business.

There was an indifferent light left on the fifth landing

John Joy Bell

and the stair leading to it. Teddy found a point of vantage whence through the wire walls of the shaft he could obtain a view, not of Bullard's office itself, but of the corridor leading thereto. On the way up he had noted that the Aasvogel Syndicate's door was just round the corner and that it was the only one showing a light.

Calling himself a fool for his pains, he settled down to the wretched game of spying. He had not long to wait - much to his combined astonishment and gratification. "This must be my lucky night," he reflected. A man appeared on the landing - a foreign-looking person with a heavy dark moustache under an oddly shaped nose, wearing eyeglasses, and carrying a suit case - and made for the corridor. Ere he turned the corner he cast an anxious glance over his shoulder, which glance was more cheering to Teddy than a pint of champagne would have been just then. And next moment the gentle opening and closing of a door further delighted and excited him. Without a doubt the man had gone into Bullard's office!

Within the minute Teddy was again calling himself names. Ass! Was there anything even mildly extraordinary in the visitor or the visit? After a while he decided that he could not lose much if he transferred his espionage to the outside of Manchester House. Fortunately it was a fine night, for, as it came to pass, he had nearly two hours to kick his heels.

Then the Aasvogel's visitor came forth alone, and in haste, and turned in the direction of Liverpool Street. Shortly afterwards he boarded a King's Cross bus, mounting to the top. Teddy took a seat inside, still calling himself names , yet unable to abandon the absurd chase.

At King's Cross the man, along with a dozen passengers, got out and made for the main-line station. Teddy followed at a discreet distance till within the booking hall, when he put on speed and contrived to be close to his quarry as the latter stopped at a ticket window - first class - to Teddy's amaze. He heard him book "return Glasgow."

Now the Glasgow portion of this particular night train, usually an exceedingly long one, is next to the engine. Perhaps that is why the Great Northern Company has kindly placed a little refreshment saloon towards the extremity of the platform. The traveller, after a glance at the train, entered the saloon. The weary sleuth resisted the desire for a drink and proceeded to stroll up and down the Glasgow portion. Five minutes before the train was due to start the traveller reappeared wiping his mouth, and got into a vacant compartment. He placed his suit case on a seat and went out into the corridor.

"Well," Teddy said to himself, "that jolly well ends it. The old story - suspect a Johnny because he doesn't look a handsome gentleman! Serves me right!" All the same, he lingered, a few paces from the carriage. Four minutes passed and the traveller was still absent. Thirty seconds left ... fifteen ... five ... the starting signal ... the first, almost imperceptible movement of the prodigious train.

Just then the traveller reappeared in the compartment, picked up the suit case, sat down and opened at. But - Teddy sprang forward open-mouthed - it wasn't the same man! The train was gathering speed. Teddy ran alongside and stared in. The traveller glanced over his shoulder, just as that man had done on the office landing, then turned away. But again Teddy had caught a glimpse of a profile including an oddly shaped nose. Why, good Lord! it *was* the same man - only the beggar had lost his eyeglasses and moustache! ... Our sleuth had made a discovery, indeed, but how on earth was it going to profit him? Disregarding expense - no new failing on his part, to be sure - he took a cab back to Manchester House.

The Aasvogel office was in darkness. The surmise might easily be wrong, Teddy admitted to himself, yet it did look confoundedly as though Bullard had returned to the City that night with the particular object of meeting the quick-change gentleman now on his way to Glasgow. At all events the affair was interesting enough to spoil another night's rest for Teddy France.

Two mornings later Bullard received the following brief note, which was undated and unsigned, in an envelope postmarked Glasgow:

"No one on premises at night. Probably tomorrow night."

Bullard informed the chief clerk and telephoned to Lancaster that he was leaving for Paris by the night train. Apparently he reached there safely, for next morning the office received a telegram relating to some company business, not, perhaps, of the first importance, handed in at the Gare du Nord office and signed Bullard. And Teddy, calling at the Lancasters' house in the evening, just to obtain a glimpse of his beloved, who alas! was with a dinner and theatre party, learned from Mr. Lancaster, who was always glad to see the young man, that Mr. Bullard had run over to Paris. Which was naturally rather astounding news to Teddy, whose own eyes had seen Mr. Bullard enter the Glasgow sleeping car at Euston, about twenty-four hours earlier.

John Joy Bell

CHAPTER XI

Dr. Handyside was too fond of his easy-going seaside existence to be readily induced to leave home. At the same time, he had not severed all ties with Glasgow, which ties included a select coterie of kindred spirits who dined together once a month during the winter in a somewhat old-fashioned restaurant; and he would have been exceedingly loth to miss one of their cosy gatherings. But he insisted on sleeping in his own bed, and accordingly, there being no steamer connection at so late an hour, it was his custom to return by train to Helensburgh and thence complete the journey in his car which he drove himself, reaching home shortly after midnight.

To-night's dinner, however, had seemed hopelessly beyond his reach, owing to his injured foot, which as yet merely allowed him to hobble a few yards, and which would have been worse than useless in driving. But we are never too old to worry over trifles, and in the course of the morning, while in the garage, he blurted out the difficulty to Caw. It was really an appeal, and at any other time Caw would have been mildly amused. Now he was embarrassed, for while anxious to oblige the doctor, he had no intention of losing all connection with Grey House for several hours in the middle of the night.

He shook his head. "I only wish I could drive you home to-night, sir," he said, "but you see -"

"All right, Caw," said Handyside, looking ashamed of himself, and hobbled off, still hankering, however.

An hour later Caw came to him in the study, and presented an open telegram. "Will you be pleased to look at this, sir?"

The doctor read: -

"Registered letter received. Best policy.

"BULLARD."

"God bless me, Caw! - the man's in Paris!"

"Quite so, sir. I shall be glad to have your instructions for this evening, sir. Very thoughtful of Mr. Bullard, if I may say so - damn him!" - the last inaudible.

"I've been wondering whether he would acknowledge the notes," said Handyside, brightening up and hobbling to the door. "Marjorie," he called, "for Heaven's sake see if I've got a decent tie for to-night!"

* * * * *

And now it was midnight. The southerly gale which had broken out late in the afternoon was booming up the loch, bombarding the house, and gusts of bitter rain were thrashing the exposed windows.

Marjorie flung a couple of logs on the study fire and returned to her book. She had prepared sundry comforts for her father and was awaiting, not without anxiety, his arrival. She was thankful he had Caw with him. A large portion of the journey was being made in the very teeth of the tempest.

A tap on the door brought her round with a start. It was only Mrs. Butters, the housekeeper, or, to be precise, the head and shoulders of that estimable but slow-witted female, heavily swathed in a couple of grey shawls.

"What on earth is the matter?" exclaimed Marjorie. "Why aren't you in bed?"

"Please, miss, do you think I might do something to stop the alarum clock of that Mr. Caw?" Mrs. Butters was not yet at all sure of Caw. "It's been ringin' for close on an hour, and I can't -"

The girl was up like a shot - her face set, her hands clenched. What was she to do? It would take an age to explain to the housekeeper, who, when she did under-stand, would in all probability simply howl helplessly.

"Close on an hour," she said to herself. "Oh, Heavens, the thing must have been done long ago!" Still, she could not be absolutely sure. She glanced at the clock. No, her father and Caw were not even due yet.... "Mrs. Butters," she managed to say in a fairly steady voice, "please go back to bed. I - I'll attend to the alarum immediately. Go at once or you'll catch your death of cold."

Left alone, she grew pale, but within the moment she had crossed to a bureau - her own - and was taking out a purchase made in Glasgow the previous day. "Oh, why didn't I practise in the wood this morning, as I said I would?" she sighed, fumbling with a little ivory-handled revolver. She shuddered. "Oh, I can't ... I daren't ... I *must*!" And ran from the room.

Marjorie will never forget that journey through the passage, her light a flickering taper, for the electric illumination was no longer in operation. At the end of it she had literally to force her limbs to mount the narrow stairs. At the top, with her ear to the closed door, she could hear nothing save her pounding heart. There was no keyhole, no crevice whereby she might know whether it was light or dark on the other side. Caw had spoken that morning of making a peep-hole in the door. She would have given much for one now. And the taper was burning fast.

"They must have gone," she thought, "yet how can I be sure? On such a night they might be tempted to stay awhile from the storm." Hand with revolver pressed to breast, she listened again. Not a sound. But the silence might be explained by the presence of a solitary man, she told herself, not necessarily one of the two she had seen that other night. A rough brute, perhaps, who would stick at nothing in that empty house. Yet the very thought pricked her courage even at the moment when the descending flame stung her finger. Unlike Caw she was under no obligation to his late master. If a thief was there, she would shoot before she would let the Green Box go.

She dropped the taper, trod on it, and gasped to find herself in utter darkness. Once more she laid her ear against the panel, and this time, surely, a sound reached the straining nerves - a faint noise of something solid though not ponderous falling upon something less resonant than wood, less dulling than carpet. She felt like collapsing. But her will, her pride, came to the rescue. "If I don't open that door," she said to herself, "I'll be ashamed of myself for the rest of my days."

Her finger fluttered on the spring-button and pressed; her hand pushed. As the door gave she perceived that the room *was* lighted, though not brilliantly; she heard nothing but a howling of wind and a rattling of rain. A whiff of smoky coal met her nostrils. The silent moving door was now half open. She took a couple of steps inwards and halted, her left hand clinging to the door's edge, her right clutching the pretty weapon. And she all but screamed....

Under the lights of two candles on the mantel, in an easy-chair drawn up to the recently kindled fire, reclined a man, his head thrown back, his eyes closed. His legs were outstretched, his boots on the hearth, steaming, one of them in dangerous proximity to a large coal evidently newly fallen. On another chair lay a drenched greatcoat and cap.

The man was young, somewhat slight of build, of fresh and pleasing countenance, clean shaven, of indeterminate colouring. His crisp hair was so trim in spite of its dampness as to suggest the attentions of a barber within the last twelve hours. His hands were rough and bore traces of scars; the fingers, though slender for a man, might have belonged to a labourer's; the first and second of the left hand resting on the chair-arm held a cigarette - unlighted. The expression of his countenance was happy - contentedly so.

" Oh!" thought Marjorie, "he *couldn't* steal!" and in the

same breath perceived that he was not asleep. He moved slightly, with a lazy grunt.

His hand wandered to a pocket, felt within, came out empty, and wandered to another, with like result. "Hang it!" he muttered, and opening his eyes, tried, absurdly enough, to see what might be on the mantel without the trouble of rising.

Neither bold nor fearful now, simply fascinated and wondering whether he would get up or do without matches, Marjorie watched him. And the next thing she knew was that his eyes were staring into hers. Then fear, suspicion and sense of duty returned with a rush. The men who had already attempted to steal the Green Box had been just as well dressed - better, indeed. She was taking no chances. With firm determination, but also with a wavering hand, she raised the revolver.

"Great Heaven!" shouted the young man, "be carefull or you'll hurt yourself!" He wriggled up and sprang to his feet.

"Who - who are you?" Marjorie demanded with a regrettable quaver. "Have you come after the Green Box? Because, if so -"

"Would you mind," he said very gently, "putting down your pistol? Those things are so apt to go off unexpectedly, and at the moment you appear to be aiming at my uncle's best beloved Bone - "

The revolver fell softly on the thick carpet. Marjorie felt like falling after it.

"Thank you," he said gratefully. "You have mentioned

a Green Box, but having brought no luggage, I don't seem to grasp -"

"Your uncle!" she whispered.

"Mr. Christopher Craig." He regarded her for a moment and his expression changed. "Good Lord!" he exclaimed, "is it possible that he is no longer tenant of the house? You see, I arrived late, and deciding not to disturb any one, just proceeded to make myself comfortable for the night, and -"

Marjorie pulled herself together. "You are not -"

At that instant Caw, breathing hard, sprang from the darkness, then stopped as if shot.

"Well, Caw," said the young man, "I'm jolly glad to see you."

"Oh, my good God!" gasped Caw, "it's Mr. Alan!" He began to shake where he stood.

"Confound me!" said the young man under his breath, "I clean forgot I was supposed to be dead a year." He strode over to the servant. "Shake hands, Caw, just to make sure I'm of ordinary flesh and blood. I'm sorry to have upset you like this," He turned to the girl. "And to you I make my apology for having alarmed -"

"You didn't!"

"- for imagining I had alarmed you," he corrected himself with a bow and twinkling eyes.

The latter drew her smile despite her still jangling

nerves. "I suppose I have to apologise, too," she said, "for taking you for a - a burglar."

"Not at all, because - I may as well confess it at once - no burglar can be more anxious to avoid discovery than I am - or was."

Caw found his speech. "Mr. Alan, sir, I - I haven't words to express my feelings at seeing you alive and well - I really haven't." He turned away with a heave of his shoulders as Dr. Handyside, limping painfully, appeared in the doorway.

It was his turn to be astounded, but his welcome when it came was of the heartiest. "I take it," he went on, "that Marjorie, my daughter, and you have already made each other's acquaintance."

"If Miss Handyside will have it so," said Alan, repressing a smile as Marjorie, with a decided return of colour, stooped and secured the revolver which had escaped her parent's eye. "Naturally Miss Handyside was a little surprised to find me here until I explained who I was." His gaze travelled to the servant who stood apart in meditative regard of the clock. "Caw, how is my uncle?"

Handyside prevented a pause. "There is so much to tell you, Mr. Craig, that I propose an adjournment to my study where we shall find some refreshment which I fancy you can do with. You are not aware, I believe, that your uncle had a private passage built between our two houses, which not only explains our appearance here, but provides a short route to food and warmth."

" Then my uncle - " began Alan , evidently a

little puzzled.

"Your pardon, Mr. Alan," said Caw, coming forward, "but it is necessary to ask you one question. How did you get into the house?"

The young man laughed. "I suppose you don't think it worth while locking doors in these unsophisticated parts. After I had rung twice, and was wondering what was going to happen to me, I found that the outer door was unfastened and that the inner door was not locked. So I came in and made myself at home, unwilling to disturb - What's the matter. Caw? And you, doctor? Why, Miss Handyside, what have I said?"

But none of the gravely concerned faces was looking in his direction.

With a heavy sigh Caw went over to the writing table, stopped and drew out the deep drawer on the right.

For a moment or two there was no sound save that of the storm. Then, with a gesture of hopelessness, Caw slowly raised himself.

"Yes," he said, in a small, bitter voice, "it is gone!"

CHAPTER XII

Alan Craig, as he afterwards stated, had entered Grey House at a quarter before midnight; the clock had attracted his attention as soon as he lit the candles. The candles, he had noticed, had been used not long previously, for the wicks were softish, and he had been aware of an odour of tobacco, not stale, in the atmosphere of the study. These two little discoveries had been sufficient to end the incipient idea induced by the stillness and chilliness that the house might be temporarily uninhabited.

Less than half an hour prior to Alan's arrival, the man Marvel left by unbolting the outer door. He had entered by cutting through a lightly barred window at the back, and would have retired by the same way but for the fact that he had wounded one of his hands rather severely, and could not risk disturbing his rough and hasty bandage.

But though injured and drenched to the skin, and facing a long tramp in the vilest of weather, he turned from the gates of Grey House in a fairly cheerful temper. He had done the job and done it easily. The Green Box reposed in his suit case, and would fetch four hundred pounds on delivery. Only four hundred pounds? Well, Mr. Bullard had named that sum, but perhaps - and Mr. Marvel grinned against the

John Joy Bell

gale - Mr. Bullard was not going to get off quite so cheaply. To Marvel's sort, possession is not just a miserable nine points of the law: it is all the law and as much of the profits as trickery can extract.

No, no! - he stumbled in the almost pitch darkness, and cursed briefly - Mr. Bullard was not going to handle his Green Box for much less than a thousand pounds! If only the key had been available, reflected this choice specimen of humanity, he would have had a look at the contents. Papers, Mr. Bullard had said - more incriminating documents, no doubt! Mr. Bullard was a very nice man, he was, but he could not always have it his own way. Mr. Bullard ...

A sound in, but not of, the storm, muttered in Marvel's ears. Peering ahead, he descried a small light. He was passing a wood at the time, and the windy tumult as well as the roaring from the loch made confusion for his hearing; but presently he recognised the intruding sound as the throbbing of a motor. "Some silly fool got a breakdown," he was thinking sympathetically, when a terrific gust caught and fairly staggered him. Ere he fully recovered balance and breath something cold and clammy fell upon his face, was dragged down over his shoulders and arms, blinding, pinioning him. The suit case was rudely wrenched from his hand; he was violently pushed and tripped; and with a stifled yell he fell heavily on the footpath and rolled into the brimming gutter.... By the time he regained footing, the use of eyes and ears, there was no light visible, no sound save that of wrathful nature.

*　*　*　*　*

In the doctor's study it was the host who undertook the

duty of breaking to Alan the news of his uncle's death; it was Caw who informed him of the old man's thought for him during the last year of life, on the very last day of it.

"You must understand, sir," the servant added, "that from the day after you went away my master was living not in his own house, but in yours. It pleased him to think of it that way, sir. 'I am not leaving my nephew anything,' he used to say to me; 'I have given him what I had to give.' He always believed in your safe return, though to others it seemed so impossible. There are many things to be told - you have already witnessed something that must have puzzled you, sir - but with your permission I will say no more till tomorrow, when I have got my wits together again, as it were."

"I think I can keep my curiosity under till then, Caw," said the young man, "and, to tell the truth, I don't feel equal to talking about my Uncle Christopher's affairs just yet. But if Dr. Handyside isn't too tired, I'd like to explain without delay why I made a secret of my existence, also why I came home - well, like a thief in the night." He glanced a little quizzingly at Marjorie, who blushed and retorted good-humouredly -

"Don't you think you owe me - us - the explanation, Mr. Craig?"

"Mr. Craig owes us nothing," Handyside said; "and I ought to remind him that while we were his uncle's friends - his most intimate friends, I might say, these five years - we are now, in a sense, intruders who have no claim whatever on Mr. Craig's confidence. Further" - the doctor's tone became rueful - "I fear I am greatly to blame -"

Alan interposed, "I want you to accept my confidence. I came home expecting to find myself as poor as when I went to the Arctic, and now I find my good uncle has altered all that, and in my new circumstances I may decide to change certain plans I had made. But I must first put myself right with my uncle's friends as well as his trusted servant. I'll make a short story of it - just the bare facts."

"As you will," said the doctor. "Caw, take a chair."

"If I may say so, sir, I prefer to stand."

"Caw," said Miss Handyside, "take a chair."

"Very good, miss," said Caw, and seated himself near the door.

"As I learned by consulting old newspapers on the other side," said Alan, "the expedition returned home safely at the time appointed; but I was reported lost - lost while out hunting. I'll start from that hunting episode, though trifling incidents had happened before then, which ought, perhaps, to have put me on the alert. One of the best shots, if not the best, in the expedition was a man named Flitch. Like myself, he joined in place of another man, almost at the last moment. He was a rough character, and his position was merely that of an odd-job man, but I must say he did most things well, especially in the mechanical line. He and I had frequently made hunting excursions together, but always with one or two other members of the party. And now, for the first time, we went out from the camp alone."

"Oh!" murmured Marjorie.

"We tramped an unusually long way from the camp - at Flitch's instigation, as I recognised afterwards; but in the end we were rewarded by coming on a fine bear. 'You take first shot,' said Flitch, in his curt, sullen fashion. I did, and was lucky. But the gun was not down from my shoulder when Flitch deliberately shot me in the back - not with his gun, but with a revolver he had never shown before -"

"The dirty hound!" growled Caw.

"I fell, feeling horribly sick, and as I lay I saw him toss the revolver into a seal hole. Then, as he stood staring at me, I must have fainted."

"The beast!" cried Marjorie.

"When I came to myself - how long I remained unconscious, I never learned exactly - I was on a sort of bed, and an aged Eskimo was bending over me. I had been picked up by a couple of his party out after seals. I must have lain there for weeks under the care of that queer old medicine man who, somehow, contrived to doctor or bewitch me back from the grave, for the wound was rather a bad one. The Eskimos treated me very decently, and it was not till I was convalescent that I realised I was their prisoner. I rather think they must have fled with me from the search party mentioned in the newspapers. The tribe, as far as I could gather, had a grudge against white men in general, though not against any person in particular. Well, I practically became one of them for the winter that followed. In time I grew fit and ready for anything, but they had annexed my gun and other belongings, which left me pretty helpless. However, I had the luck to save one of the young men during a tussle with a bear, and he was absurdly grateful. Eventually he planned a way of escape and guided me, after a good many mishaps, to an American whaler that had been compelled to winter in the ice. I told the skipper most of my story, but begged him to keep it quiet from the others, and between us we invented a plausible enough tale for the crew. The ship came out of the ice all right, but was wrecked, by running ashore, on the homeward trip. Some of us got to land and found our way into British Columbia. I had enough money to take me across Canada, but when I got to Montreal I was penniless. I took any jobs that offered until I had scraped together enough for a steerage ticket home -"

"But my master would have sent anything you had asked for!" exclaimed Caw.

"I did not doubt it. Only, you see, I was desperately afraid of my existence getting known, and -"

"But why?" - from the impulsive Marjorie.

"An obsession, if you like," said Alan with a grave smile. "During all the time of my convalescence, and in all the periods of leisure that followed, I kept wondering what on earth had made Flitch want to kill me. We had never had anything like a quarrel, and what had he to gain by my death? He had robbed me of nothing. It's a great big 'Why,' and I've got to find the answer to it. But I'm keeping you from bed."

"Go ahead," said Handyside. "Have you no suspicions?"

"I have; but they seem a bit far-fetched, especially now that I'm home. At any rate, I dare not mention them yet.... I arrived in Glasgow this afternoon, and got made as civilised-looking as was possible in a couple of hours. I had intended coming on here by rail and steamer, but an out-of-date time-table deceived me, and too late I found that the winter service just started gave no train after five. At the hotel they suggested motoring, and after a meal I started on what seemed a first rate car. But we had a breakdown lasting an hour, a dozen miles out of Glasgow, and then, running down Garelochside in the face of the storm, we smashed into the ditch. After making sure that the car was hopeless, I left the man at a wayside cottage and tramped the rest of the way. Hence my late arrival, and you know the rest."

"May I ask," said Caw, "if you met anybody on the road - near home, I mean?"

"I passed a person who seemed to be intoxicated, if judged by his violent language, but in the darkness and the rain we must have been practically invisible to each other."

"If he was using bad language, sir," said Caw, rising, "he was certainly not the party I am thinking of. May I retire, gentlemen?" he inquired, glancing towards Miss Handyside.

"Yes, Caw. You will have much to tell Mr. Craig to-morrow," said the doctor. "I leave it to you to explain why you were absent to-night. I doubt I shall never get over it."

Caw made a stiff little inclination, saying, "My fault

alone, sir," and went out.

"There goes a good and faithful servant," remarked Handyside; "and a good chauffeur, too," he added with a heavy sigh.

"Mr. Craig," said Marjorie, breaking a silence, "do you wish us to regard you as non-existent - I mean to say, do you wish your return to be kept a secret?"

"I'm going to sleep on that question, Miss Handyside," he replied.

"I can keep a secret rather well, and I believe father can, too, " she said. "Won't you tell us whom you sus -"

"Marjorie," the doctor interposed, "the lateness of the hour is telling on your discretion."

"I'm afraid it is." She got up, went to her bureau, scribbled something on a half sheet of paper, folded it neatly, and presented it to Alan. "Don't look at it till you are in your room," she said softly. "Good night, and sleep well."

Ten minutes later, in the guest's bedroom, Alan opened the paper and read the words -

"Mr. Bullard?"

CHAPTER XIII

By ten o'clock next morning Caw, who had risen at five, had Grey House in a fair state of comfort for the reception of its new master, if not its new owner. The producers of warmth and electricity were at work again; the elderly housekeeper, who in Christopher's time had never been upstairs, was recalled from a near village just when she was beginning to wonder whether, after all, perfect happiness was included in retirement with an ample annuity, in the garden a man was already reducing the more apparent ravages of the gale. Caw himself quietly repaired the moderate damage done by the thief of the Green Box. Following the instructions written by his late master, he had sent a telegram to the Glasgow lawyer. He was in the study dusting the thick glass protecting the clock when, about ten thirty, Alan arrived via the passage.

"An odd place for a clock," the young man remarked. "I had a look at it last night. But why 'dangerous,' and what's that green stuff?"

"Mr. Craig intended that the clock should not be interfered with before it stopped - nearly a year hence, sir. I understand the liquid is something stronger than water, but whether explosive or poisonous, I could not say, sir."

John Joy Bell

"Curious notion!" Alan pointed to the pendulum flashing gloriously in the sunlight now breaking through the racing clouds. "Are they diamonds?"

"Yes, sir. Worth, I have heard, about two thousand pounds."

"Then, of course, they would account for the precautions."

"Very likely, sir. Only I have a feeling that this clock has a meaning which we shall not learn until it stops. The maker constructed it in a locked room in this house, of which my master had the key, and I think my master knew even more about it than Monsoor Guidet did. Is the temperature here agreeable to you, sir?"

"A trifle warm, don't you think?"

"It shall be regulated to suit you, sir. Mr. Craig was sensitive to a degree, one way or the other."

Alan turned abruptly from the clock which, somehow, he was finding fascinating. "Well, now, Caw," he said, dropping into an easy chair by the fire, "hadn't you better begin to explain things?"

"At once, if you wish it, sir. But I'm hoping that Mr. Craig's lawyer from Glasgow, Mr. Harvie, will be here at noon, and as he may have fuller information than I can give, I was wondering if you would not care to hear him first. Indeed, Mr. Alan, I think it would be worth your while to wait, I could tell you a good deal, but my master did not tell me everything, though I have sometimes thought he meant to tell me more -"

"Very well, Caw. I'll ask only one question for the present. Did my uncle see anything of Mr. Bullard within the last few months of his life?"

Caw let fall the duster and recovered it before he answered: "Yes, sir. On the afternoon of the day of his death Mr. Bullard and Mr. Lancaster sat in this room with him."

"Mr. Lancaster, too!"

"Yes, sir."

"Thanks; that will do for the present. Now I have a letter to write. By the bye, do you remember my friend, Mr. France, being here once? I am going to send for him."

"I remember Mr. France very well indeed, sir, and I will do my best to make him comfortable. I think you will find everything here," Caw moved the chair at the desk.

Alan got up, then hesitated. "Do you know, Caw, I can hardly bring myself to take possession in this cool fashion right away."

"My master would have wished for nothing better. You will remember, sir, that all has been yours for the last eighteen months." Caw made the stiff little bow that betokened retiral.

"A moment. Caw," said the young man. "I take it that you would have done anything for my uncle."

"That is so," was the quiet reply, "and, if I may say so,

Mr. Alan, I am here to do anything for you."

He was gone, leaving Alan perplexed and not a little touched, for he could not doubt the man's sincerity. Presently he sat down and wrote to Teddy France, disguising his writing as much as possible.

"My dear Teddy:

"Before you go further, get a grip on yourself, then turn the page very slowly and look at the signature. Have you done so? You see, I want firstly to avoid giving you a sudden scare, and I hope it has been at least modified, old man; secondly, though I'm very much alive, I'm not advertising the fact at present and trust you to help me in keeping it dark. My story is too long to put on paper, but you shall have it all as soon as you can come to listen. Is it possible for you to get leave at once and come here for a couple of days? I badly want to see you again and ask your help and advice. Wire me on receipt of this. Relying on your secrecy,

"Yours as ever,

"ALAN CRAIG.

"P.S.: I'd like Doris to know, but only if you can find a way to tell her secretly. Ask her to trust me for a little while."

The visit of Mr. Harvie, the lawyer, who arrived at noon, meant little but disappointment for Alan. After a few polite words of congratulation, the lawyer dived into business, explaining Alan's position as the result of his uncle's deed of gift, and reciting a short list of securities mixed up with money figures.

"All very simple and satisfactory so far as it goes, Mr. Craig," he said, "and, of course, I am always at your service should you think I can be of the slightest help. Your uncle's will provided only for a legacy and an annuity to the male and female servants, also a thousand pounds to Dr. Handyside, the residue, about four thousand pounds, falling to yourself. My duty for the present ends with the delivery of this" - he handed an envelope to Alan - "though my responsibilities do not cease until the clock stops."

"I wish you would explain the clock, Mr. Harvie."

Mr. Harvie wagged his head. "My knowledge concerning the clock is confined to written instructions of my late client, whereby I shall be present when it stops, but my duties then will depend on circumstances. The significance of the clock itself I do not yet comprehend. All I know it that the clock will run a year from the date of my client's death, and that, at least twenty-four hours prior to the stoppage, I shall be warned and informed of the hour at which I must be present." He paused to purse his lips and continued: "I do not think you will resent my remarking, Mr. Craig, that for as sane a business man as ever I met, your uncle had some of the oddest ideas - which, nevertheless, you and I are bound to respect. Possibly a chat with Mr. Caw may dispel some of the fog you have stepped into on your otherwise fortunate and happy return home. I feel that Mr. Caw knows a great deal more than I, but in this case, at any rate" - Mr. Harvie permitted himself to smile - "what I do not know is none of my business."

"You can assure me that absolutely everything in this house belongs to me?" said Alan after a short silence. "You know of nothing which my uncle intended to make over to friends?"

"Nothing whatever. Mr. Craig was absolutely clear on that point when I drew up the Deed of Gift. Still, as I have said, in any new difficulty I am at your service. I liked your uncle, Mr. Craig. I once mentioned a sad case of unmerited poverty to him, and his generosity astonished, nay, shamed me. You have a good man's place to fill."

Mr. Harvie stayed to lunch - Caw performed wonders in the circumstances - and caught the two o'clock steamer. As soon as he was gone, Alan opened the envelope. If he had looked for revelations within, he was bound to be once more disappointed. The enclosure consisted simply of a letter, and not a lengthy one at that.

"GREY HOUSE,

"26th October, 1913.

"My dear Alan:

"It is written that we shall not meet again. My malady grows daily worse, and the end may come at any moment. But I am of good cheer because of my faith in your ultimate return. Whence comes that faith I cannot tell - but whence comes any great and steadfast faith? When you come into this house and the little fortune that has been yours since you left for the Arctic, you may meet with some puzzling things; you may even be tempted to say, or think, that the old man must have been a little 'cracked.' But one must amuse oneself, especially when thought gnaws and time hangs heavy; and if there happens to be a way of attaining one's chief desires which is not altogether a tiresome and conventional way, why not choose it, as I have done? Should my whims cost you trouble or annoyance, forgive me. Let things take their course, if at all possible, till the Clock stops. Trust Caw, who knows as much as I care for any one to know; Lawyer Harvie, who knows next to nothing; Handyside and his daughter who may, or may not, know anything. In my latter days my trust in human nature has been shaken, though not destroyed; yet I say to you: Rather a host of declared enemies than one doubtful friend. Farewell, Alan, and may God send you happiness. A man can make pleasure for himself.

"Your affectionate uncle,

"CHRISTOPHER CRAIG."

*   *   *   *   *

After a little while Alan rang for Caw.

The servant's eyes held a glimmer of anticipation induced by the lawyer's visit. Surely Mr. Harvie had been able to divulge something that would render his coming task a little easier, for Caw had still to tell of the Green Box and at the same time conceal the fact that Christopher Craig had died at bitter enmity with his two old friends - or at all events, the grounds of that enmity. As though Christopher had wished to lay particular stress on his desire for such concealment, Caw had found among his written instructions the following words: " At all costs, my nephew is to be spared the tragedy of his parents' ruin."

At Alan's first remark the glimmer went out.

"No, Caw, I'm no wiser than I was this morning. Mr. Harvie knows nothing except that he is to be present when the clock stops, and a letter written to me by my uncle, which he gave me, leaves me as much in the dark as ever. My uncle's letter says, however, that I am to trust you, and that you know more than any one."

Caw made a slight inclination. "May I ask if the letter makes mention of Dr. Handyside and Miss Handyside, sir?"

"I am to trust them also," Alan replied, with a smile, "as well as Mr. Harvie."

"Thank you, sir. As you have seen, sir, I have ventured to trust Dr. Handyside and Miss Handyside a bit of my own; in fact I was forced into so doing; and, though I had my master's word for it, if necessary, I am glad to hear it again from you, sir. As for Mr. Harvie, I take leave to hope we shall not require to trust him."

"Why on earth -?"

"Well, sir, he's a lawyer - "

"Good lord, Caw! What are you driving at? My uncle trusted him, and his letter -"

"If you'll excuse me, sir, you have just been telling me that Mr. Harvie knows next to nothing. Mr. Harvie, I beg to say, is a very nice gentleman, and as honest as any lawyer need hope for to be; but a lawyer is the last sort of human being we want to have in this business, sir."

"I'm afraid I don't quite grasp -" began Alan, amused by the other's earnestness.

"Well, sir, did you ever go to a lawyer to ask a question?"

"I can't say I have, that I remember."

"Then, sir, I have. I once asked a lawyer one question, and before he could, or would, answer it, sir, he asked me fifty, and then his answer was rot - beg pardon, sir - unsatisfactory. But what I mean is just this, sir. With all due deference to Mr. Harvie, we don't want outsiders asking questions. My master himself would have been against it, and I'm hoping you will understand why before very long, sir."

Alan sat up. "Before we go any further," he said, "will you tell me what you were looking for last night when you opened a drawer in that writing-table and - well, go ahead."

Caw took out his handkerchief and wiped his brow. "A green box, sir, that had been there a few hours earlier."

"The contents?"

"Diamonds, sir."

"What?"

"Diamonds, sir."

"I didn't know there were diamonds - except in that pendulum."

The other gave a faint sigh.

"Were those in the box of any great value?"

Caw moistened his lips. "Six hundred thousand pounds -"

"Oh, nonsense!"

"My master's words, sir."

"Then - why should they have been left lying there?"

"My master's orders, sir."

Alan opened his mouth, but found no speech. Said Caw: "You find it difficult to believe, sir, but there are other things just as difficult. For instance, I was forbidden to use any violence to prevent the box being taken away - that is, taken away by certain parties. A horrid position for me, sir."

"Yes," assented Alan, absently. Presently he went on: "Don't imagine that I doubt anything you have said, Caw - except that the diamonds, whose value there must surely be some extraordinary mistake about, were in the box."

"But, Mr. Alan, I can swear they were! It was I who closed and put the box in the drawer for the last time, at my master's request. He had been admiring them, as he often did -"

"Who were the parties who were to be allowed to take the box?"

After a moment's hesitation, - "Mr. Bullard, sir, and Mr. Lancaster. They were the only persons besides myself who knew about the diamonds. I should tell you that my master showed them the diamonds that afternoon."

"Good God!" said Alan under his breath. Aloud: "Are you telling me that you suspect those two gentlemen of st - taking the box?"

"They came here late on the night after my master's death, with that object, sir."

"But the box was taken last night."

"I can't swear that it was they who were here last night, but I can swear they would have had the box on the night I have named, sir, but for Miss Handyside."

"Miss Handyside! ... Sit down, man, and tell your story. I'll try not to interrupt."

"Thank you, sir." Caw drew a chair from the wall; for once he was glad to be seated. He told his story in a crisp, straightforward fashion, avoiding side issues, and his listener heard him out in silence.

There was a pause before the latter spoke.

"You've given me something to think about, Caw," he said gravely. "Meantime I'll ask only three questions. Have you any doubt that the box and its contents belonged entirely to my uncle?"

"None at all, sir. I remember his getting the box made - twelve years ago, I should say. Also, I knew he had made a great deal of money and was putting it into diamonds."

"He hadn't a duplicate box?"

"If he had, sir, I should have seen it. For the last two years of his life, I had to look after everything for him, even open his safe."

"I see. Now tell me: Did my uncle and Messrs. Bullard and Lancaster part on good terms that afternoon?"

Caw could have smiled with relief at the form in which the enquiry was put. "Why, sir," he said, with ill-suppressed eagerness, "they shook hands, and my master bade them a kind farewell. Mr. Lancaster was visibly affected."

"And they were back the next night!"

"Six hundred thousand pounds is a lot of money, sir."

Alan got up, strode to the window, and looked out for a minute's space.

"What would you say, Caw," he asked, turning abruptly, "if I told you that for the last eighteen months I have regarded Mr. Bullard and Mr. Lancaster as my best friends?"

The servant, who had risen also, replied respectfully: "I would say I was very sorry, sir."

"Indeed! - And if I told you that they had helped me

with a large sum of money - what then?"

"I should take the liberty, sir, of wondering what you gave them for it."

"Good Heavens!" the young man exclaimed, "the thing is impossible!" Controlling himself - "Thanks, Caw, I'll not trouble you more for the present."

"Very good, sir. When will you take tea?"

"I'm taking tea with Dr. Handyside."

"Very good, sir. I had better show you how the door works from this side."

*　*　*　*　*

It was a much worried young man whom Caw presently left alone. Until last night, when he had looked at Marjorie Handyside's note, it had never occurred to him to connect the crime in the Arctic wastes with the will he had signed in the Aasvogel Syndicate office, on that fine spring morning, eighteen months ago. His only suspicion, which in nine thoughts out of ten he had almost rejected for its absurdity, was against the man Garnet whose place he had filled in the Expedition. Garnet, who was an author and a vile-tempered fellow even in good health, had gone half crazy because the Expedition was not postponed for a year on his account. He had cursed Alan as a scheming interloper, and so forth, and had actually expressed the wish that he might leave his bones "up there." And last night, the girl's note had given his mind nothing more than a nasty jar. Bullard? - why, that idea, he had thought, was still more absurd than the other!

But now what was he to believe? Caw's revelation seemed to leave him no choice. And yet the thing appeared preposterous. Bullard and Lancaster were rich men, and while his acquaintance with the former had been comparatively slight, memories of the latter's frequent kindnesses and hospitality had warmed his heart many a time during his exile in the Arctic. Lancaster a trafficker in murder? - Lancaster the delicate, gentle father of the girl who had promised to wait for him? No, by Heaven, he would not believe it! As for Bullard -

The sinking sun shot a ray against the clock, and the glitter of diamonds roused him from his brooding. It was the Handysides' tea hour. He must try to get a quiet word with his hostess. He had met her at breakfast, but the doctor had been present. There were several things he wanted to say - must say - to her. She was brave - much braver than he had given her credit for a few hours ago - as well as bonny. As he descended to the passage he thought of how she had outwitted Bullard. Fortune was with him; he found her alone in the drawing-room.

"I always give father ten minutes grace when he's cleaning his car, and it's pretty messy after last night, while he has got to be careful with his foot," she explained. "By the way, Mr. Craig, I have to apologise for my curiosity of last night, but I'm not used to stories like yours."

"My apology is about a more serious matter," he replied. "I've just been hearing from Caw of how you rescued the Green Box at the first attempt to remove it.

It was the pluckiest thing I ever heard of, and I'm under a tremendous obligation to you."

"Oh, please don't!" she said, with a laugh and a blush. "You must understand that I hadn't a pistol that night. The pistol was an awful failure, wasn't it? You weren't a bit afraid - for yourself, anyway - and I was terrified. I'd have been far more effective if I'd just opened the door an inch and called 'boo!'"

"I fancy that would have finished me, Miss Handyside! But do you want to learn to shoot? If so, and you'd allow me, I'd give you a lesson or two, with pleasure."

"Would you? - But you mustn't tell father. Luckily he didn't notice the horrid thing last night. Now, I think I'd better give him a hail to come to tea."

"One moment, please," said Allan. "Would you mind telling me why you wrote down that name last night?"

She became grave at once. "Was it the wrong one, Mr. Craig?"

"I can only hope so. But what made you think it a possible one? Had you ever seen the man before that night?"

"No." She paused, then said slowly: "Mr. Craig, if he wanted your uncle's diamonds that night, it is likely that he wanted them long before then, and it must have occurred to him that your life stood in his way of ever getting them as a gift or legacy." She halted, and then asked: "Well?"

"This is for your ears alone, Miss Handyside," he said

on an impulse. "When I wanted very much to go to the Arctic and could not find the necessary money, Mr. Bullard and - and another man advanced it, and I made a will in their favour."

"Oh, how horrible!"

"And yet all that proves nothing with regard to the man Flitch."

"No more does this," she quickly rejoined. "But when I saw that Bullard man's face as he laid the Green Box on the table, I felt that there was a being who would stick at nothing. I'll never forget his expression. It was as if the humanness had fallen from a face. It was - devilish.... That was what made me write down his name last night." She held up her hand. "Hush!"

Dr. Handyside hobbled in, looking far from happy. "Has Caw told you how he came to be absent from his charge last night, Mr. Craig?" he asked.

"In the same circumstances I'd have been absent myself," said Alan.

Marjorie gave him a grateful glance. "Poor father feels as if he owed you over half a million," she said.

The guest laughed. "Well, he can easily feel that he has paid the debt - by taking the Green Box as seriously as I do!"

"In other words as a joke?" said Handyside sadly. "That's very generous of you, Alan, if I may say so, - to quote Caw - but the Green Box is too hard and cold a fact to jest about."

"Then let us ignore it, if you please. My uncle's letter, which his lawyer handed me to-day, requests me to let things take their course, if at all possible, until the Clock stops; and that's what I'm going to do so far, at least, as that blessed Green Box is concerned. As a matter of fact, the Clock interests me far more than the box."

"Why?" said Marjorie.

"I don't know, but there it is!"

"Have you any hope," asked Handyside, "that there is any chance of recovering the box or, rather, its contents? Forgive my harping on the subject?"

"No," answered Alan, thinking of Doris Lancaster. "And pray believe me, doctor, when I say that I care as little as I hope."

For which saying Marjorie could have kissed him.

CHAPTER XIV

The unspeakable Marvel reached London shortly after seven p.m., - nearly an hour late. A sleet storm had descended on the Metropolis. He took a four-wheeler to the City. It crawled, but he was glad of the time to rehearse once more the part he had decided to play, during the latter hours of the railway journey. Here was a desperate idea inspired by a desperate situation. A hundred other ideas had offered themselves only to be rejected. He shivered with more than cold, fingered the flask in his pocket, but refrained from seeking its perfidious comfort. There must be no slackening wits in view of what was coming.

At last the cab stopped at his destination. With stiffened limbs he ascended the weary flights of stairs, paused on the fourth landing to blow into his hands and flap his arms. Then, after a glance round, he turned into the corridor on the left. The door of the Aasvogel Syndicate offices was still unlocked, by arrangement. He opened it quietly, stepped in, and as quietly closed it, turning the key. With a fairly firm and confident step he advanced to the lighted room at the end of the passage. His old foolish, ingratiating smile was on his face when he entered.

Bullard swung round from his desk.

"Hullo!" he cried genially. "Got back! Beastly weather, isn't it? Just returned from Paris an hour ago. Sit down and warm yourself."

"Thanks, Mr. Bullard." Marvel took a chair at the fire and proceeded to chafe his hands. "Paris, did you say? Coldish there, I suppose?"

"Felt like snow this morning. By the way, I didn't get your note till my arrival here to-night."

Marvel began to feel that things were shaping nicely. "I sent it as soon as I could, Mr. Bullard. Awful weather up there last night - something ghastly. Wouldn't take on the job again for ten, times the money."

"Well, it's over, and I take it that you were quite successful."

"Oh, that part of it was easy, Mr. Bullard."

"Good!" With that Mr. Bullard's geniality vanished. "I say, where's the Green Box?"

Mr. Marvel grinned pleasantly. "Always in such a hurry, Mr. Bullard! But don't be alarmed; the Green Box is all right - very much all right."

"Look here, Marvel. I'm not in the humour for any humbug. I want that box - now!"

"And I want that four hundred pounds before I produce the box -"

"Well, the money's ready."

"- and another five hundred when you touch the box -"

"You impudent swine!" cried Bullard viciously. "So that's your game!"

"Well, Mr. Bullard, when I came to think it over in that ghastly blizzard, I saw you had inadvertently under-estimated the value of my services, and considering that I had already parted with those valuable papers of mine for one -"

"Oh, shut it, man! Do you take me for a fool?"

"On the contrary, Mr. Bullard! You want that box badly, and an extra five hundred is neither here nor there to you."

Bullard's expression was so ugly then that the pretender wavered. "Where is the Green Box? Answer!"

"Give me the four hundred, and I'll take you to it."

"Take me to it? I think not!"

"Oh, Mr. Bullard, surely you don't distrust me."

Bullard appeared to reflect, and said harshly: "One more chance. Bring the box here at ten to-morrow morning, and I'll give you two hundred extra, you dirty little thief!"

"Five hundred, Mr. Bullard," said Marvel gently. He could have hugged himself.

Again Bullard appeared to be lost in thought, his fingers toyed with the nugget on his chain. At last he said sullenly: "I might have known you would try it on, you scoundrel. But I must have the box first thing in the morning. It's awkward enough not to have it tonight." He turned to his desk and picked up an envelope with a typewritten address. He sat staring at it as though he had forgotten Marvel's presence.

Suddenly he wheeled and spoke. "You shall have five hundred in the morning -"

"And four hundred to-night, Mr. Bullard."

"Yes - an hour hence. Do you know the Victoria Docks? - Of course you do. Well, the street named here" - he tapped the envelope - "is close to them. Deliver this letter and bring me back an answer - and the four hundred are yours. Hold your tongue! The thing is too private for an ordinary messenger. It's entirely owing to your vile behaviour that this letter must be delivered to-night. Will you take it, or must I take it myself? Mind, if I do, you can go to the devil for your four hundred, ay, and the five hundred to boot. I've stood the limit from you, Marvel, and I'm quite equal to locking you up in our strong-room here till you're ready and eager to give up the box for nothing!"

"Come, come, Mr. Bullard," said Marvel, rising, "there's no need for all this - this roughness. I'll take the letter with pleasure if you'll give me a couple of hundred to go on with."

Bullard tossed the letter back on the desk, and proceeded to light a cigar.

Marvel took a step forward. "I was only joking, Mr. Bullard. I'll take your message, and trust you."

"Very well," growled the other, handing it over. "Take care of it. You ought to be back in an hour. You'll find me here."

"Eight you are!" said Marvel, and went jauntily from the room.

Bullard sank back in his chair. "The blind fool!" he murmured, and grinned.

An hour later he was dining in the Savoy restaurant.

About ten o'clock he was shown into Lancaster's library. He was in evening dress. He carried a suit case bearing, in the midst of many old labels, his own initials. The moment the door was shut he said -

"Where's Mrs. Lancaster? Didn't she get my note?"

Lancaster, his weary eyes blinking in the sudden rousing from a troubled nap, replied: "Yes, it caught her as she was about to leave the house with Doris. Is anything the matter?"

"Did Doris go alone?"

"Yes, but -"

"I wish you would tell Mrs. Lancaster -"

At that moment the lady entered, gloriously attired, her eyes smouldering.

"What's the matter, Mr. Bullard?"

"Thanks for staying at home in response to my request," he said suavely. "I have hopes that you won't find it a wasted evening. By the way, can you get rid of the attentions of your servants at so early an hour?"

Her sullen eyes brightened with curiosity. "I daresay I can, Mr. Bullard, but may I ask -"

"Please add the favour to the one already granted, and rejoin us here as soon as possible."

When she had gone, Bullard laid the suitcase on a chair, opened it, and took out the Green Box which he placed on the table. Then deliberately, and with a steady hand, he helped himself to a cigarette from his host's silver box, and lit it carefully.

"Well, Lancaster," he said, after exhaling a long whiff, "how's that?"

"Great Heavens!" Lancaster stopped staring and sat down feebly. "How did you get it? Where? Surely not in the same place as before!"

"That I can't tell you. The point that interests me is that it is here now. My story will keep - it's quite good enough for that. By the bye, where are your congratulations?"

Lancaster stretched out a shaking hand. "Take it away, for God's sake," he said. "Don't - don't let my wife see those stones. I tell you again, Bullard - I swear it - I don't want one more than will clear me of that one debt."

"Don't talk rot," was the light retort. "Mrs. Lancaster is going to choose one or two for luck. Between ourselves, as her prospective son-in-law I naturally desire to win her favour, as well as her entire confidence in my ability to provide suitably for her daughter. Besides, you must see that for your own sake it is better that she should be invol - pardon - interested. Why groan, my friend? Your troubles are over."

Mrs. Lancaster came in, gazed, and pounced. "What is it? What's wrong with Robert? What is all the mystery about?"

"This little box," said Bullard, patting it, "contains what I may call the Christopher Collection. No more questions now, if you please. Pray be seated. Are the servants -?"

"Yes, yes! Open it! I must see -"

"Unfortunately we lack the key. However, my expert tin-opener ought now to be waiting outside. I'll fetch him in, apologising for his uncouthness, which he can't help. He might like a little whisky, Lancaster. Ah, I see it is already provided. Better have some yourself, old man."

With these words, Bullard left the room to return a minute later with a rough-looking man in garb that might have been termed semi-sea-faring. There was nothing particularly sinister about his reddish-bearded face, but his eyes were full of fears and suspicions, and the ordinary person would have shrunk from his contact. His conductor having locked the door, said -

"This is Mr. Flitch, who -"

"Damn ye!" muttered the man with a start and a scowl.

"Or, rather, Mr. Dunning, who is going to open the box for us. But you will please excuse me while I first ask him one or two personal questions. Well, Dunning, you got my note?"

"Ain't I here?"

"You attended to the messenger?"

A mere grunt of assent.

"Under lock and key?"

A nod.

"Any papers?"

"Not a scrap."

"Money?"

"Never you mind about that. I done what ye wanted. He's safe enough. Come to business!"

For an instant Bullard looked like striking the fellow, but he laughed, saying: "Well, it wasn't my money. Now you can go ahead. That's your job on the table. Want a refreshment first?"

"No," growled Flitch, alias Dunning, with a suspicious look at Mrs. Lancaster. He slouched over to the table and seated himself. From a big pocket he brought a cloth bundle, unrolled it on the table, and disclosed an array of steel implements of curious and varied shapes. His fingers were coarse and filthy, but his touch was exquisite; it was something worth seeing, the way he manipulated his tools in the lock of the Green Box. In a little while he seemed to forget the existence of the spectators. He even smiled in the absorption of his work. There was no forcing or wrenching: all was done in coaxing, persuasive fashion. But it was no simple task, and thirty minutes went past.

Bullard, seated by the table, rarely shifted his gaze from the busy fingers. Mrs. Lancaster, on the couch, a little way off, devoured the casket with brilliant, greedy stare. As for Lancaster, in his chair by the hearth, he had turned his face from the scene of operations, and sat motionless, one hand gripping the chair-arm, the other shading his eyes.

At last the worker paused, drew a long breath, and made to raise the lid. But Bullard's hand shot out and held it.

"That will do, my man."

The worker let go with a shrug of his shoulders, and proceeded to bundle up his tools.

"I could do wi' a drink now," he grumbled. "Neat."

Bullard turned to the small table at his elbow, and poured out half a tumbler of whisky. The other, having stuffed the bundle into his pocket, rose, seized the glass, and gulped the contents. He set the glass on the table and held out his hand. Bullard laid a heap of sovereigns in it, and it closed as if automatically.

"Report when he's really hungry," said Bullard in an undertone, and the man nodded. "Mr. Lancaster," he said aloud, "would you mind showing this man to the door? I'll do nothing till you come back."

"Eh - what's that?" quavered Lancaster, exposing a dazed-looking countenance.

"Oh, I'll do it," said his wife, rising impatiently. "This way, my man."

He slouched out after her. There was silence in the room till she returned.

"What a loathsome creature," she remarked. "Flitch, you called him. Is not that the name of the man who went out hunting with Alan Craig, Mr. Bullard? No wonder -"

"Look here!" said Bullard, and lifted the lid.

The woman's breath went in with a hiss. Unable to resist, her husband crept from his place and stood peering over her shoulder.

Bullard lifted out the shallow trays and laid them side by side. The room seemed to be filled with a new light.

"Six hundred thousand pounds," Bullard murmured.

"Oh!" exclaimed Mrs. Lancaster in a reverential whisper. Then she started violently. "Nothing - nothing," she added quickly, and went on gazing. She had remembered that she had not re-locked the door, though she had drawn the heavy curtain. But she could not tear herself yet awhile from that delicious spectacle of wealth.

They were all three fascinated.

After a while Bullard moved slightly. "May I choose a lucky one for you, Mrs. Lancaster?" he asked, and picked out a fairly large stone.

He dropped it as though it had stung.

"What's this?"

He took up another and paused - paused while his face grew old.... A third he took from another tray and touched it to his tongue.... A fourth from the third tray.... A fifth....

Then his fist flew up and fell on the edges of two trays so that the contents shot up like a spray in sunshine and scattered over the room. In a strangled voice he yelled -

"Paste, by God! We're tricked!"

The door opened; the curtain was drawn aside.

"Father! Who was that dreadful man who -"

In the stifling silence, Doris, home hours before her time, stood there in dance gown and white cloak, a latch-key in her hand, her eyes wide with wonder - wonder that gave place to horror.

CHAPTER XV

It would have been beyond Teddy France to describe clearly his own feelings as he waited in the Lancasters' drawing-room late on the following afternoon. His dearest friend was alive; his dearest hope was dead. Yet how could he be otherwise than glad, if only on Doris's account? Early in the day he had sent her a note, express, begging her to be at home at five. This meant questionings and reproaches from Mrs. Lancaster, for she and her daughter had what she deemed a most important social engagement; but the girl was firm, and eventually the mother went off alone in a sullen temper.

In any case, Doris would have revolted from tea and tattle that afternoon. She had suffered a great shock the previous night. And since Teddy's note had suggested something most urgent, but told her nothing, she entered the drawing-room to meet him with foreboding added to a consuming fear. At the sight of him, so honest and kindly, she could have gone to his arms out of sheer longing for peace and comforting.

Teddy thought he had himself well in hand for his delicate task, but he was pale, and she noticed it.

"What is it?" she asked, all apprehension.

John Joy Bell

"Something good, Doris, but I can't tell you until you sit down."

"Good!" She forced a smile. She would not hurt his feelings, though apparently he had nothing very important to tell her after all. Poor Doris! all the big things in her life nowadays were of the evil sort. "Well, why don't you tell me, Teddy?"

"Because it's so tremendously good.'"

"Oh!" There was no mistaking his earnestness. Her mind turned quickly to Bullard. Had Teddy found out something?

"Doris, if you were given one wish, what would you wish for? You know, you can say anything to me."

She did not hesitate. "I'd wish that father were free from a great and terrible trouble."

"Well, we may hope for that, I'm sure. But if - if the wish would bring about something that - that you had believed past hoping for - what then?" He did not wait for her answer. "Doris," he said gently, "somebody has come home, safe and sound.... I had a letter from Alan Craig this morning. He is at Grey House now." He paused, puzzled. She was taking it so much more calmly than he had expected. The room was dusky and the fire-light deceptive, so he could hardly read her face. But presently he descried the glint of tears, and next moment she drooped and hid her eyes in her hands.

He spoke again. "For a reason which I don't yet know, Alan has come home secretly. He asks me to beg you to trust him for a little while. He must have a very strong reason for the secrecy. He wants my advice and help, so I'm leaving for Scotland to-night. If you have any message, please give me it now, Doris, and I'll leave you. You must want to be alone."

He waited, leaning against the mantel, watching her bowed head, torn betwixt loyalty and longing. Minutes passed before she uncovered her eyes and sat up. "Teddy," she said, "please sit down. There are things I must tell you before you go to Scotland." She wiped her eyes and put away the handkerchief as if for good. "You must be thinking me a very strange and heartless girl. You must be asking yourself why I am not over-joyed at the wonderful news. Don't speak. I suppose I don't properly realise it yet. Alan is alive and well! - I never was so glad of anything; I'll never cease to be glad of it. And just for a moment nothing else in the world seemed to matter. But - but I can't escape - I am like a prisoner told of a great joy which she can never look upon -"

"Doris, what are you saying? You don't for a moment imagine that Bullard -"

"Let me go on while I can. It's not easy to make my story coherent, so be patient... Something most awful happened last night. You know I was at the Lesters' dance, but I only stayed an hour - I got so worried about father. I pleaded a headache, and they got a taxi for me. It would be nearly eleven when I left. The fog was lifting. Just as the cab was reaching home I looked out and saw a dreadful-looking man coming from our door. He stared at me so horribly, so suspiciously, that I waited in the cab till he was well away. I had a latch-key and let myself in quietly. I went into the drawing-room. The lights were on, but the fire was low and no one was there. Mother had spoken of going early to bed, and I thought she must have done so. I went along to the library. There was no sound, but as I opened the door I heard a hoarse voice, though what it said I did not catch. It was followed by a smash. I drew back the curtain - you know how it hangs across the corner - and I saw -"

"Doris," the young man cried, "you're distressing yourself -"

"I must tell you, or go mad. Mr. Bullard was sitting at the table with his back to me. Father and mother were standing on the other side. They were just ghastly. On the table was a dark green roundish box, open, and some trays of diamonds. There were diamonds on the floor, too." Doris paused and wet her lips. "When I was a young girl," she continued, "before we came home, you know, Christopher Craig took me into his house one afternoon to give me some sweets, as he often did, and after bidding me not tell anybody, he showed me a dark green box, and in it were trays of diamonds. I never forgot it."

"But my dear girl -"

"Almost at once mother ordered me to go away. I went up to my room, and thought till I began to understand. I asked myself questions. What were those sudden journeys to Scotland for? Why was father so nervous afterwards? Who was the dreadful-looking man I saw? What made father and mother look so - so awful when I found them in the library?"

A heartsick feeling possessed Teddy, while he said:

"But, Doris, all those apparently ugly things may be capable of explanation."

"Wait! ... Of course I could not sleep. I didn't know what to do with myself. At three in the morning I went down to the library for a book, though I knew I should never read it.... And before the cold fire he - father was sitting alone, like a - a broken man. Oh, Teddy, you always liked father, didn't you?" Ere lie could reply she proceeded: "He was so lonely, poor father! I loved him better than ever I had done.... And after a while he told me things - things I can't tell even to you. But the box of diamonds was Christopher Craig's - now Alan's. Father would not blame Mr. Bullard more than him- self - but *I* know.... And now here is a strange thing: all those diamonds are false, and of little value compared with the real. And, do you know, father was glad of that, though it means ruin. Father supposes it was a trick of Caw's - Caw was Mr. Craig's servant - I used to like him - and he was really very fond of me when I was a little girl - and so I thought of a plan." She sighed.

"Am I to hear your plan, Doris?"

"Oh, it can never be carried out now. It was just this: I would make a journey to Scotland, with the box in my dressing-case - it's there now; but let me go on. Then I would hire a car for a day's run round the coast, and I would call at Mr. Craig's house - quite casually, of course - just to see how my old acquaintance, Caw, was getting on. That would be - or would have been - the most natural thing in the world. Of course Caw would ask me into the house, and would offer to get me tea. And while he was getting it - well, I know where the box used to be kept -"

"You brave little soul!"

"Oh, I'd risk anything for father," she said simply. "Once the box was back in its place, he would be safe from one horror, at any rate. The stones, though they are imitation, are worth several thousand pounds. Even if Caw found me out, I don't think he'd do anything terrible."

"But why should Caw suspect your -"

"He doesn't suspect - he *knows*! There are things about it I can't understand, but this morning my plan seemed the best possible. Before we went to bed father and I got slips of wood and jammed the box so tightly shut that you would have said it was locked - there was no key, you understand. Then - it was my idea - I got a little earth from a plant in the dining-room and made a few dirty marks on the carpet and window-sill. And I took the decanter and poured a lot of the whiskey out of the window, which I left open; and I put a soiled tumbler on the floor. And we broke the door of the cabinet where the box had been, and then we went up to bed, and I took the box with me."

Teddy stood up. "You perfect brick!" he cried; "I feel like cheering!"

She smiled the ghost of a smile. "And now you've guessed that there was a fuss about burglars in the morning, and Father 'phoned Mr. Bullard that the box was gone - which was not quite true, but as true as Mr. Bullard deserved - and Mr. Bullard came furious to the house, and left vowing vengeance on the dreadful-looking man who had unlocked the box the night before. So you see my poor little plan worked so far - only so far."

"What you mean," said the young man softly, "is that Alan must not know -"

"Caw is bound to tell Alan, has probably told him already. Don't you see how hideous the situation has become for father - and Alan, too?"

"I do see it. But now - you know there's not a bigger-hearted chap in the world than Alan Craig - suppose your father were simply to tell him everything -"

"Oh, never!" she exclaimed. "That would mean betraying Mr. Bullard, and father is - no, I can't tell you more. And I'm terrified that Mr. Bullard may yet discover that the box was not stolen last night after all - he's so horribly clever."

Teddy considered for a moment. "If the box were back in its old place," he said slowly, "that would end the matter in one way -"

"In every way, for Alan and I would never meet again -"

"You know Alan better than that, Doris. It is possible that Alan is not yet aware of the - the loss; even possible that Caw has not discovered it."

"Oh! if I could only hope for that! - not that I could ever face Alan again. But, Teddy -"

"Well," he said deliberately, "it might be worth while to act on the possibility. If you think so, I'm your man, Doris."

"You - you would take the box?" Her suddenly shining eyes gazed up at his face in such gratitude and admiration that he turned slightly away. "You would risk your friendship with Alan -"

"Nonsense! Don't put it that way, Doris; and don't talk of never facing Alan again. All this will pass. The thing we want to do now is to make it pass as quickly as possible. Give me the box and the necessary directions, and I'll do my best."

"Oh, you are good! I confess I thought of your doing it, but the idea came all of a sudden and I hated it. I still hate it. It's making you do an underhand thing; it's cheating Alan in a way."

"It's returning his property, anyway," said Teddy, not too easily. "But the more I think of it, the more necessary it seems. For we do not know that the box belongs to Alan alone; and supposing others were interested in the diamonds, false though they are, Alan might be forced to - to act. So let me have it now, and I'll clear out, for I can tell you I'm pretty funky about meeting Mrs. Lancaster with it in my hand. And, Doris, it's plain to me that your father is somehow bound to Mr. Bullard. If you can, find out how much - excuse my bluntness - it would take to free him. I'm a poor devil, yet I might be able to do something in some way -"

"Oh, Teddy, Teddy, what am I to say to you?"

"Not another word, Doris, or we'll be caught!" He laughed shortly, strode to a switch and flooded the room with light. There was a limit even to his loyalty.

Five minutes later he left the house with a tidy brown-paper parcel under his arm.

In her room Doris fell on her knees, and when thanksgiving and petitions were ended remained in that position, thinking. And one of her thoughts was rather a strange question: "Why am I not more glad - madly glad - that Alan is alive?" And she remembered that she had sent no message.

CHAPTER XVI

About four o'clock Bullard came into his private office full of ill-suppressed wrath. Lancaster, who had been waiting for him in fear and trembling, looked a mute enquiry.

"Yes," said Bullard harshly, "I found the beast after losing all those precious hours, and I may tell you at once, he had nothing whatever to do with the disappearance of the Green Box from your cabinet. He accounted for all his doings after leaving Earl's Gate, and I was able to verify his story. He went straight to a filthy gambling hell, lost a lot of money and got dead drunk. He's not decently sober yet."

"Then who could have done it?" Lancaster forced himself to say.

"Spare me idiotic questions! What I want to know is why on earth you did not take better care of the box."

"I daresay I ought to have put it in my safe," the other stammered, "but you left it with me as if it was nothing to you, and it - it really had become of so little value - comparatively -"

"Of little value! Why, its value to us might have been immense. The stones are paste, but what does that prove? Simply that Christopher's real stones are elsewhere. Christopher wasn't such a fool after all, and Caw has not tricked us wittingly. Caw imagines we've got the real stones right enough. At first I thought it might be otherwise, but my new theory is the one to hold water. The stones we saw that afternoon in Grey House were the stones we looked on last night -"

"Then - oh, my God! - Christopher was suspecting us, playing with us, all the time!"

"Keep calm. Remember, Christopher told us we should have our reward -"

"And this is it!" Lancaster groaned.

For the moment Bullard's self-confidence was shaken - but only for the moment. "Listen, Lancaster," he said steadily. "Christopher trusted no man absolutely - and who would, with half a million involved? He may even have doubted Caw. But Christopher was as friendly as ever, and he did not tell us, without meaning something, that the diamonds would be divided into three portions when his cursed clock had stopped. And so I believe that we shall yet get our shares - on a certain condition. - Are you following me?"

Lancaster nodded in vague fashion. " But the condition ..."

"Oh, Lord! hasn't it dawned? Why, the shares shall be ours when the clock stops, provided the Green Box, its contents intact, is then in its place in Christopher's study. Doesn't that hold water up to the brim?"

Lancaster turned away his face. He could have

cried out.

"And now," said Bullard bitterly, "you've let the Green Box slip through your fingers!"

"Why didn't you tell me all that last night?" cried the ill-starred Lancaster. He dared not tell Bullard that the Green Box was safe in his house. Bullard would never, however great the compensation, forgive trickery against himself; and Bullard's theory remained to be proved. Lancaster's soul now seized on its last hope: that Doris would be able to carry out her plan of conveying the box to Grey House. "Why didn't you tell me last night?" he repeated.

"Is that all you've got to say?" Bullard asked, a sort of snarl in his voice: "And I suppose you still expect me to put you right over that twenty-five thousand pounds!"

"My God, Bullard, but you *promised*! Oh, surely, you don't mean to fail me!"

Bullard threw himself into the chair at his desk. While he chose a cigar he regained something of his customary control. "I beg your pardon, Lancaster," he said presently. "I ought not to have said that, seeing that I have your daughter's promise, and do not doubt it. But the thing has hit me - both of us - hard.... Now don't you think you had better go home? Don't work yourself into an illness again. The Green Box is gone - for good, I fear. We can't call in the police, you know. But there are still things to be done - for instance, find out whether the real diamonds are in Grey House - and, mark you, I think they are! If I were only certain, I'd act on the will at once. That beast Flitch has been restless lately. Wants to leave the country. His evidence might be necessary in proving the loss of Craig. But we'll talk it out to-morrow. Are you going?"

Without a word Lancaster went out; but he sat in his own private office for several hours.

"What prevents me," asked Bullard of himself, "from throwing the worthless fool overboard and letting him sink?" And the only answer was "Doris. I believe he'd sell his rights in the will for -"

The telephone on his desk buzzed. Next moment he was listening to the voice of Mrs. Lancaster.

"I'm just going out," it said, "and I thought I ought to let you know about Doris. She had an express letter from young France this morning, and insists on staying at home now to receive him. You asked me to keep an eye on him. Any news? ... Why don't you answer?"

"Pardon, my dear lady. No; there is no news, except that I've been on the wrong track and have small hope of getting upon the right one. Thank you for letting me know; at the same time, I must keep to my bargain with Doris - no interference, you understand. By the way, has Doris referred to last night?"

"Not with a single word."

"Ah! ... I may call to-morrow. When does Mr. France arrive?"

"Five. But what's to be done about -?"

" To-morrow , please , to-morrow. Look after your

husband, will you? Good-bye."

The woman's soul was still seething with resentment against the man on account of the diamond fiasco, as she called it; at the same time, she was acutely sensible of the fact that now more than ever his friendship was essential to her interests.

Bullard lay back in his chair, frowning thoughtfully. Odd that Doris had made no reference to her glimpse of the scene in the library last night. Odd, too, that she should be receiving France at such an hour. And there were other things that struck him as odd. Lancaster's manner during their recent talk, for instance.... Francis Bullard had made the bulk of his fortune through unlikely happenings; it had become a habit with him to deal, as it were, in "off chances." At all events, he felt he would like to secure a sight of young France's face as the latter came from the house. It might tell him something. Before long he left the office and the City. Rain was beginning to fall.

It was falling heavily when Teddy came down the steps of 13 Earl's Gate. He was wondering which way would take him the more speedily to a cab, when a taxi appeared moving slowly towards him out of the streaming gloom. He whistled, and the chauffeur replied, "Right, sir," steering towards the pavement. The cab came to rest midway between two lamps. The man reached back and threw the door open. Teddy gave his address, and got in. At the same moment the opposite door was torn open; the parcel was snatched from his possession; the door banged. The cab started. Teddy had a mere glimpse of some one muffled to the mouth, hat brim drawn low. He turned and sprang out, staggered badly, almost fell, recovered his balance, and beheld a figure leaving the step for the interior of the retreating cab. He ran after it with a shout, - and remembered the dangers in publicity. Still, he continued to run, seeking to make out the number which had got plastered with mud. Hopeless! Travelling now at a high speed the cab disappeared round a corner, and Mr. Bullard had secured considerably more than he had come for.

At that moment the most wretched young man in London was Teddy France. What was he to do? He could not go North without informing Doris of the calamity. He could not trust the information to a letter. There he stood in the rain, cursing himself and imagining the cruel blow it would be to the girl. Suddenly he realised that no time must be lost. To wait until later in the evening would doom his chances of seeing Doris alone. He must return to the house at once - and as he took the first step, a car purred softly up to No. 13, and deposited Mrs. Lancaster. It was all up! To call now for the second time would rouse all manner of suspicions.

An hour later, drenched and in despair, he entered a post office and telegraphed to Alan, postponing his visit for twenty-four hours. Then he went home, and after worrying his mother by making a miserable dinner, went forth again, and, having changed his mind, returned to Earl's Gate. Mrs. and Miss Lancaster, the servant informed him, had gone out for the evening. Thereupon he determined to resume his shadowing of Bullard, whom he could not help connecting, directly or indirectly, with his late assailant. On this occasion he went about the business with some boldness. At Bright's Hotel he made enquiry at the office, after assuring himself that Bullard was not in the lounge or its vicinity.

"Mr. Bullard has gone to Paris for a couple of days," the clerk told him. "Left here twenty minutes ago."

Teddy had his doubts. He visited a number of stations and spent a good deal of money on cab fares, but failed to obtain the smallest satisfaction. He finished up at the midnight train from King's Cross. Had he been able to be in two places at the same time, he would have got what he wanted at St. Pancras.

In another part of the Midland train that carried Bullard North, sat the man Flitch, alias Dunning. Once more Bullard had need of his skill. He was decently clothed in ready-mades and almost recovered, roughly speaking, from his bout of the previous night. But he was full of melancholy. Bullard's fee for the opening of the Green Box, not to mention the small fortune annexed from Mr. Marvel, was all gone. What he had not lost over the cards had been stolen while he lay fuddled. Thus he had been ready enough for another job from his patron. The hapless Marvel, by the way, had been left secure in a dungeon-like cellar, with enough bread and water to keep body and soul together for a couple of days. Bullard had not had time to decide what to do with the creature.

In the seclusion of his sleeping berth Bullard examined the Green Box, forcing it open with a bright little tool. He would get a new key for it in Glasgow on the morrow. He cursed his luck and Lancaster. It would have gone hard indeed with Lancaster but for the existence of Doris. But Bullard was an optimist in his way. He was far from being beaten. Before the train was twenty miles on its journey his head was on the pillow; two minutes later the busy, plotting brain was at rest - recovering energy and keenness for the next act.

John Joy Bell

CHAPTER XVII

The night was fine but still very dark. An hour or so hence the moon at its full would make many things visible, and chiefly for that reason but also because he desired to return to London the same night, Bullard with his unsavoury companion, had arrived thus early at the gates of Grey House. Yet now it looked as though his programme would have to be abandoned, or, at any rate, drastically altered. For the house, as was plain to see, was occupied. There was no great display of lights, but a ruddy glow shone through the glazed inner door, and a thin white shaft fell from a slit between the drawn curtains of the familiar upper room.

"Caw taking a look round, no doubt," remarked Bullard, recovering from his first annoyance. "Wonder where the beggar has his lodgings and how long he is likely to hang about.

"Is the game up, mister?" asked the man at his elbow. "Cause if so, I'll just remind ye that I got to get paid, results or no results. Ye brought me here to open a door for ye, and 'tisn't my fault if the door's open already."

"Shut up till I've thought a bit." After a pause, Bullard began: "Pay attention, Flitch -"

"Not that name, damn ye!"

"Idiot, then. I was going to say that I could have done with an hour or two in that house, but that a couple of minutes would be better than nothing -"

"Couple o' minutes? That's easy - if ye don't mind a little risk."

"I'm used to risks," said Bullard, shifting the Green Box to his other arm. "But it is vital that I go in and out without being seen."

"Can't guarantee anything in this blasted rotten world," said Flitch, "but I think I can do the trick for you."

"How?"

"By bringin' whoever's in the house out at the back door while you slips in at the front."

"Do you mean that you will knock at the back -"

"Cheese it, mister! It's your turn to listen now. I've got in my pocket here a couple o' useful little articles which I never travels without when engaged on a job o' this sort - as I was pretty sure it was goin' to be. Them little articles is noisy, but ye can't have everything, even in Heaven, and as things has turned out now, they're just *it*." Mr. Flitch, at last in his element, paused to chuckle hoarsely.

"Oh, hurry up. You're talking of explosives."

"Go up one! Well, now, mister, suppose I sneaks up round to the back premises and fixes the pretty things all serene and comfortable to one of the outhouses, then lights the fuses and retires. In a little while - bang! bang! What price that for fetchin' yer friend out at the back door just to see if something hasn't maybe dropped off the clothes-line?"

"I believe you've hit it," said Bullard after consideration. "How long do the fuses burn?"

"Two minutes to a sec. The moment I've seen 'em go off proper I'll come back and wait for ye here, unless there's a chase, when I'll bolt for the car. Meanwhile you'll ha' crept up to near the house, ready to do yer bit as soon's ye hear yer friend movin'. It's chancey of course, but that's the sort o' trade it is. Better take this" - Flitch brought something from his breast-pocket - "in case the key's turned in that front door."

"Thanks; I've got one. Now say it all again so that we have no misunderstandings."

A few minutes later Bullard was crouching at the side of the steps beyond reach of the rosy light, his nerves taut, his whole being waiting for the signal. Smartly it came, and the stillness of the winter night was shattered.... Again!

The sound of some one running downstairs reached his ears; next it came from the oak-floored hall, diminishing; then a door - possibly one with a spring - went shut with a smash. Silence for a brief space, then noise from the back of the house. It was now or never.

Up the steps he bounded, yet halted to clean his boots on the mat. At that moment he thought he heard a cry, but nothing could stay him now. The shining tool in his clutch was unnecessary: the handle turned, the door opened. He sped across the hall and upstairs. Lights were burning in Christopher's old room; the pendulum of the clock scintillated as it swung. The fire burned cheerfully. There was a smell of Turkish tobacco. A book lay open on the writing table. Bullard noticed all these things and for an instant wavered and wondered. Without further pause, however, he placed the Green Box in its old refuge, carefully closed the drawer, and rose to go. Just for a moment the clock held him. Then he shook his fist at it and bolted. Closing the front door noiselessly after him, he went softly down the steps and across the gravel till he stepped upon the grass border, when he made swiftly, recklessly, for the gates.

A yard from them he all but fell over Flitch. That gentleman was lying face downwards, in a perfect agony of terror, scrabbling the gravel, mumbling to the Almighty to save him.

Bullard shook him, whispering savagely: "Get up, you fool! It's all right; we've done the trick -"

"O God, don't let his ghost get me! He was the first I ever killed, O God, and I wanted the money bad -"

"Curse you, Flitch! What the devil's the matter? If you won't come now, I must leave you to get caught - and that's the end of *you*!" Bullard gripped him by the collar and dragged him to his knees.

And now Caw's voice was heard calling: "Mr. Alan, Mr. Alan, wait till I get another lamp."

At that on Bullard's face the sweat broke thickly. With a gasp he let Flitch drop like a heavy sack, and started to run.

Not far beyond the gates Flitch overtook him.

Between thick sobs Flitch was moaning: "I heard his voice. 'Twas clear and strong. He's alive! ... I didn't kill him after all. Oh, God, I'm that thankful. I heard his voice. He's alive...."

Bullard swung his hand backwards and smote the babbling mouth. "Idiot! Do you think there's no punishment for attempted murder?"

"I'll confess - I'll confess to himself - and he'll forgive -"

"Will you! Is attempted murder your only crime? Shut your crazy mouth now, or it will be the worse for you."

And so, panting with exertion and passion, the fearful twain came to the car hidden in the wood. But Bullard was already recovering.

*   *   *   *   *

"No damage that I can see, except to the door of the garage," said Caw at last. "The car's all right."

"We'd better take a turn round the house," answered Alan, "though it's a search-light that's wanted tonight."

"Be careful, sir!"

"Oh, nonsense! Whoever it was has cleared out long ago." He moved off in advance, and was turning the corner, flashing his torch into the shrubbery, when a pale figure flew out of the darkness.

"You're safe!" cried a voice in tones of supreme relief. "Oh, but I was terrified for you!"

"Miss Handyside!" A flash had shown him a white-face, wide eyes, parted lips - also a hand gripping a pretty revolver. His finger left the electric button. Impulsively he softly exclaimed: "Does it matter to you, my safety?"

Darkness and a hush for the space of a long breath, and something happened to those two young people. Then Caw joined them.

"What was it?" the girl enquired, almost coldly. "We heard shots, and I ran through the passage - father is following - and I came out by the front door, and -"

"Weren't you afraid, miss?" Caw asked on a note of admiration.

"Yes, but -" she halted.

"The only thing that has happened, Miss Handyside, so far as we have discovered, is that some ass has been setting off fireworks against the garage door," said Alan. "Anyway, we can't do anything to-night. Let's go in and find Dr. Handyside. He'll be horribly anxious about you."

"There will be a moon shortly," Caw remarked, "and I'll take a look round then, Mr. Alan."

"Right! Let us have something hot - coffee and so on - upstairs."

"Very good, sir. Your pardon, miss, but that nice pistol -"

"Oh, *would* you take it away from me, Caw?" she sighed. "Keep it till I ask for it."

"Thank you, miss." Caw received the little weapon.

It was, of course, utterly absurd, but at the moment Alan felt annoyed with his servant.

They found the doctor starting to negotiate the stair.

"Ah," he cried, "glad to see you! What the dickens are your friends after this time, Alan? Stealing your coals for a change?" He laughed, but one could have seen that he was immensely relieved by the sight of his daughter.

Together they spent a couple of hours in the study and discussed a dozen theories. Perhaps Alan had least to say for himself. He was inclined to be absent-minded. On the other hand, he discovered, after a while, that he was disposed to look rather too frequently in the direction of his girl guest. Left to himself, he became aware that his plan for the immediate future was not altogether satisfactory. It was too late now to ask Teddy to delay his already postponed visit, but had that been feasible he would have made up his mind to start for London in the morning. Doris was in London, and his desire was towards her - or was it partly his duty?

CHAPTER XVIII

"So that's my story up to date," said Alan, and took out his pipe.

"And a very pretty story it is," returned Teddy, "if only there didn't need to be a sequel, old man. Of course, you can't possibly let the matter drop. I wouldn't myself."

The two friends were seated in the study of Grey House. The November twilight was failing. Teddy had arrived early in the day, and since then they had spent few silent moments together.

At the outset Teddy had forgotten all his troubles in the joy of the resumed intercourse, but before long even the tale of Alan's adventures had not served to keep them in abeyance - especially the thoughts of Doris. Teddy would never forget that interview when he had confessed to the losing of the Green Box. It had been a stunning blow to the girl who had considered only the disaster it entailed for her father. For Teddy she had had no reproaches, only gentleness. "You must have had a very wretched night," she said kindly. "Now we can only wait and see what happens. You must not worry too much."

" If I were sure Bullard had it, I'd go this minute and

John Joy Bell

offer every penny I have," Teddy desperately declared.

"I cannot imagine Mr. Bullard wanting the box for what it might be worth in money," she said; "I'm afraid he may use it in some way against father - and poor father was almost happy last night. - Oh, Teddy, I didn't mean to hurt you, you've done your best." He had turned away because there were tears in his eyes.

"Has Mr. Lancaster told you," he asked presently, "whether money would break the power of Bullard over him?"

After a little while her reply came in a whisper: "Yes; but it's an impossible sum - twenty-five thousand pounds." Teddy let out a groan, and just then Mrs. Lancaster had intervened.

"Yes," Alan was saying, "I'm going to make a big effort to find Mr. Flitch."

"He isn't by any chance a smallish dark man with a queer nose?"

"He's a huge, ruddy man - but what made you ask, Teddy?"

"I'll come to that when I'm telling you my little story of how I tried to shadow Bullard."

"Shadow Bullard! Good Heavens! - you!"

"Something to do in my spare time," said Teddy with a feeble smile.

The host eyed him in the firelight. "You don't feel like

telling it just at once, do you?" he enquired kindly. He had been thinking his friend was looking none too fit.

"Oh, I don't mind, Alan, if you care to have it now."

"I admit curiosity. Is there anything to prevent your telling it in Caw's presence? Be quite candid -"

"Caw is welcome to it."

"Thanks," Alan rang the bell. "Caw and I have a good many gaps in our knowledge, and it's just possible that you may be able to fill some for us."

"I've found out next to nothing definite except that Bullard is a rank liar; but I'm determined to go on with the shadowing -"

Caw appeared, and was about to remove the tea-tray.

"Never mind that just now," said Alan. "Give us lights, sit down, and listen to what Mr. France has to say.... Go ahead, Teddy. We'll keep quiet till you've finished."

Teddy's, as we should have expected, was not a very long story. At its conclusion Alan turned to the servant.

"Well, Caw?"

"Am I to speak, sir? Very good. Then I will only say two things. Firstly, I was a very great fool to be taken in by Mr. Bullard's wire from Paris: I ought to have considered the chance of his having an assistant over there. Secondly, the man with the nose, sir, is Edwin Marvel, an uncommon bad egg, if I may say so, known to my master in the old days; and I am inclined to think that Mr. Bullard employed him to pinch - beg pardon, obtain - the Green Box, though I do not believe for a moment that Mr. Bullard trusted him far with it."

"You are convinced then that Bullard has the box now?" said Alan.

"If I hadn't been convinced before - which I was, Mr. Alan - Mr. France's remarks would have satisfied me. If I may ask, Mr. France, what do you think about it yourself?"

Poor Teddy! He would fain have abandoned concealment there and then, but all he sadly permitted himself to say was: "If Bullard hasn't got it, who has?" In the same breath he asked: "But why was the confounded thing not kept in a safe place'?"

"By my uncle's orders it was kept in a drawer in that table. One might be pardoned for fancying that the whole affair is a sort of game - and rather a silly one at that," Alan said, a trifle irritably. "But for Caw's assurance to the contrary I'd refuse to believe that the box contained anything worth having. My uncle was not a fool, and yet -"

Caw, who could not endure hearing his late master's methods called in question, interrupted gently: "Pardon, sir, but possibly Mr. France might care to see where the box was kept."

"Show him, then."

The servant got up and went to the writing-table. "In this drawer , " he began, stooping, and drew it open.... "Good God, Mr. Alan, the box is back!"

Alan jumped while Teddy sat down on the nearest seat.

Alan was first to speak. "What we want at once," said he, "is a locksmith."

"A locksmith, sir!" ejaculated Caw, his countenance expressing the liveliest horror.

"Of course! We must have the box opened, though we can hardly expect to find anything in it at this time of day."

"But - but my master's wishes, Mr. Alan!"

Alan suppressed a strong word. "You mean that we ought not to open it until the clock stops?"

"Sir," said Caw, "if my master meant anything when he bade me throw the key into the loch, I am sure he meant the box to remain closed until the time appointed for the ending of my service to him. Besides, he told me -"

"But hang it all! he did not foresee an emergency like this!"

"I cannot say, sir. At any rate, it is not for me to question his wisdom. I am in your service, Mr. Alan, and proud of it, but I am also in his, until the clock stops - and so I beg of you very kindly, sir, not to put me in a position that might make me seem disrespectful to the wishes of yourself or him." The little speech was delivered with such quiet dignity and withal in such frank appeal that Alan was touched.

John Joy Bell

"Upon my word, Caw," he said warmly, "you're the right sort! All the same, it's a horribly annoying situation. I must think it over." Suddenly, with a laugh, he turned and shook his fist at the clock. "Confound you! can't you get a big move on?"

"If I may say so," said the servant, "I sympathise with you, Mr. Alan, regarding that clock. The only reason, I think, for its being made to go for a year was to allow time for your return. And now within a fortnight of its starting, here you are, sir, safe and sound!"

Teddy roused himself. "Is there any reason why it should not be stopped before its time?" he enquired.

Caw's mouth opened. "My master's orders" was on his tongue. And yet, as he had just said in other words, the object of the clock's existence, so far as he knew it, had been already attained. "So far as he knew it!" - that was the clause that stuck.

"Well, Caw?" said Alan, "what were you going to say?"

Caw shook his head. "I haven't knowledge enough to answer either 'yes' or 'no.' I have imagined, Mr. Alan, that that clock may be doing more than just telling the time. Sometimes, indeed, I think it - it *knows* something."

At that moment a bell rang in the distance. "Excuse me, sir," said Caw and went out.

"What's the man driving at?" said Alan with natural enough impatience.

"Well," his friend replied slowly, "doesn't it seem queer that the clock should have been put there simply to proclaim when the year was up? A grocer's calendar could have done that much -"

"By Jove!" Christopher's nephew strode across the room and stood staring at the timepiece. "Teddy," he said at last, "if it weren't for that blighted Green Box, I'd be imagining all sorts of -"

Caw entered with a telegram on a tray. "For you, Mr. France," he said, presenting it. "The messenger waits."

Teddy read and went rather pale.

"Not bad news, old man?" Alan asked, coming over.

"Yes, it's bad - and yet it might have been worse. Read it. Don't go, Caw - or rather, ask the messenger to wait -"

"We'll ring for you, Caw," said Alan.

The message in his hand ran on to a second sheet, and was as follows:

"Father has heard of Alan's return from B. The shock was too much, but though weak he is very glad. But I fear for him. Tell Alan whatever you think desirable. This is a last resort. Reply Queen's Road P.O.

"DORIS."

In Alan's heart an angry question flared up and went out. Why this appeal to Teddy? Nay, enough that she needed help. Besides, she might not have felt at liberty to address him direct. He looked up with a tender expression and met his friend's eye - good honest eyes that were bound to betray a secret such as Teddy's.... It struck Alan then that his return to home life might have consequences more momentous than he had dreamed of. With a slight flush on his tanned skin he went back to his chair by the fire, and, motioning Teddy to one opposite, said: -

"Just do what Doris says, old man. Tell me whatever you think desirable, and no more. And before you begin, I'll remind you that in all our talk to-day I have never once uttered a word against Lancaster. The man has been simply the victim, the tool, of Bullard. Caw thinks the same, and my uncle said as much just before he died. You and I know that he is no villain. And why delay sending an answer to this wire? There can be only one answer. You'll find forms on the table."

"Won't you send it, Alan?"

"I'll send one to Lancaster himself."

"Better not."

"Why?"

"Mrs. Lancaster is on Bullard's side."

"Ah!"

"Besides," Teddy continued, rather awkwardly, "I feel that you ought to hear what I have to say before you promise Lancaster -"

"I was merely going to ask him not to worry

about anything."

"Exactly! But I had better tell you at once that in order to follow your advice Lancaster would require to have twenty-five thousand pounds."

Alan gave a soft whistle. Then he laughed pleasantly. "You may tell Doris to tell him not to worry about anything. I'm owing him fifteen hundred and interest as it is."

"Alan!" cried Teddy, incredulous; "you don't really -"

"Oh, shut up! Put it any way you like, but don't keep Doris waiting. Listen! How will this do? 'Tell father with Alan's regards, no cause for anxiety in any direction, and he hopes to see you both almost immediately. Guard this from B.' ... Anything else?"

"I - I'd like to mention that the box is here."

"The box! But what in creation does Doris know -"

"I'll be telling you in a minute," Teddy interrupted, looking hot and miserable.

"All right. Go ahead."

Teddy added to the message: "Surprised to find box safe here." Then, with his pencil dabbing the blotting-paper, he said: "Alan, if you don't mind my suggesting it, I think she'd like a word from you - for herself." He had evidently forgotten that he had brought no "word" for Alan.

The latter did not reply at once. "You might put," he

said slowly, his gaze on the fire, "'Trust Alan,' or words to that effect - No, don't say anything."

Teddy gave him a puzzled glance, sighed, and completed the message.

Alan rang the bell, remarking: "Caw will be interested to know that it was Bullard who was here last night with his petards. Pretty clever chap, Bullard. But what on earth made him return the box?"

"I can tell you that also," said Teddy, as Caw came in for the telegram.

"Quick as you can, Caw," Alan said. "Mr. France has more to tell us."

The friends smoked in silence till the servant came back.

This time Teddy reserved nothing save Doris's promise to marry Bullard at the end of a year. That, he felt, was for Doris herself to tell. Beyond an occasional exclamation his recital met with no interruption. When he had made an end there was a long pause while Alan and Caw filled up mentally a few more of the gaps in their knowledge. The latter was sadly upset by the revelation of the stones being paste.

"I wonder," said the former, "who the man was who opened the box for Bullard?"

"Lancaster, I fancy, will be able to tell you. Bullard seems to have rather a choice set of assistants. Doris described him as a dreadful-looking man!"

"May I ask you a question, Mr. Alan?"

"Certainly - as many as you like."

The servant was gazing at the carpet. "When Mr. France informed us that the diamonds in the Green Box were false, why, sir, did your eyes jump to the clock?" He rose without waiting for the answer. "And may I remind you, gentlemen, that you are dining at Dr. Handyside's in twenty minutes from now?" He was going out when Alan recalled him.

"Have you the address of the chap who made the clock, Caw?"

"I have, sir."

"Then wire him now asking him to come here in the morning. And, by the way, Caw - " Alan hesitated.

"Sir?"

"You don't mind being left alone this evening?"

"No, sir. I hardly expect that anything will happen *this* evening. Besides, it is evidently known now that you are at home. Also, which I omitted to mention before, there is the bell wire to Dr. Handyside's study."

"Then that's all right," Alan said, not without relief, "and you'll have that big dog by to-morrow or next day."

Caw bowed and went out.

" You didn't answer his question about the clock ,"

remarked Teddy.

"Confound the clock!" Alan laughed and got up. "For a moment I had a mad idea that - well, never mind for the present. We don't want to be late next door."

CHAPTER XIX

Bullard was still in Glasgow. The return of Alan Craig - for he had soon come to laugh at Marvel's story - had been a staggering blow. The will, by which he had reckoned to win, should all other means fail, was become a sheet of waste paper. Moreover, the "other means" were almost certainly rendered impracticable by the presence of Alan at Grey House. Those, however, were only his first thoughts.

The car bearing him and the shivering Flitch from the scene of their success and consternation was not ten miles on its way when his nerves and mind began to regain their normal steadiness and order. Another five miles, and the germ of a fresh plot began to swell in his brain - perhaps the ugliest, grimmest plot yet conceived and developed in that defiled temple. It was a crude plot, too, and quite unworthy of Francis Bullard, as he would have realised for himself had he not been obsessed by the new conviction that the real diamonds, now virtually Alan's, were hidden in the clock in that upper room. Further, it contained a serious flaw, in that it allowed nothing for the possibility of Alan's making a fresh will. And finally, if one may be permitted to put the primary objection last, it depended on the possession of the Green Box which had just passed from his keeping.

John Joy Bell

Nevertheless, commonsense like conscience failed to condemn the scheme, and Bullard drove into Glasgow with his mind made up.

An awkward situation was now created by the presence of Flitch. Bullard dared not, for more reasons than one, let the creature go his own ways, and eventually, swallowing his disgust, he took a double-room in a third-rate temperance hotel, giving the landlord a hint to the effect that he was shepherding a semi-reformed dipsomaniac. It was a long night for Bullard, and probably the same for Flitch who between dozes either prayed for Heaven's mercy, or groaned for anybody's whisky.

On the morrow, fortunately for Bullard's plans, the wretch had apparently got over his penitence and was certainly none the worse of his short spell of compulsory abstinence. All the same, Bullard on going out, after Flitch's breakfast, to enjoy his own elsewhere, locked the latter into the bedroom, which was on the third floor. First of all he despatched to Lancaster a telegram brutal in its curtness: "Alan Craig is at Grey House." Later he made a number of purchases in places not much patronised by the general public, then took a room at the North British Hotel wherein he shut himself until lunch time. Having enjoyed a carefully chosen meal, he returned to his inferior lodging and permitted the captive to feed. Thereafter a hushed and lengthy conversation took place in the frowsy bedroom. At times Flitch objected, at times he pleaded, and in the end was bullied into sullen acquiescence.

"And I've got to stick in this hole till it suits ye, have I?" he grumbled.

"Just so. Pity you're not fond of reading. I see there's a Bible on the dressing-table," Bullard said airily. "But it won't be for more than a day or two - three at the outside. I must be back in London on Monday morning whether we pull it off or not."

"Monday! But look here, mister, what about that chap we left chained up in the cellar?"

Bullard had forgotten, for the time being, about the ill-starred Marvel, but the reminder did not trouble him. Marvel out of the way for good would not be a happening to regret. "I daresay our friend will have an appetite by Monday," he remarked, playing with the nugget.

"He'll be dead! I'd bet anything he's eaten his bit by now, and yon's a hellish cold place in this weather. If I'd known murder was yer game, Mr. Bullard -"

"That'll do. You can leave the matter to me. Do you want to get out of this country or not, Flitch?"

"God knows I do!"

"Then you know who is the only person who can help you to go. Don't be a fool. Good afternoon!"

He took a cab to the North British Hotel. On alighting, a newsboy offered him a paper. He was passing on when his eye was caught by the bill - "Serious Rioting on the Rand." He bought a paper and with set countenance made his way to the writing-room off the lounge. At that hour the place was deserted, and in the furthest corner he seated himself and opened the paper. Trouble had been threatening on the Rand for some time, but Billiard was quite unprepared for a catastrophe such as he was now called upon to face. The details were few but fateful. Thus: -

"The group of mines controlled by the Aasvogel Syndicate are the chief sufferers so far. Dynamite was freely used, and power-houses, batteries and cyanide-houses present scenes of hopeless ruin. The shafts, it is stated, are destroyed. Several persons on the staff of the Lucifer Mine are unaccounted for. At the moment of cabling fires are raging in several quarters."

For several minutes after he had mastered the significance of it all, Bullard sat perfectly still. There was a curious pallor about his mouth and he had a shaken, shrunken look generally. Letting the paper slip to the floor he rang the bell, and, when the waiter arrived, ordered tea. "But first fetch me some telegraph forms," he said.

A busy hour followed. Keenly considered and reconsidered messages had to be written for despatch to his private brokers as well as to those who acted for the Syndicate, and to the Syndicate's secretary. By prompt action something - a good deal perhaps - might be saved from the wreckage - for himself. For others he had no thought. "This finishes Lancaster," he said to himself; "he'll have to face the music, after all." He sighed. "Means losing Doris, perhaps...."

The fates, it seemed, were conspiring to force his hand. It was now imperative that he should be in London by the following night, at latest. He foresaw a journey to South Africa, a long stay there. Was he going to be compelled to abandon his greatly daring new scheme? Why, the new scheme was a hundred times more urgent, more vital than it had been a couple of hours ago! And yet it would be sheer madness to attempt to carry it out to-night - unless the unlikely happened. He looked up at the clock - five-twenty already! - and murmured "impossible."

His reflections were disturbed by the sing-song voice of a page-boy coming through the lounge.

"Number one hundred and seventy-four," it droned, "number one hundred and -"

Bullard darted to the door. "Here, boy," he called a trifle hoarsely, holding out his hand.

A moment later he was opening an envelope. There was nothing in it. He dropped it upon the fire, took his coat and hat, and left the hotel by the station door.

At a corner of the bookstall, at which hurried suburban passengers were grabbing evening papers, a youngish man in a bowler hat, of wholly undistinguished appearance, was apparently engrossed in the study of picture postcards, but he turned as Bullard approached, and presently the two were strolling up No. 3 platform.

"Well, sir, I've hardly had time to do much, but I thought I had better report what little I've gathered," said the youngish man. " It doesn't seem very important -"

"Go ahead," said Bullard impatiently.

"Right, Mr. Warren. Mr. Craig and his friend -"

"His friend?"

John Joy Bell

"Sorry I didn't get the name to-day - but -"

"Never mind! Go on!"

"Mr. Craig and his friend are dining to-night at the house next door - Dr. Handyside's -"

"Ah! How did you learn that?"

"The doctor's housekeeper. She wouldn't have her photo taken, but she didn't object to a chat." The youngish man smiled to himself. Evidently his news was worth more than he had anticipated.

"Sure it's to-night?"

"Absolutely, Mr. Warren."

"Anything further?"

"I'm afraid not, sir. You must understand -"

"Thanks. Well, Mr. Barry, I've decided to let the matter drop for the present."

The private detective's face fell. He had been congratulating himself on having secured a "good thing." But he brightened at his patron's next words.

"Will ten pounds satisfy you?"

"Why, sir, it's very good of you!"

Bullard passed him a couple of notes. "I may want your services later. Good-bye."

Re-entering the hotel he passed through to the door opening on the Square, had a cab summoned, and drove to his lodging of the previous night.

"Wake up, Dunning! I've remembered your name this time, you see! We'll be in London to-morrow! Meanwhile, to business! If you're hungry, you can have something to eat in the car."

* * * * *

Alan and Teddy took the long way to the doctor's; a breath of fresh air was desirable after so many hours indoors. Though dark the night was fine, with a suspicion of frost in the air. Having seen them depart, Caw turned the key in the glass door. He went upstairs and methodically switched off all unnecessary lights and supplied the study fire with fuel. He was meditating on the return of the Green Box and the no less startling revelation concerning its contents, and just to reassure himself he opened the deep drawer. There it lay, the familiar, maddening thing! "I guess they won't bother their heads about *you* again," he reflected, "but I wonder what they'll go for next?" He paused before the clock and wagged his head. "We'll have to keep an eye on you, my friend," he muttered, then switched off the last light, and went down to his supper.

He was enjoying his first pipe when the bell rang.

"Another wire, I should say," he sighed, getting up reluctantly. "Wonder whether I should ring or take it along. They can hardly have finished dinner yet," He put his hand in his pocket and felt his revolver. "Shan't be caught napping, anyway."

He went briskly down the hall and opened the door. He had a bare glimpse of a big, burly figure - and then a dense fine spray of intense odour caught him full in the face. Blindly he sought to bang the door, but staggered sideways in an agony of gasping and weeping. He fell, clawing at the wall, and lay stupefied, at the mercy of the unknown, who promptly proceeded with whipcord to truss him up both neatly and securely. Then he was gagged, drawn into the room on the right, the dining-room, and locked in.

Flitch went back to the front door and waved his hand, and Bullard, carrying a small black bag, appeared out of the darkness.

"Get back to the car," he said. "I shan't be long." He closed and locked the door on his assistant and went swiftly upstairs. He was not thirty seconds gone, when Flitch followed stealthily in his wake. It was nothing to Flitch to turn an ordinary key from the other side.

In the study Bullard switched on the light over the writing-table. Opening his bag he took out the con-tents - an oblong package in waterproof paper sealed with wax in several places, with the short ends of three broad tapes protruding from the top, and a tube of liquid glue. He opened the deep drawer, and after noting the precise position of the Green Box, drew it forth and set it on the table. He wrought rapidly but without flurry. Opening the box with the key he had procured in Glasgow the previous day, he transferred its contents, trays and all, to his bag. "Looks as if they hadn't discovered it yet," he thought. Then over the bottom of the box he squeezed a goodly quantity of glue. He placed the package in the box, cautiously pressing it down. He lowered the lid and found that a slight pressure was required for its complete closing. This seemed to please him. Raising the lid again, he placed a sheet of notepaper between the tapes and the waterproof paper and smeared the tapes thickly with glue. For a brief space he regarded his handiwork, then put down the lid, forcing it gently until the key turned. Withdrawing the key, he replaced the box exactly as he had found it, and finally, after consideration, dropped the key in beside it.

He wiped sweat from his forehead. He felt faintish, and perhaps conscience was whispering for the last time. But without lingering, taking his bag, he turned away from the table and stood gazing at the clock. The flashing pendulum exasperated him with its suggestion. He was tempted to smash the thick glass there and then. Only that mysterious, sluggish, iridescent fluid deterred him. The cruel man is usually exceedingly sensitive about his own skin. But with an inspiration he made a note of the words minutely engraved on the rim surrounding the dial - "A. Guidet, Glasgow." Then with a curse he departed.

On reaching the car he found Flitch in a dismal state.

"Mr. Bullard," moaned the creature, "will ye tell me what was in the bag that ye carried it so careful? Will ye swear this is the last job ye'll ever make me do?"

"Oh, shut up!" was the answer, followed by the unspoken words; "I must get rid of this swine, somehow."

They made good time to Glasgow and caught the late express for London. Before the train started Bullard posted a note to Barry, the detective: "Find out and

John Joy Bell

wire me the address of A. Guidet, a clockmaker, in Glasgow. - Warren."

CHAPTER XX

Morning brought a telegram from Monsieur Guidet, and a couple of hours later the little Frenchman arrived at Grey House in a sorry state of apprehension. The clock! - impossible that he could have failed in any way! - there must have been gross and deliberate ill-usage! ... and many more words to the same effect. When he stopped for breath Caw assured him that there was nothing wrong with the clock and mentioned why and by whom the summons had been sent him. Whereupon Monsieur went frantic. "Stop the clock - nevaire! - what crime to think of! - the clock must not stop till he stop himself!"

"All right, Monsoor, you can explain all that to Mr. Alan Craig. The clock, like everything else here, belongs to him now, - and I happen to have a headache this morning."

"Hah! you have rejoice at the return of the young Mr. Craik," said Guidet, controlling himself and sympathetically considering Caw's red eyes and husky voice. "Good! - but you look upon the wine when he was wheesky, and there is not so much jolly good fellow in the morning - eh, Mr. Caw?"

"Oh, yes, we've been doing a lot of rejoicing - I don't think," returned Caw with weary good humour. Thanks

John Joy Bell

to Handyside's attentions he was not much the worse of the spray which had been more efficacious than virulent. Within half an hour he had managed to attract the attention of the house-keeper who had given the alarm. What had puzzled every one concerned was that the attempt should have ended as it had begun with the assault on the servant. Nothing had been touched. "Must have taken fright," was the only conclusion arrived at after a thorough search and rather a discursive consultation.

Caw ushered the clock-maker into the study. Handyside and Marjorie were present by invitation.

"You had better wait, Caw," said Alan. "Be seated, Monsieur Guidet. Many thanks for coming so promptly."

Monsieur bowed solemnly to each person, looked for a moment as if he were going to bow to his masterpiece also, and took the chair preferred by Caw.

"It was my dutiful pleasure to come with speed, Mr. Craik, for sake of your high respectable uncle, and I am at his service, I hope, when I am at yours."

Alan gave the embarrassed nod of the average Briton listening to an ordinary observation elegantly expressed. "Very good of you, I'm sure. Well, I suppose Caw has told you why we have troubled you - simply to have your opinion as to stopping the clock now, instead of allowing it to go on for nearly a year."

Obvious was the effort with which Monsieur Guidet restrained his feelings while he enquired whether the clock had been annoying anybody.

"By no means," Alan answered, wondering how much the man knew. "But my friends and I have come to the conclusion that certain annoyances will not stop until the clock does. I hesitate to ask you questions, Monsieur Guidet -"

"I beg that you will not do so, Mr. Craik. I have leetle knowledge, but it is discreet and confiding. But in one thing I am sure: your reverent" (possibly he meant "revered") "uncle did not mean the clock to bring annoyance to you and your friends. No, sir!"

"In that case, I should imagine he would have wished it to stop as soon as possible. Caw assures me that the main object in making the clock to go for a whole year was to allow time for my return before certain wishes of my uncle took effect. You take my meaning?"

"I do, sir; and though the late Mr. Craik did not remark it so to me, I can believe such a thing was in his brains at the time. But to stop the clock before he has finished his course - that is another story, sir!"

Teddy put in a word. "Dangerous, Monsieur?"

"Why do you ask such a question, sir?"

"My friend probably refers to the notice and to the green fluid," said Alan.

"Monsieur," cried Marjorie, "may I guess what the danger is?"

"Hush, Marjorie!" muttered her father.

Monsieur gave her a beautiful smile and a charming

bow. "Mademoiselle," he said sweetly, "is welcome to one hundred thousand guesses."

With that there fell a silence. It was broken by Caw.

"If I may say so, Monsoor seems to have forgotten that the clock is the property of Mr. Alan Craig, and therefore -"

"Mr. Caw," said Guidet quickly, "because I remember that, I say what I say; I refuse what I refuse."

"Come, Monsieur," said Alan, "it is an open secret that that clock is more than a time-keeper."

"Myself would almost suspect so much." He said it so quaintly that a smile went round. Caw alone preserved a stolid expression.

"Monsoor," he said very quietly, "I respectfully ask the lady and the gentleman here present to bear witness to a promise which I am ready to put in writing. ... If I am alive when that clock stops, about a year hence, I will pay you, Monsoor, a thousand pounds."

Guidet sprang up and sat down again. He appealed to Alan. "What does he mean, Mr. Craik?"

"He means," Alan answered, "that whatever possible danger there may be in stopping the clock, there is very probable danger in letting it go on. Is that it, Caw?"

"Yes, Mr. Alan, and I hope you will believe that my remark was not entirely selfish."

" The trouble , Monsieur , " added Alan , "is that like

yourself I cannot answer questions."

"One, if you please, Mr. Craik. Is the danger for you also?"

Alan smiled. "I'm not worrying much - "

Marjorie interposed. "Yes, yes, Monsieur!" she exclaimed, and hastily lowered a flushed face.

The Frenchman was plainly distressed. "This," he said at last, "was not expected. I perceive that you have enemies, that my esteemed patron had enemies also. Not so bad did I understand it to be. I imagined Mr. Christopher Craik was humourist as well as clever man -"

"So he was," the host interrupted; "but the ball he set rolling is nowxde doing so more violently than I can believe he intended. Still, if stopping the clock before its time is likely to stultify his memory in any way - why then, Monsieur, I, for one, will do my best to keep it going. What do you say, Caw?"

"If that is how you feel, sir, then I say, 'long live the clock!'"

"Hear, hear!" murmured Teddy.

"Caw," cried Miss Handyside, "you're simply splendid!"

Caw had not blushed so warmly for many years.

Guidet, pale and perturbed, had taken a little book from his pocket and opened it at a page of tiny figures

John Joy Bell

close-packed. Now he rose. "If I may go to a quiet place for one half-hour, I - I will see if anything can be done, Mr. Craik, but I promise nothings."

"See that Monsieur Guidet has quietness and some refreshment," said Alan to the servant, and the two left the room.

"Let's go for a walk," remarked Teddy. "This clock business is getting on my nerves. I shall never again wear socks with -"

"But I do think," said Marjorie hopefully, "the funny little man means to do something."

Dr. Handyside got up and strolled over to the clock. "Monsieur Guidet," he observed, "has evidently the sensibilities of an artist as well as the ordinary feelings of humanity. Caw has appealed to the latter. If I were you, Alan, I should appeal to the former by suggesting to Guidet the probability of an attack on the clock itself."

On the way out-of-doors, Alan looked into the room where the Frenchman sat staring at a diagram roughly drawn on notepaper. He wagged his head drearily.

"I fear I can do nothings," he sighed.

"Perhaps I ought to mention, Monsieur," Alan said, as if the idea had just occurred to him, "that my enemies are just as likely to attack the clock as my person - more likely, it may be."

"Hah!" Guidet bounded on his seat. "My clock! - They dare to attack him! -"

"Possibly with explosives -"

"Enough! Pray leave me, Mr. Craik. I - I may yet find a way. Give me a whole hour."

During the walk up the loch Teddy actually forgot the clock. Alan and Marjorie were in front, and he noted his friend's bearing towards the girl with a pained wonder, and thought of Doris.

On returning to the house they found Monsieur waiting for them. He held a sheaf of papers covered with queer drawings and calculations. And he hung his head.

"Mr. Craik," he said sadly, "I have struggle, but it is no use. I see an hour, thirteen days after to-day, when perhaps I *might* stop him without disaster - but only perhaps - only perhaps. And so I dare not, will not risk. One leetle, tiny mistake of a second, and" - he made an expressive gesture - "all is lost."

The silence of dismay was broken by Handyside.

"But bless my soul, Monsieur Guidet, if you stop him at the wrong time, you can easily set him going again."

"Not so! He stop once, he stop for ever."

"But," cried Marjorie excitedly, "although you stop him - the clock, I mean - it will still be there; it won't fly away."

The little man regarded her for a moment. "Mademoiselle," he said and bowed, "he will be done - finished - dead. I will say no more." He turned to Alan. "Mr. Craik, I am sorry to be not obliging to you. Yes;

and I confess I am nearly more sorry for myself. But I hope the time comes when you will understand and excuse. The good God preserve you and him - and Mr. Caw - from enemies." He bowed all round. "Adieu."

And so ended the little company's great expectations.

"I suppose there's nothing for it but to hang on," said Alan with a laugh, "and get used to the situation. I think you, Teddy, had better chuck your berth in London, live here, and help me to write that book on my Eskimo experiences."

"Very pleased," replied Teddy, "if you don't mind my having the jumps once a while."

"Oh, do come and stay with Mr. Craig," said Marjorie in her impulsive fashion, which annoyed Teddy chiefly because he was forced to confess it charming. He disapproved of the proprietary interest she seemed to take in his friend, and yet had circumstances been a little different, how he would have welcomed it!

"A very good notion," observed Handyside. "The clock can't have too many guardians, and I don't imagine you would care to bring in strangers."

"Not to be thought of," replied Alan. "But I'm sorry for Caw. Teddy and I must leave him alone for a few days. We're catching the two o'clock steamer. Things to see about in Glasgow, and on to London in the morning. I'm hoping the big dog may turn up to-day."

Marjorie gave her father a surreptitious nudge.

" I don't like intruding my services," said the doctor,

"but I should be very glad to spend the nights here during your absence -"

"Me, too," said Marjorie.

"Be quiet, infant! Just be candid, Alan."

"I'd be jolly glad to think of Caw having your support, doctor," the young man heartily answered, "but it would be accepting too much. I have no right to bring you into my troubles -"

"Then that's settled," said Handyside. "I hope you don't mind my saying it, but I've felt a new man since I learned that the stones were false. Marjorie and I must be going now, and there's only one thing I want to be sure of before we part."

"What is that, doctor?"

"I want to be sure that the Green Box is in its place."

They all laughed. "That's easy!" Alan opened the drawer. "Behold! - just where it was last night."

Marjorie's hand darted downward. "What key is this?" she cried, holding it up.

"By Jove!" he exclaimed. "I could swear that wasn't there last night."

"Might have been lying in the shadow," Teddy suggested. "It's a new key."

"Oh, do try it in the box!"

"I think we may do that much." Alan lifted the box to the table. "Try it yourself, Miss Handyside."

"It fits! - it turns! Oh, Mr. Craig, just one little peep inside!"

"Against the rules," said Teddy, burning with curiosity.

"What rules?"

"We decided that it would be against my uncle's wishes to open the box before the clock stopped," Alan said reluctantly. Then brightly - "But, I say! we didn't take into account the fact that it had been already opened, though not by us - which alters the position considerably. Don't you agree, Teddy?"

"Oh, confound the thing, I'm dying to see inside, and yet -"

"I rather think - " began the doctor.

"Oh, don't think, father!" said Marjorie, her fingers on the edge of the lid. She looked to Alan. "May I?"

A tap, and Caw came in with a telegram for Alan.

"Excuse me," the host said, and opened it.

Caw caught sight of the key in the box, forgot his manners, and leapt forward, laying his hand on the lid.

And Alan went white as death. "Turn the key, Caw," he said hoarsely, "and take it away." Partially recovering himself, he apologised to the girl. "It was too rude of me, but something reminded me that I should be betraying a trust by opening the box now. Please try to forgive me."

She was very kind about it, for there was no mistaking his distress.

Presently she and the doctor departed. Alan dropped into a chair and handed the message to the wondering Teddy.

"Read it aloud. Listen Caw."

Teddy read: -

"Handed in at Fenchurch Street, 11:20 a. m. Alan Craig, Grey House, Loch Long. *For life's sake don't ever try to open Green Box - Friend.*"

CHAPTER XXI

In the train, nearing London, Alan and Teddy yawned simultaneously, caught each other's eye, and grinned.

"We've had a deuce of a talk," said Alan, "and I hope you feel wiser, for I don't. How much simpler it would all have been had my uncle refrained from those explicit instructions respecting Bullard. We've actually got to be tender with the man until that blessed clock stops."

"But oh, what a difference afterwards! - though I doubt if we'll ever get anything like even with the beggar. By the way, about the Green Box -"

"Don't return to it!"

"I must, old chap. Do you still take that warning wire seriously? You don't think now that it was sent by Bullard for purposes of his own?"

"I feel that the warning was genuine and not Bullard's. Yet who could have sent it? Lancaster? Doris? ... But how should they know there was anything changed about the box? Also, was it Bullard who was in the house the night before last? It was certainly not he who went for Caw.... Oh, Lord, we're beginning all over again! Let's chuck it for the present. And, I say, Teddy, won't you come with me to Earl's Gate after we've had some grub?"

"Thanks, no. I've made up my mind to have another dose of shadowing our friend. Ten to one I have no luck, but instinct calls."

"It's jolly good of you, and I'm afraid it's going to be a filthy night of fog. Well, when shall I see you?"

"Depends. Don't wait up for me. To-morrow is included in my leave, and the next day is Sunday, so we are not pressed for time."

"Consider what I said about your coming to Grey House for the winter. You could help me in many ways. Of course, I don't want you to risk your prospects at the office, not to mention your person, and you must allow me to -"

"I'll see what can be done. You know I'm keen to see the thing through. By the way, I needn't remind you to be mighty slim to-night so far as Mrs. Lancaster is concerned. She represents Bullard in that house. You spoke of inviting Lancaster to return North with you for a change of scene, and Heaven knows the old chap must need it; but don't you think such an invitation might simply mean upsetting the whole boiling of fat into the fire? Bullard -"

"And don't you think that the sooner we have the flare up the better? - Oh, hang! I keep on forgetting about that clock!"

"Lucky blighter! However, it's your affair, and the change might be Lancaster's salvation. He'll never get any peace for his poor weary soul where he is."

"You are fond of the man, Teddy?"

"Always liked him," Teddy answered, a trifle shortly. "Not so fond as you are, judging from what you're doing for him."

"Oh, drop that! I suppose there's no likelihood of getting them all to come North?"

"Can you imagine Mrs. Lancaster existing for a week without crowds of people and shops and theatres?"

"Well, we'll see," said Alan. "I - I'll consult Doris about it."

Ten minutes later they were in the Midland Hotel. Alan found a telegram from Caw - "Nothing doing," - and received a legal-looking person who had been awaiting his arrival.

*   *   *   *   *

Time, the kindly concealer, is also the pitiless exposer. How often in the Arctic had Alan imagined, with his whole being athrill, this reunion with the girl who, in the last strained moment of parting, had promised to wait for him! How often had Doris, in the secrecy of her soul, even when the last hope of reunion had failed, repeated the promise as though the spirit of her lost lover could hear! And now fate had set these two once more face to face, and - neither was quite sure. Emotion indeed was theirs, joy and thankfulness, but passionate rapture - no! A clasping of hands, a kiss after ever so slight a hesitation, and the embrace that both had dreamed of was somehow evaded.

"You haven't changed, Alan, except to look bigger and stronger," she remarked, after a little while.

"And you are more lovely than ever, Doris," he said; and now he could have embraced her just for her sheer grace and beauty. He was angry with himself and not a little humbled, for he had never really doubted his love for Doris. Her comparative calmness troubled rather than wounded him, for his faith in her was not yet faltering like his faith in himself, and he wondered whether her calmness was born of girl's pride or woman's insight. Nevertheless, amid all doubts and questionings his main purpose remained unwavering: he was here to ask Doris to marry him as soon as possible, so that he might rescue her and her father from the difficulties besetting them.

As for Doris, her mind was working almost at cross purposes with his. Apart from the double barrier created by her father's unhappy position and her promise to Bullard, she knew that she could not willingly marry Alan, for at last it was given her to realise why the first news of his safety, as told by Teddy France, had failed to glorify her own little world.

She had seated herself, bidding him with a gesture to do the same, and now they were placed with the width of the hearth between them. She was the first to break the silence that had followed a few rather conventional remarks from either side, and it cost her an effort. She was pale.

"Alan, I wish to thank you for your message to father

in Teddy's telegram. I - I think it saved him. But - please let me go on - I want to be quite sure that Teddy told you everything that mattered."

"Everything I need know, Doris. I wish you wouldn't distress yourself. It's going to be all right, you know. How is your father to-night?"

"I think he will be well enough to see you to-morrow," she replied, and went on to ask a number of questions very painful to her. When he had answered the last of them in the affirmative, she sighed and said: "Then, Alan, I think, I hope, you do know nearly all, and I can only beg you to believe that father never meant to injure *you* in any way. It was not until there was no hope left of your being alive that he - "

"Doris, I implore you not to talk about it. Mr. Lancaster was my good friend in the old days, and I trust he is that still. When I see him to-morrow I shall have to depend on that friendship, because, you see, Doris, I shall want - with your permission - to ask a great favour of him."

On the girl's tired lovely face a flush came - and went. "Alan, this is no time for misunderstandings," she said bravely, "and when you have a talk with father, I wish you to - to try to forget me."

"Forget you! ... Ah! you mean you do not wish me to refer to your part in helping him -"

"Oh," she cried hastily, "I was afraid, after all, Teddy would not tell you one thing - "

"It can't matter in the least, dear Doris. What I want to

ask your father is simply his blessing on us both in our engage -"

"For pity's sake, no! Listen, Alan; and don't think too unkindly of me, for I have promised to marry Mr. Bullard -"

"Doris!"

"- a year from now." She bowed her head.

He was on his feet, standing over her. "Bullard!" he exclaimed at last, "Bullard! Good Lord, Doris! Had that fat successful gambler actually the impudence to ask you to marry him?"

"Oh, hush!" she whispered. "The fact remains that I gave my promise."

He drew a long breath. "Of course you gave your promise, and the reason's plain enough to me! You gave it for your father's sake!" As in a flash he saw what she had suffered. Teddy's story had told him much, but this! ... His heart swelled, overflowed with that which is so akin to love that in the moment of stress it is love's double.

And this young man, casting aside his doubts of himself, caught in a passion evoked by beauty in distress and hot human sympathy, fell on his knees, murmuring endearments, and took this young woman, with all her doubts of herself, to his breast.

And Doris let herself go. Doubts or no doubts, right or wrong, it was sweet and comforting, after long wearing anxiety and and loneliness, to find refuge in the strong, gentle arms of one who cared. But it was a lull that could not last.

"Dear," he was saying when she stirred uneasily, "you shall never marry him! Why, you don't even need to break your promise, for we will see to it that he shall never dare to ask you to fulfil it. Leave Mr. Francis Bullard to Teddy and me."

"Alan, this is madness!" She drew away from him. "How could I forget? Father is so completely in his power."

"But we are going to rescue him, you and I, thanks to good old Teddy."

She shook her head. "Ah, no, Alan, you are too hopeful."

Alan was puzzled. "Didn't you and he understand my message to him in Teddy's wire?" he asked at length.

"We understood that you - you forgave everything. Oh, it was kind and generous of you!"

"Was that all?" Alan got up and stood looking down at the fire. "I didn't want to say a word about it," he said presently. "I hoped Mr. Lancaster at least, would take my meaning. It's horrid having to discuss it with you, Doris, but Teddy mentioned something about a - a debt -"

"Oh!" It was a cry of pain. "Teddy must have misunderstood me. I never meant - "

" Teddy did it for the best, you may be sure, and I'm

grateful to him. Let me go on, dear. It is this debt that gives Bullard the upper hand - is it not? Twenty-five thousand, Teddy mentioned as the amount."

"Don't! - don't!" She hid her face.

"And so - and so I just brought the money along with me." He cleared his throat. "And Mr. Lancaster will be a free man to-morrow. Doris, for God's sake, don't take it like that!"

She was not weeping, but her slim body seemed rent.

"Doris, since you are going to marry me, what could be more natural than that I should want to help your dearest one out of his trouble? I've more money than I need - honestly." He laid his hand on her shoulder. "Dear little girl," he continued, with a kindly laugh, "you've no idea how difficult it is to speak about it. And I can't carry the thing through myself; simply couldn't open the subject to him and offer the money. I want you to help me - and at once. I suppose he is strong enough to bear a small surprise. So I want you to go now and tell him, and - and give him these. I brought notes, you know, because they are more private." His free hand dropped a packet into her lap. Amazing how little space is required for twenty-five thousand pounds in Bank of England notes! "Doris!"

She did not raise her head, but her hands went up to her shoulder and took his hand between them. Hers were cold.

"My dearest!" he cried softly.

"Oh, Alan, Alan," she said in a dry whisper. "I shall

never get over this, I will never forget your goodness. But I can't - I *can't* do it."

"Yes, you can, dear. I know it's hard. I know it means sinking your pride -"

"Pride! - have I any left?"

"Plenty - and plenty to be proud of! Help me to remove your father's trouble, and we shall all be happy again. Just think that you are putting freedom into his hand -"

"Have mercy, Alan!"

"Dearest, is it too hard? Well, well, I must do it myself, after all. Only that will mean so many more troubled hours for him.... Doris, you will do it, for his sake and mine? After all, what does the whole affair signify? Simply that you and I will have so much less to spend later, - and do you mind that?"

He had won, or, at all events, filial love had won. It is the other sort of love that pride may withstand to the last.

She did a thing then that he would remember when he was an old man: drew his hand to her lips. The colour rushed to his face. "Not that, dear!"

She rose and he supported her, for she was a little *dizzy* with it all. "What am I to say to him, Alan?"

"Just say that it is merely what my Uncle Christopher would have done, had he known. And tell him to get well quickly, because I want him to come to Grey House for a change, at the earliest possible day. I want you and Mrs. Lancaster also, Doris. Will you come?"

She shook her head. "I'm afraid -"

"Never mind now. I'll write to Mrs. Lancaster to-night, and perhaps I may see her to-morrow."

"You - you won't tell her about this, Alan?"

"Certainly not. I've forgotten about it," he said, with a smile intended to be encouraging. "And I'll go at once. Perhaps that will make it a little easier for you. As soon as you've seen your father, you ought to turn in. Will you?"

She attempted to smile, but her voice was grave. "I will do anything you wish - now and always. I can't thank you, Alan dear, but God knows -" She could say no more.

"You dear little girl," he said, rather wildly, "there's just one thing you must be quite clear about. This miserable money may buy your father's peace of mind, but it has not bought one hair of your beautiful head." He took her in his arms and kissed her. "Sleep well ... till to-morrow!"

Her mind was still in turmoil as she went up the broad staircase, clutching against her bosom the precious packet, but her eyes were wet at last. Her father was saved! For herself she had no thought.

She halted at the door of his room, listening. It was essential that he should be alone.... She started violently.

Another door on the landing opened and Mrs. Lancaster came forth.

"Surely Mr. Craig has not gone already," she said. "I am just going down."

"He has gone, mother, but he hopes to see you tomorrow."

"Too bad! He can't have told you all his adventures, Doris." Thus far Mrs. Lancaster had learned nothing beyond the bare facts of Alan's return and his intention to call.

"I think he is keeping them for you and father," said the girl, striving for composure. "He wants us all to go to Grey House as soon as father is well enough to travel."

"At this time of year? - absurd, or, at all events, impossible! - for you and me, at any rate. Has Mr. Craig not been made aware of your engagement to Mr. Bullard?"

"I thought we had agreed not to talk of that." Doris laid her fingers on the door-handle.

Mrs. Lancaster came a little closer. "Is that a letter for your father? The last post must have been late?"

The strain was telling on Doris; she gave a nervous assent.

"Ah, it has not come by post, I see! Why it is not even addressed to him!"

"It is for him."

"From Mr. Craig?"

"Yes."

"If it is anything exciting, he ought not to have it to-night. It will spoil his chances of getting to sleep."

"I - I don't think so, mother."

"My dear girl, you ought to be perfectly certain, one way or another. I simply cannot trust you. Leave it with me, and you can give it him in the morning."

Doris felt faint. "I can take care of it, but I'm sure it won't do him any harm. I will -"

With a swift movement of her supple body and arm the woman possessed herself of the packet. At the feel, the almost imperceptible sound, of it her eyes gleamed, her dusky colouring darkened.

"Mother!" gasped Doris.

"I cannot risk having your father upset. You can ask me for it in the morning."

"Mother!" Impelled by a most hideous fear the daughter sprang, clutched, missed - and fell like a lifeless thing.

Mrs. Lancaster rang for her maid.

When Doris came hazily to herself she was in bed.

"Drink this, my dear," said her mother gently.

It was a powerful sleeping draught, and soon the girl's brain was under its subjection.

*　　*　　*　　*　　*

About ten o'clock Mrs. Lancaster, in her boudoir, rang up Bullard, first at his hotel, then at his office, whence she obtained a response.

"Can you come here at once?" she asked him.

"Impossible! Anything urgent?"

"Alan Craig has been here."

"... Well?"

"He knows about - things. I'm sure he does."

"For instance?"

"Robert's difficulties."

"No special harm in that, is there? He won't be alone in his knowledge for long, you know -"

"What do you mean?" she cried in alarm.

He ignored the question and asked another. "Was Craig in any way unpleasant? Quick, please!"

"I didn't see him, but I should imagine he was quite the reverse. The servant Caw must have kept back things. Doris tells me he wants the three of us to go to

Grey House -"

"What? To Grey House?"

"Of course, I should never dream -"

"Great Heavens, how extremely fortunate for you! My dear Mrs. Lancaster, you must accept the invitation at once. Don't let it slip. Have your husband well enough to start in the beginning of the week."

"Are you crazy? What should I do at Grey House?"

"I'll tell you precisely what you may do - but not now. For the present I should inform you that it may be your last chance of salvation."

"What on earth do you mean? Not the dia -"

"Listen carefully! I have already told you of the disaster to the mines -"

"But all that will come right in time."

"One may hope so. In the meantime, however, the Syndicate will require all its available funds, and, as you know, there is a matter of nearly twenty-five thou-sand pounds, which Mr. Lancaster -"

For a moment the woman was incoherent. Then - "Mr. Bullard, we have your promise that you would see that matter put right."

"My dear lady, this calamity was not to be foreseen. I am unspeakably sorry, but I have been hard hit, and the plain truth is that I am quite powerless for the present.

Of course I shall do what I can to delay - er - discovery, but unfortunately I must leave for South Africa on Friday, this day week."

"Then all is lost! Ruin - disgrace -"

"Not so loud, please. Be calm. All may not yet be lost - if you at once accept young Craig's invitation. Now let us leave it at that. To-night I am distracted by a thousand things, but I will call in the morning to enquire for your husband and, incidentally, to make things clearer to you."

"Can't you explain now? I shan't be able to sleep -"

"No.... But, by the way, it would do no harm were your husband to ask Craig, if he is really friendly, for a loan. If I'm any judge of men, Craig is the sort of silly fool who, because he has come into a bit of money, is ready to give lots of it away. However, you can suggest it to your husband, if you like. How is he to-night?"

"I think he is better, but he was so excitable a little while ago that I had to give him some sleeping medicine. He is sleeping now."

"Sooner or later, you know, he has got to be told of the Johannesburg disaster. What about getting Doris to break it?"

After a pause - "I'll see," said Mrs. Lancaster, "but I do wish you would give me some idea -"

"You really must excuse me. I hear some one coming in to see me. Till to-morrow - good-bye!"

Mrs. Lancaster, her handsome face haggard, lay back in her chair and for a space of minutes remained perfectly motionless. At last her lips moved -

"Whatever happens, I shall have twenty-five thousand pounds."

CHAPTER XXII

As Bullard replaced the receiver, Flitch came slouching in.

"Couldn't help bein' a bit late, mister," he remarked. "Fog's awful to-night. Got lost more'n once."

"Fog that came out of a bottle, I suppose," said Bullard sarcastically.

For an instant resentment flamed on the hairy countenance, but Flitch seemed to get it under control and answered nothing. There was a certain change in the man's appearance. His hair and beard were freshly trimmed, and he had a cleanlier look than we have hitherto noticed; moreover, his expression had lost a little of its habitual sullen truculence.

"All right; sit down till I'm ready for you," said Bullard, and proceeded to clear his desk of a heap of newspapers. They were mostly Scottish journals of that and the previous day's dates. Earlier in the evening he had searched their news columns for a heading something like this: "Mysterious and Fatal Explosion in a Clydeside Mansion." Mrs. Lancaster's news had, of course, informed him that nothing of the kind had taken place, and had also raised doubts which he would have to examine later. Sufficient for the present that the Green Box plot had failed. Contrary to his calculations, the key had remained undiscovered; otherwise Alan Craig and Caw, who would surely have opened the box together, would have ceased to exist. Their destruction, however, was perhaps only postponed - unless he became fully persuaded that the new plan suggested by Alan's invitation to the Lancasters was a more feasible one.

He turned sharply from the desk to his visitor, who was still standing.

"Come for your second and final hundred - eh?"

Flitch stared at the carpet, crushing his cloth cap in his hand, and uttered the most unexpected reply that had ever entered Bullard's ears.

"No, mister."

An appreciable time passed before Bullard's gape became modified to a grin. "I see! You want me to keep it till you sail. Wise man! But upon my word, you took me aback - refusing money! - you! When do you want it, then? You had better tell me where to send it, as next week I may -"

Flitch, having moistened his lips, interrupted quietly with -

"I don't want yer money, mister, - now or ever."

"What the devil do you mean?"

"I've joined the army."

Bullard burst out laughing. "Was the sergeant sober?"

Flitch made an attempt, not very successful, to draw himself up and face the scoffer. "The Salvation Army, I was meanin'," he mumbled.

Bullard stopped laughing. Flitch spoke again awkwardly and in jerks. "That night up yonder about finished me. I've turned over a new leaf. The Captain said it wasn't too late, if - if I repented of all my many sins."

"It'll take you a while to do that, won't it?" said Bullard, sneering to cover his perplexity.

"No doubt, mister."

"And so you are above money! How beautiful! Going to pay me back that one hundred pounds you got from me the other day, I suppose!"

"Haven't got it now, mister. Fifteen bob and coppers in me pocket - that's all."

"Crazy gambler! How do you imagine you are going to get out of this country without my help?"

"Goin' to stay and face any music that likes to play. That" - said Flitch, still quietly - "is what I'm going to do, mister."

Bullard took to fiddling with the nugget on his chain. "Well," he said, "as it happens, I haven't got many hundreds just now to throw about, but I expect you'll change your mind when the first tune begins to play - only I warn you, it may be too late then. That's all!

Now, what about your prisoner? How did you leave him?"

Flitch hesitated before he said: "That's one o' things I'm goin' to tell ye about, mister ..."

"Well, hurry up."

Flitch took a long breath and faced his patron, fairly and squarely.

"Mr. Marvel's gone," he said.

"What?"

"I was fearin' ye meant ill by him, and this mornin' I gave him back his money and let him go free."

Grey and ugly was Bullard's face; his body was rigid; his jaw worked stiffly. "You - you damned fool!"

The other drew his crumpled cap across his sweating forehead. "I was thinkin' ye wouldn't be extra pleased," he said, "but I'm for no more blood on me hands - no, nor other crimes, neither. Now," he went on, and his voice wavered, "now for the second thing. Mr. Alan Craig -"

"Idiot of idiots, he's in London at this moment! You'd better clear - that is, after I'm done with you."

"Ye give me good news, mister, for now I know for certain I've put meself right wi' Mr. Alan Craig - wait a moment! - and saved *you* from another dirty sin. I knows what ye had in the parcel that night, mister; I saw ye fixin' up the infernal -"

"Curse you! what are you drivelling about?"

Flitch, his face chalky, continued: "And so I sent Mr. Alan Craig a wire warnin' him that - oh! for God's sake don't look at me so! I didn't give *you* away!" His voice rose wildly as Bullard's hand stole to a drawer behind him. "No, no; ye shan't shoot me! I must ha' time to repent proper." He took a step forward. "I'm not goin' to hurt ye, but I'm not goin' to let ye kill me till -"

From his desk Bullard whipped a long, heavy ruler, sprang to his feet and lashed out at the other's head. "You two-faced swine!"

Flitch reeled backward, sobbing with pain and passion. "Ye devil's hound! ... But I'll go for ye now!" Recovering his balance, he plunged furiously at the striker.

Bullard struck again - a fearful blow with a horrid sound.

This time Flitch did not go back, but toppled forward, clawing at Bullard's waistcoat, and reached the floor with a thud and a single gasp.

And there was a silence, a period of petrifaction, that might have lasted for one minute or ten: Bullard could not have gauged it. At last he came to himself. His teeth were chattering slightly. He examined the ruler, drew it through his fingers; it was quite clean, and he replaced it on the desk, softly, as though to avoid disturbing any one. Yet he wiped his hands on his handkerchief before he crossed the room to an antique ebony cabinet where he helped himself to a little brandy. Then he came back to the desk and for a while stood lax, staring at the blurs of white paper thereon.

Stiffening himself, he turned and for the first time looked down on his handiwork....

Bullard had not meant to kill, though his heart had been murderous when he struck. It was without hope that he knelt to examine his victim. Flitch's time for repentance had been short indeed. He lay sprawled on his side, his hands clenched, yet his countenance was not so repulsive. Well, he had escaped human judgement, and worse men have lived longer.

Bullard got upon his feet. His mental energies were working once more. He must act at once. The simplest way out was simply to 'phone for the police and give himself in charge for killing a man in self defence. But that would mean, among other things, a trial! ... Out of the question! There must be another and safer if less simple way out. He thought hard, and it was not so long before he found it. The fog! - if it were still there.

He shut off the lights and passed to the window. The sill was low; the sash opened inwards. Outside was a narrow balcony, with a foot-high stone balustrade. Presently he was peering out into the bitter, filthy night. The fog was denser than ever; he had never seen it so thick. The presence of lamps in the deserted street below was betrayed by a mere glow. Across the way the dark buildings could scarce be distinguished. The sounds of human life seemed to come from a great distance.

Leaving the window open, he gropingly moved back to his desk, struck a vesta and kneeling, went carefully through the dead man's pockets. A scrap or two of

John Joy Bell

paper he took possession of. With the aid of another vesta he found his way to the cabinet for more brandy. Physically he required stimulant. Flitch had been a big heavy man ... he was no smaller nor lighter now.

*   *   *   *   *

And so, at long last, the ponderous, inert, uncanny thing lay balanced across the balustrade and sill, the legs sticking into the room. Breathing hard, Bullard grasped the ankles. A heave, a jerk, a twist, a push.... Hands pressed hard over his ears, Bullard waited for an age of thirty seconds. Then action once more. He closed the window, switched on the lights, and inspected the floor. Finally he rang up the police station.

"I'm Bullard, Aasvogel Syndicate, Manchester House. A man attempting to enter by the window has fallen to the street. I'll remain here till you come."

CHAPTER XXIII

The spiritual glow in which Alan left Earl's Gate had cooled considerably by the time he reached the Midland Hotel. It was not that he actually regretted his actions of an hour ago; rather was it as though an inward voice kept repeating, "Why aren't you happier, now that you have lifted a crushing load from an exhausted fellow-creature? Why aren't you in the seventh heaven since you are going to marry that most desirable girl?" There was never yet human exaltation without its reaction, but in Alan's case the latter had followed cruelly fast.

In the smoke-room, almost empty at so early an hour, he dropped into a chair and lit a cigarette. "What the deuce is wrong with me?" By the time the cigarette was finished he could, with a little more courage, have answered the question. For he could not deny that his thoughts had gone straying, not back to the brightly lighted drawing-room and the beautiful hostess, but to a dark garden and a terrified girl with a little revolver in her hand. Ordering himself not to be a cad as well as a fool, he removed to one of the writing-tables. There he set himself to compose a nicely worded note of invitation to Mrs. Lancaster. After that was done he drew a couple of cheques for the same amount and wrote the following letter to Mr. Bullard:

"Dear Mr. Bullard:

"You will no doubt be surprised to see my writing again, and I take this way of announcing my return home lest you should hear of it before I can find time to call upon you, which, however, I hope to do before long. To-night, on my arrival here, I called upon Mr. Lancaster, and was sorry to learn that he was too ill to receive me. But I do not wish to delay an hour longer than necessary the settlement of my debt to you both, and so I ask you kindly to receive on his behalf and your own, the enclosed two cheques in payment of the amounts of, and interests on, the advances which you and he so generously made to me in April of last year. I daresay you have almost forgotten the incident which meant so much to me, and still does. Until we meet,

"Faithfully yours,

"Alan Craig."

"A bit stiff and formal," was his comment after rereading it several times, "but I don't think it gives much away."

The two hours that followed were perhaps the dreariest he had ever spent in civilised circumstances. London had given him enough to think about in all conscience, but his mind would not be controlled; as surely as a disturbed compass needle it kept moving back to the north.

Teddy's arrival, half an hour after midnight, he hailed as a great relief. Teddy wore a tired and soiled aspect, but his eyes glinted with repressed excitement.

"Let's go up to my room, Alan," he said at once; "I've got something to shew you."

The moment they were there, with the door bolted, Teddy's fingers went to his waistcoat pocket.

"Recognise it?" he asked, holding up an inch of fine gold chain bearing a small nugget.

"No I don't. Stay! it's not unfamiliar - but no; I can't place it. Whose is it?"

"Bullard's."

"Oh! Where did you pick it up, Teddy?"

Teddy sat down on the edge of the bed. In a voice not wholly under control he replied -

"I took it from the hand of a dead man, a couple of hours ago."

"A dead man! Good -"

"He seemed to fall out of the fog, but it was actually from the window of Bullard's office, in New Broad Street. I was watching from the other side of the street when he fell. I - I was the first person to reach him. He was quite dead - awfully smashed, poor chap. There was a lamp near. One of his fists was slightly open. I noticed a glitter in it. It was this thing. I took it. - I must have a smoke."

"Better ring for something to drink."

" No. I want all my wits to make a clear story of it.

Look here, Alan! The long and short of it is: Bullard committed murder to-night -"

"Oh, I say!"

Teddy ignored the interruption. "Of course I went with the crowd to the police station, and, though not as a witness, managed to get in. Bullard with an inspector turned up before long, but I kept out of his way. He had called the police himself. The man, he stated, had been trying the window of his private room while he was in another part of the premises; on entering his private room and switching on the lights, he had caught a glimpse of a face and hands falling backwards. That was all a lie. The lights had been out for some time when the man fell. The fog was horribly thick, but I can be sure of that much. And then - this!" he dangled the nugget.

Alan broke the silence. "It looks bad, certainly, but still, you know, Bullard might not - and quite naturally, too - have liked to admit that after a struggle he pushed the man from the window - if that's what you mean."

"No, that's not what I mean. About twenty minutes earlier, I saw the man enter Bullard's office by the usual way -"

"Ah!"

"And note this, Alan! At the police station, I saw his fingers go to the nugget - he has a habit of playing with the thing when he is talking - and when he realised that it wasn't there, I thought he was going to faint. He soon pulled himself together, but -"

"The police didn't suspect him, did they?"

"Bless you, no! They were all sympathy! Oh, he's safe enough - for the present. The poor chap he murdered was certainly rough looking enough to be a burglar."

"What was he like?"

"A big strong man, with an ugly red-bearded face, and - it's queer how one notices trifles - his ears were pierced for - "

"Good Heavens, it was Flitch!"

Teddy jumped. "The man who shot you -"

"The same - I'm sure of it, even from your slight description. And - and Bullard has killed him!"

"Your revenge, Alan."

"No, no, old man, I never wanted his life. It was only his employer I was after."

"You've got his employer now - if you want him."

Alan stared at his friend. "Why do you say *if I want him*? Don't you imagine I want him?" - he cried - "not for anything he may have done or tried to do to me, but for what might have happened had Mar - Miss Handyside opened that infernal Green Box -"

"The telegram may have been a hoax. The box may or may not contain an infernal contrivance, but even if it does, you can't convict Bullard any more than you can arrest the soul of the man who is dead."

"I don't understand you," said Alan. "Tell me why you used those words, 'if I want him,' meaning Bullard."

"Simply because," answered Teddy, "I'm pretty sure you don't want him. Think a moment!"

The other sprang to his feet. "Come along, Teddy! There's no thought required. That nugget has got to be handed to the police before we're an hour older."

Teddy rose slowly and slipped the nugget into his pocket. "Alan, my son," he said gently, "that nugget does not leave my possession - no, not for all your uncle's genuine diamonds. Think again!"

"Oh, rot! If you're afraid of the police, Teddy -"

"Perhaps I am -"

"Well, give the thing to me, and I'll -"

"One moment." Teddy's face went ruddy. "I'd like you to answer a question, though it may strike you as abominably impertinent. Are you - are you as fond as ever of Doris Lancaster?"

Alan was also flushed as he replied: "Doris and I settled that to-night, Teddy. But what has it to do with Bullard's nugget? I'm aware it has something to do with Bullard -"

"Hold on!" said Teddy, pale again. "I think I can put it so plainly that you'll wonder why you didn't see it for yourself right away. Listen! Put this nugget into police hands, and Bullard goes into the dock. If Bullard goes into the dock, ugly things, not all connected with this murder, will surely come out. Lancaster will be involved; Doris -"

Alan threw up a hand. "God forgive me, Teddy," he cried, "and thank God it wasn't I who found the nugget!"

*   *   *   *   *

"Besides," said Teddy a good deal later, "your Uncle Christopher was most desirous that nothing should happen to Bullard before the clock stopped. And now, old chap, I think we had better turn in."

Left to himself, Teddy sighed. "He's going to marry Doris, and, whether he knows it or not, he's in love with that Handyside girl. Surely I have the devil's own luck!"

CHAPTER XXIV

Never a heavy sleeper, Mrs. Lancaster was fully aware of her daughter's entrance before Doris reached her bedside. She affected neither drowsiness nor ignorance of the latter's quest.

"You ought not to have got up so early, Doris," she said. "Why, it's not eight yet. Not that light - the far away one, if you insist. Are you feeling better?"

"Yes, I think so. I've had a long sleep." The girl's eyes were shining strangely, and the shadows beneath them were deep; but she did not look ill. "Father is awake now," she said.

"Indeed! I suppose you have come for that packet." Mrs. Lancaster raised herself a little on the pillows. "I suppose, also, you are aware what the packet contains, Doris."

"Yes, mother."

"Is it a gift or a loan to your father?"

"A loan - I hope. Please let me have it -"

"One moment, my dear. Am I right in further supposing that your father intends to pay a particular debt with all this money?"

Doris's head drooped in assent.

"Has it not occurred to you that your father would be treating me very badly if he used all this money for such a purpose?"

"Mother!"

"You fancy I have said something very dreadful, but - listen! Things have gone wrong at Johannesburg. There has been rioting. Mines have been wrecked and ruined. For a long time to come - years, perhaps - your father's income may be next to nothing. What is to become of me? You, of course, have your Mr. Bullard - not so rich as he was; but he is not the sort of man to remain long poor. You had better sit down, Doris. I have kept the newspapers of the last few days from your father."

The girl was clutching the brass rail of the bed. "Do you mean that father is ruined?" she whispered, aghast.

"Not far from it, I'm afraid. Now don't make a fuss. I rely on you to break the news of the mines to him before Mr. Bullard arrives this morning. Mr. Bullard will give him the details, no doubt. Another thing; you must persuade Mr. Bullard to get rid of that debt we have mentioned. He has his own difficulties at present, I should imagine, but he is not the man to be beaten by a sum like twenty-five thousand pounds. We cannot have scandal - disgrace. You have done much for your father already - that I freely admit - but at this crisis you must do more. - My smelling salts are behind you."

Doris had swayed, but she recovered herself, though her face was white and desperate.

"Mother, that money you have - "

"I'm afraid you are going to be shocked, Doris, but I had better tell you at once that the money is mine."

"Yours!" It was a shock, a dreadful shock, and yet Doris had come to her mother's room full of ghastly apprehensions. "Oh, but you can't mean it!"

"My dear girl, can I be franker? Call it anything you like, theft, if you fancy the word; but the money is mine. I decline to go into the gutter for any one."

"But - dear God! - don't you realise what your keeping it will mean to father? Yes, you do! You know too well -"

"I have shown you a way out of that difficulty. Mr. Bullard will do anything you ask -"

"And what am I to say to father?"

"Nothing! - unless you wish to kill him. For Heaven's sake, take a reasonable view of the matter. A year hence your father will probably bless me for what I have done. A thousand a year is always something. As for Mr. Craig, he will have helped even more practically than he thought. Of course, your taste in accepting money from one man while engaged to another is open to question."

With a soft heart-broken cry Doris let go her hold and fell on her knees at the bedside.

"Mother, in the name of all that is right and good, give me back the money. I don't want to - hate you."

Mrs. Lancaster touched a wisp of lace to her eyes, "Really, Doris, you are making it very painful for me, but some day you will see that I was wise. For the present, I would rather die than give up the money. I have no more to say."

In some respects Mrs. Lancaster was a stranger to her daughter, but Doris always knew when her mind was immovable. She knew it now. She rose up from her knees. Out of her deathly face her eyes blazed. Had she spoken then, it would have been to utter an awful thing for any daughter to say to the one who bore her.

"Doris!" exclaimed the woman, shrinking under her scented, exquisitely pure coverings.

The girl threw up her head. "If father goes down," she said bravely, "I go down with him. And I don't think the money will make you forget, mother. There are two sorts of gutters." She turned and went quickly out.

But in the privacy of her own room she fell on the bed, a crushed and broken thing, a creature of despair, writhing, groping in the darkness of an unspeakable horror. If there was a sin unpardonable, surely her own mother had committed it. If there was a bitterness beyond that of death itself, surely she herself was drinking thereof.

Well was it for the mind of Doris Lancaster that she was not left long to herself. A maid tapped and said that Mr. Lancaster was asking for her. She arose immediately and removed the outward signs of misery, telling herself that whatever happened, he must be spared until the last moment; also, the divulging of the disaster on the Rand must be postponed, whether Mr. Bullard liked it or no. For the present she had to give her father his breakfast and tell him of Alan's visit. She prayed Heaven for a cheerful countenance.

Mr. Lancaster had rested well and was looking better, but anxious.

"You didn't come in to see me last night, after all," he said.

"Mother told me you were asleep, so I didn't disturb you - and I was unusually tired, dear."

"But he came?"

"Oh, yes. Alan came, and he's coming again this evening, when he hopes to see you."

"Aren't you well, Doris? You shivered just now. ... What did he say?"

"Nothing that wasn't kind, father. He wants you to go to Grey House for a change the moment you feel able for the journey. He wants us all to go. What better news can I give you than that, dear?"

Lancaster's eyes grew moist. "God bless the boy for shewing that he bears me no ill-will," he said. "What did he talk about?"

"It was a very short visit last night," she replied, "but, as I told you, he is coming again to-night. You think you will be able to see him?"

"I shall have no peace till I can thank him for his big heart.... Doris, I wish you had not promised Bullard -"

"Oh, hush! We agreed not to speak of that."

He sighed heavily. "What a woeful mess I've made of my life; and I've had so many chances, my dear, that I dare not hope for one more. And I don't blame anybody but myself -"

"Dear, don't think of it that way. You have simply been deceived in people, or, at least, in one person."

"Your mother made me believe in him, and certainly he knew how to make money. No, I don't blame your mother, Doris. I've been a disappointment to her -"

"Father, I can't bear your talking so, for I believe in you with all my heart. And think of Alan Craig, and Teddy France, too - oh, they would do anything for you!"

He shook his head, smiling very faintly. Then, suddenly, he became grave and a strange look - strange because unfamiliar - dawned.

"Doris, give me your hand. Will you say again that you believe in me?"

"I believe in you with all my heart," she answered, striving for control.

"Then - then you are *not* going to marry Bullard."

"Oh, please -"

"You and I," he went on, "are both longing, dying for freedom, and I know of a way out. Doris, will you believe in me, continue to desire me for your father, though I bring ruin and shame on you? Answer me!"

"Nothing could change me, dear."

"Then I will take the way out wherever it may lead, for prison itself would be freedom to me, and marriage with Bullard would be worse than prison to you. Doris, Lord Caradale, the chairman of the Syndicate, arrives from America on Tuesday. I will tell him the truth -"

She caught him in her arms. "No - no - not that," she sobbed. "He is a hard, cruel man; he -"

"It is the one way to freedom for us both. For my own poor sake, my girl, don't seek to weaken my resolve. I would like to do the right thing once before I die." He kissed her. "Now leave me, and don't fret. Don't let any one come to me for an hour or two."

Lest she should break down utterly, Doris obeyed. The thing had got beyond her strength physical and mental. She could have cried aloud for help. And in a sense she did, for she went to the telephone and rang up Teddy France at the Midland Hotel.

"Can you meet me at the Queen's Road Tube in half an hour?" she asked.

"Certainly. I'll start now," said Teddy, who had not breakfasted. Alan was not yet downstairs. "Something wrong, Doris?"

"Just come, please. Good-bye."

He was there before her, his heart aching.

What had happened that she could not tell to Alan? Before long he knew. She told him all as they walked in Kensington Gardens, in the brilliant sunshine. It seemed to Teddy far more horrible than the gruesome business in the fog of twelve hours ago.

"And you feel there is no hope of inducing Mrs. Lancaster to - to change?" he said at last. Knowing Mrs. Lancaster as he did, he recognised the futility of the question.

"If you don't mind, Teddy," she answered, "we won't speak about that again. The shame of it sickens me. But what about - Alan? He and father will meet tonight. I don't for a moment imagine that Alan will mention the money, but naturally he will think it very strange if father doesn't. And, oh! how *can* I explain to Alan? It's too dreadful!"

"Alan," he said, "would only be sorry - as sorry as I am. But, Doris, it isn't to-night yet."

"You mean that I have time to - to see Mr. Bullard? He is coming to the house this morning - may be there now - and I don't want him to get near father. Yes," she said, in a lifeless voice, "I will speak to him - plead with him, if necessary -"

"No, you shan't!" said Teddy, who doubted very much whether Mr. Bullard would reach Earl's Gate that morning. The inquest was at noon.

"It's the only way out. Father must not be allowed to trust himself to the tender mercies of Lord Caradale

John Joy Bell

next week. I know Lord Caradale. He doesn't mind how money is made; but he does mind how it is lost. Oh, Teddy, don't you think father has suffered enough?"

"More than enough - and so has his daughter." Teddy gritted his teeth. Every moment this girl grew dearer; every moment she seemed further away. "Doris," he went on, "I want your promise that you will do nothing at all till I see you again. Should Bullard come to the house, keep him from Mr. Lancaster, but tell him nothing. Meet me here again at three o'clock." Gently he stopped her questions. "And forgive my leaving you at once. Don't hope too much, dear, but don't altogether despair. There's just a chance that there may be another way out."

The hour that followed was the most thronged of this young man's life. Fortunately he had left a note for Alan, explaining his sudden departure on the score of some forgotten business which had to be overtaken before the inquest, so he was free to go direct to a certain legal office in the city. As for Doris, she went home in that numb condition of mind and spirit which comes upon some of us while we wait for a great surgeon's verdict. Her mother informed her that Mr. Bullard had telephoned, postponing his call till the afternoon, also that she had received and accepted Mr. Craig's invitation to Grey House.

"We shall travel on Tuesday, Doris, so you must see that your father has no relapse."

Doris turned away without answering. Tuesday! That was a long, long way off - in another life, it seemed.

CHAPTER XXV

The inquest was over. A suggestion for an adjournment, half-heartedly expressed by one juryman, had been briefly discussed and withdrawn. Bullard had come through his ordeal without a spot of discredit. He looked pale and fagged, but what was more natural in the circumstances? A horrid experience it must have been, those present agreed, to behold a face and clutching hands fall away from a fourth-story window! And he was going to pay for a decent funeral for the abandoned wretch who might have murdered him! There was a gentleman for you!

Nevertheless, more than once Bullard's nerve had been at breaking point. What was young France doing at the inquest? He was to know soon enough.

Teddy was waiting for him just outside the door.

"I have a taxi here, Mr. Bullard," he said, "so we can go to your office together. I have a little business to discuss - financial, I should say."

"I'm afraid it must keep, Mr. France," Bullard managed to reply fairly coolly. "This is Saturday, you know, and after business hours."

"You will see for yourself presently, Mr. Bullard, that

John Joy Bell

it won't keep. In fact, if you don't step into that cab at once -"

Bullard got in, Teddy followed, and the cab started.

"Wow," began Bullard, "what the - "

"Hope you don't mind my smoking," said Teddy, lighting a cigarette. "Rather an uncomfy corner you've just come out of, Mr. Bullard."

"Kindly choose your words more carefully - 'corner' does not apply to my recent unpleasant experience - and name your business."

"We shall be in your office in a very few minutes, and I prefer to name it there."

"Very well." Bullard restrained himself and fell to thinking hard. What had brought France to the inquest? The question repeated itself maddeningly. The tragedy had not been mentioned in the morning papers - their early editions, at any rate.

Teddy gave him a minute's grace, then casually remarked -

"You heard from my friend, Alan Craig, this morning, I believe. Miraculous escape, wasn't it?"

"Very.... Yes, I have a letter from Mr. Craig - to which I shall reply - direct."

"Alan is an odd chap," Teddy pursued. "No sooner is he home and in safety than he makes his will. Did it at his lawyer's in Glasgow, the day before yesterday."

After an almost imperceptible pause - "Indeed!" said Bullard, a little thickly. "Only I'm afraid I don't happen to be interested in Mr. Alan Craig's affairs."

"Sorry," Teddy murmured, and gave him another minute's grace. Then -

"Awful end that for poor old Flitch, Mr. Bullard."

The man's face, nay, his whole body, contracted for an instant; yet he was still master of himself.

"Who?"

"Flitch - the dead man, you know."

"The man's name was Dunning, as you must have heard, and as the police discovered for themselves."

"Really, I must go to an aurist! I've got it into my head as Flitch."

"Confound you!" said Bullard, on the verge of a furious, crazy outbreak, "will you hold your tongue? I've business to think of. Lost a whole morning with that cursed inquest."

"All right, Mr. Bullard. Don't apologise."

There was no more talk till they reached the office. The clerks had gone.

Bullard led the way, not to his own private room, but to Lancaster's.

"Say what you've got to say quickly," he snapped.

"This," said Teddy, looking leisurely about him, "is surely not the room where it happened. - What's the matter, Mr. Bullard?"

Again Bullard caught and held himself on the verge. "I can give you five minutes, if you will talk sense," he said, taking the chair at Lancaster's desk, which had been left open. "Either you are drunk or you fondly imagine you have got hold of something. Now, go on! Come to the point!"

"I will," said Teddy. "How much exactly does Mr. Lancaster owe the Syndicate?"

Bullard started, but not without relief. The relief would have been fuller, however, but for the questioner's presence at the inquest.

"What business is that of yours, Mr. France?"

"Simply that I'm going to see it paid."

"May I ask when?"

"Within the next few minutes."

Bullard saw light. Alan Craig's money!

"Really?" he said. "But would it not be better if Mr. Lancaster were to make the payment personally?"

"Does it matter to the Syndicate who pays the money?"

"Of course not."

" Thanks." Teddy brought forth a couple of bundles of

bonds and share certificates. "How much is the debt?"

"Twenty-four thousand and seventy-five pounds."

"Wish I had that much," said Teddy, "but I can only give what I've got." He rose, placed the bundles on the desk, and sat down again. "There's a trifle over five thousand pounds in my little lot," he went on, "and with each certificate you'll find a signed transfer in your favour, Mr. Bullard. To save time" - he glanced at his watch - "I'll ask you to take my word for that."

Bullard put out his hand and touched the bundles. "Your securities, you say, are worth a little over five thousand pounds?"

"Right!"

"Well?"

"Well, Mr. Bullard?"

"What about the balance of twenty - or say nineteen - thousand?"

Teddy smiled. "That's your affair, Mr. Bullard."

"I should be obliged," said Bullard slowly, "if you would talk sense."

"I've written it down," Teddy said, and passed him a sheet of paper bearing these words:

"I, Francis Bullard, London Managing Director of the Aasvogel Syndicate, hereby acknowledge that I have this day received the sum of ... being the full amount due to the Syndicate by Mr. Robert Lancaster, whose debt is hereby discharged."

"What the devil is this?"

"Now don't frown and crumple it up and throw it away, as if you were on the stage, Mr. Bullard," said Teddy. "You were never more in real life than you are now. Take your pen, fill in the blank, sign at foot, and return to me. And listen! The man you lied so well about at the inquest, entered your office by the door, at ten-seventeen last night."

Bullard's countenance took on a curious shade. Almost in his heart the young man pitied him.

"If the man entered by the door, you know more about his movements than I do," came the retort. "Why didn't you say so at the inquest?"

"Mr. Bullard, I give you two minutes by my watch to complete and sign that receipt."

"You cursed young fool, do you think to black-mail me?"

"If you like to call it that - well, I'm afraid I must accept the word," said Teddy, watch in hand. "But somehow one doesn't mind so much blackmailing a blackguard. - Sit still! You can't afford two inquests in a week-end."

"What do you imagine it proves if the man did enter by the door, you prying, sneaking puppy?"

"Thirty seconds gone."

"Oh, get out of this! I'm not afraid of you. I've a good mind -"

"There was no light in your window when the man fell. At the inquest you said you had just switched on the lights."

Bullard's clenched fists relaxed; his face became moist and shiny.

"Do you want to hear any more?" said Teddy. "One minute left."

Bullard writhed. "Suppose I haven't got the money," he said at last.

"You can find it."

"And what guarantees do you give in return?"

"I promise silence so long as you keep clear of crime and make no attempt to communicate, by word or letter, with Mr. Lancaster or his daughter -"

"Hah! I see! ... But, by God, I'll destroy the lot of you yet!"

"Thirty seconds left, Mr. Bullard.... Twenty.... Ten...." Teddy stood up.

Two minutes later he stepped, almost jauntily, from the room. His little private income had disappeared, but he had a document worth all the world to him in his pocket. As he opened the door Bullard's face was that of a fiend; his hand went back to a drawer ere he remembered that he was not at his own desk.

*   *   *   *   *

Teddy was a little behind time in reaching Kensington Gardens, and he looked so haggard that the girl's heart failed her.

"Everything's all right, Doris," he said, rather huskily. "Let's sit down here for a minute."

"Teddy, you're ill!"

He shook his head, and gave her the paper, saying, "Take care of it. I don't think Bullard will trouble you or Mr. Lancaster again, Doris."

She read and began to tremble. With a sob she whispered, "Teddy, Teddy, *is* it true?"

He did not answer. He had a queer sleepy, ghastly look.

"Teddy dear! What is it?"

He appeared to pull himself up. "Upon my word," he said, with a feeble laugh, "I was nearly off that time. I wonder where I could find some breakfast."

*   *   *   *   *

In the nearest tea-room he revived considerably.

"Perhaps I may tell you all about it years hence, Doris," he said. "Not now. Just make your father happy and be happy yourself. And remember that, so far as your father is concerned, it was Alan's money. So that makes everything nice and tidy, doesn't it?"

"But father ought to know that it was you who -"

"Now, don't go and spoil everything! I assure you that I did nothing worth mentioning except miss my breakfast - which is, perhaps, a good deal for an Englishman to do."

"But, Teddy, what am I to say to you?"

"Nothing. Just smile, and say I made you."

She smiled.

"Ah!" he said softly, "you haven't smiled like that, Doris, for months! I'm a great man, after all! Now, what about moving along to Earl's Gate? I mustn't keep you longer from giving him the good news. Have you got it safe?"

She touched her breast. "Oh, Teddy, you wonderful, wonderful man! - to alter the world in a few hours!"

"Pretty smart, wasn't it? By the way, I may not see you for a while. I think Alan wants me to go back with him to-morrow night."

"We are all going to Grey House on Tuesday."

"Oh!" said Teddy of the torn heart. "Do you happen to remember how many buns I've eaten?"

* * * * *

On reaching home Doris learned that her mother had gone out. She was not sorry. She was not to know that the hour in which she gave her father his freedom witnessed a consultation between her mother and Mr. Bullard. For Bullard was not yet beaten, and Mrs. Lancaster had still to learn that her husband was safe.

CHAPTER XXVI

So the two friends returned north, Teddy with a new secret in his heavy heart, Alan in a thoroughly unsettled state of mind.

Alan's second meeting with Doris had certainly not been helpful to either. Doris, while almost assured as to her father's freedom, was at least dubious about her own, so much so that she gently but firmly refused to consider herself in any way engaged to Alan, and Alan, as any other honourable young man would have done in the circumstances, pleaded and argued.

"You will never marry Bullard," said he, for the tenth time.

"He has my promise. He might yet find another way of injuring father," she answered; "and you too," she added to herself.

Alan was handicapped: he could not think to shock her with the ugly truth about the man, unless that were necessary in order to save her from him at the last moment. He and Teddy had agreed that for the present, at least, no one - not even Caw - should be told.

"Doris, don't you really care for me?" he asked presently.

"Alan! - after all you have done! -"

"That's not the point, dear."

Quickly she turned the questioning on him. "Alan, are you *quite* sure you want to marry me?"

"What did I come home for? What am I here for now?"

And so forth. The phrase is not to be taken flippantly, but when two young people talk with the primary object of concealing their respective thoughts, the conversation is apt to partake of futility. In this case, at all events, it led to nothing satisfactory.

"It's too absurd, Doris," he cried at last. "It means practically a year -"

"Till the clock stops." She smiled ruefully. "I have to redeem my promise then - if necessary."

"Did Bullard put it that way?"

"I didn't understand what he meant till father explained," she said, and continued in a lighter tone: "I'm very curious about that strange clock of yours. I expect I'll spend all my time at Grey House watching it."

"I've a good mind to smash up the wretched thing the moment I get home! ... Doris, once more, you are not going to marry that man!"

In the end they had parted kindly, even tenderly, feeling that each owed the other something.

*   *   *   *   *

As well as an unsettled mind Alan brought with him from London a letter from Bullard, which he had received by registered post on the Saturday night. Although it must have been indited on the top of that disturbing interview with Teddy, it was frank in manner and pleasantly congratulatory in tone; moreover, it covered the will which Alan had signed about nineteen months ago. The writer concluded with regrets for the necessity which would involve his departure for South Africa within the next few days.

"Do you think he's running away, Teddy?" Alan asked his friend after showing him the letter.

"I've no doubt he's jolly glad to go, but the journey was planned, I'm sure, before the Flitch affair. Those Rand riots, you know. Poor Lancaster, did he say anything about their effect on his income?"

"Disastrous, I'm afraid. But he seems resigned to anything now that the Syndicate matter is out of the way. I wish to goodness we could lay hands quickly on those diamonds - if they exist. I want some money."

"They - or their equivalent - must exist," said Teddy. "Your uncle, situated as he was, could not have spent half a million in five years, you know."

Alan shook his head. He was depressed and disposed to be pessimistic about everything.

"Changed your theory about the clock?" the other mildly enquired.

Alan laughed shortly. "We're always doing that, aren't we?"

They reached Grey House about noon to learn that nothing of moment had happened in their absence. Possibly Caw did not consider it worthy of mention that, under agreeable compulsion, he had been giving Miss Handyside instruction in revolver shooting.

Caw was told of his arch-enemy's impending voyage.

"A good job that, sir," he remarked. "Now we'll maybe get a few months of peace."

"Oh, Bullard has ceased from troubling for good," said Teddy rather cockily.

"Indeed, sir!" returned Caw very respectfully.

His thoughts were speedily diverted, however, by Alan's intimation of the Lancasters' approaching visit.

"And you'll just forget, Caw, that you ever saw Mr. Lancaster in an invidious position here. He has suffered enough."

"I can well believe it, sir; and for Miss Lancaster's sake alone it will be a pleasure for me to make the gentleman feel at home."

"What about Mrs. Lancaster?" put in Teddy.

"If I may say so to Mr. Alan, I hope I know my place in the most trying circumstances."

" Oh , get out , Caw ! " laughed Alan. "You needn't suspect everybody!"

"Very good, sir. Only, my master did not admire her,

and he was a judge of female character, if ever there was one," said Caw, and with an inclination withdrew.

"Caw is right," said Teddy. "You know I've warned you all along about the lady."

"Rather horrid to be discussing a coming guest in such a fashion," Alan returned. "I think I know Mrs. Lancaster by this time, Teddy. She wants a lot of chestnuts, but she'd never risk burning her own fingers.... Well, I had better go round and pay my thanks to Handyside for keeping Caw company those nights. Will you come?"

Teddy excused himself on the score of correspondence neglected in London. "By the way," he added, "are your guests to know of the passage?"

"I think not," Alan replied, with a slight flush. "As a matter of fact, I'm not going to use it again except in an emergency."

Left to himself, Teddy sighed and murmured, "A private passage with a pretty enough girl at the other end - I wonder what Doris would think about it, even in an emergency."

Arriving next door Alan found that the doctor had gone out in his car. Miss Handyside, the servant mentioned, was at home. Under an effort of will he was turning away when she appeared.

Presently they were seated in the study, and he was telling her of his expected visitors.

"I wonder," he said with some diffidence, "if you could

forget that you saw Lancaster in my uncle's room that night."

There was a trace of a frown on Marjorie's brow.

"Of course I will do my best, Mr. Craig. I'm not very good at heaping coals of fire myself, but -"

"You think it strange that I should have invited him, that he should have accepted my invitation? Well, I suppose it's a natural thought. But the man has suffered terribly, and not only for his own mistakes, and I don't know that the acceptance was such an easy thing for him. Please remember that Bullard had a cruel power over him."

"And does that power no longer exist?"

"It is broken. You may be interested to know that Bullard is leaving for South Africa this week."

"I hope that is true," she said so solemnly that he smiled. "But," she went on quickly, "I'll try to be nice to Mr. Lancaster. He *did* look out of his element that night, and after all, I'm not the sort to kick a man when he's down. But I must say you're a good, kind man, Mr. Craig -"

"Please!" he protested miserably.

"Tell me about Mrs. Lancaster," she went on. "Is she very charming?"

"She is very handsome. I'm afraid she will find Grey House deplorably dull. She finds her pleasures in crowded places. But whether you admire her or not,

I'm sure you will like her daughter."

"What is her name? Is she pretty?"

"Doris is her name and - yes, she's very pretty indeed."

"Please describe her, Mr. Craig."

"Oh, no," he objected, with a poor attempt at lightness. "I'm no hand at descriptions, Miss Handyside; besides, you will see her for yourself, I hope, within the next few days. And I - I think she wants a girl friend rather badly." Thereupon he made haste to change the subject.

Conversation was inclined, however, to drag a little on both sides, and there was developed a tension just perceptible, which lasted till the arrival of the doctor.

When Alan had gone, ten minutes later, Handyside observed that the young man did not seem so bright as before his trip to London.

"I can't say I noticed any difference," said Marjorie, whose whole glad world had become gloomy within the space of half an hour; and she went away to her own room, wherein she gave herself the following excellent advice:

"Don't be silly! ... You don't really care! ... And now you know he's going to marry that thingammy girl! ... And he said she was *very* pretty, and Doris is certainly ever so much prettier a name than - no, I'm not going to cry - I'm not - I'm *not*! ... at least, not much."

John Joy Bell

CHAPTER XXVII

"I think that's everything, Caw. We shan't be much later than eleven. Don't forget that Mr. Harvie wants to catch the first steamer in the morning." Alan, in evening dress, was smoking a cigarette in the study pending the assembling of his guests in the drawing-room, all of whom had been bidden to dinner that evening by the hospitable Handyside.

"Mr. Harvie shall be looked after, sir." Caw retired to the door, closed it and came back to the hearth. "May I ask you to cast your eye over this list, Mr. Alan?" he said, presenting a sheet of notepaper.

"Why," exclaimed Alan, "this is my uncle's writing ... and it's a list of the people who are now in the house -"

"With one exception, sir. Mr. Bullard."

"That's so. Where did this come from?"

"That, sir, is one of the instructions left me by my master. Those are the names of all the people who are to be present on the night when the clock stops. I ventured to bring it to your notice now merely because it struck me as a little curious, sir, especially since Mr. Harvie, the lawyer, had not intended to stay the night."

Alan smiled. "And so we want only Mr. Bullard to make the party complete! Pity he sailed to-day for South Africa!"

"If I may say so, I should like very much to have seen him off, sir."

"Good heavens, man! Didn't that telegram of an hour ago convince you?"

"It struck me afterwards that your agent might have watched his - well, his double go on board. You will remember that wire from Paris -"

"Oh, really, Caw, your imagination carries you too far! Bullard, as you well know, is bound for South Africa on serious business: his fortune is at stake. Doesn't that satisfy you? Is it this list that has upset you?"

"Well, to tell the truth, sir, it did give me a bit of a turn, and I'm not superstitious every evening."

"You've got your big dog."

Caw smiled apologetically. "I didn't say I was afraid, sir. Perhaps you are right to laugh at me, sir; still, Mr. Bullard has always done the unexpected thing in the past, and -"

Teddy came in.

"Teddy," said Alan, "shut the door, and in the fewest words possible tell Caw what Bullard did to Flitch in the fog."

Three minutes later Caw went out, with his list, easier

in his mind than he had ever been since that midnight hour when he set the clock going.

And now Alan glanced at the clock. "Time's about up. We had better go downstairs."

In the drawing-room they found Lancaster and Mr. Harvie. Three days of the free and friendly atmosphere of Grey House had worked wonders on the former: a rather painful diffidence was still in evidence now and then, but the man was beginning to hold up his head, his nervousness was becoming less noticeable, and his old kindly manner was once more asserting itself. Once Caw had caught him watching Alan unawares, and had forgiven him much because of the gratitude in his gaze.

The lawyer had run down from Glasgow to see Alan respecting that young man's recent and serious onslaught on his capital, and had allowed himself to be persuaded to remain over night. He and Lancaster appeared to take kindly to each other, much to the host's gratification. Thus far Alan could congratulate himself on the success of his little house-party. Doris seemed to have found the friend he had hoped for her in Marjorie Handyside. As for Mrs. Lancaster, she had been a cheering surprise in her graciousness to every one and her open appreciations of her surroundings, while she had quite captivated the doctor.

It was therefore something of a blow when Doris, lovely in a wild-rose pink, but a little pale and anxious looking, appeared with the news that her mother had been stricken with a headache so severe as to necessitate her going to bed.

"I never knew your mother to have a headache before," said Lancaster, perturbed. "I hope it is nothing serious."

"She wants us not to bother about her," said the girl. "She has not been sleeping so well lately, she says, but hopes to get to sleep now, and she will ring if she requires anything. No, father; she would rather you didn't go up."

Alan expressed his regrets. "It doesn't seem right to go out and leave her -"

"I'm afraid it would just upset her if we made any difference," said Doris, "and she certainly does not look alarmingly ill."

"I will leave orders with Caw to communicate at once should she want you, Doris," Alan said at last, and presently the party went forth into the starry, moonless night.

Alan, as host, escorted Doris. As he drew her hand through his arm he felt it tremble.

"Are you troubled about your mother?" he asked.

"Just a little, Alan," she replied, after a moment. "But I'm not going to let it make me a skeleton at the feast," she added with a small laugh. She would have given much then to have been walking with Teddy; her answer to a similar question from him would have been somewhat different, for her mind was full of vague fears.

And just then Alan spoke of Teddy. "Is there anything

wrong between you and Teddy, Doris? I may be mistaken, but these last few days I have been fancying you were avoiding each other. No quarrel, surely."

"Oh, nonsense! Teddy is my oldest friend, and neither of us is quarrelsome. On the other hand, we are interested in people besides each other." Her lighter tone was very well assumed.

"That's all right then," he said, and there was a pause. Then, suddenly, he put another question: "Doris, must I go on waiting till - till the clock stops?"

Her reply was, to say the least of it, unexpected. "No, I don't think it's necessary, Alan."

"Doris!" He may have imagined his voice sounded eager as he proceeded: "Then I may speak now!"

"Please, no," she gently forbade. "I meant that you must never speak at all - to me - of marriage. For you don't really love me, dear Alan, and I - I'm really awfully glad! Now don't say another word, my friend. Who could be dishonest under such a sky?"

And having nothing to say, he held his peace till they reached the gates of the doctor's garden where the others awaited them.

*　　*　　*　　*　　*

To Mrs. Lancaster, as a matter of course, the chief guest-chamber had been allotted. Its door faced that of the study across the spacious landing; viewed from outside, its bay-window balanced that of the study and suggested an equally large apartment. It lacked, however, the depth of the opposite room, and further differed from the latter in having a window of ordinary size in the side wall, looking north. Elegance and comfort it possessed to satisfy the most fastidious senses. White walls and furniture, rose velvet carpet, and hangings, silver electric fittings and a silver bedstead. The warmed atmosphere would have been pleasant to the body without the fire, yet those glowing and flaming logs made cheerfulness for the imagination - or would have done so for the imagination of any person save Mrs. Lancaster. At intervals she shivered. She was half sitting, half reclining on the couch drawn near to the hearth. She was wearing an elaborate tea-gown which had cost her, or, to be precise, had added to her debts, more guineas than some of us earn in a year.

Her hands and neck blazed with gems, but her eyes would have made you forget the jewels, so intensely they gleamed. The finger of feverishness had touched her dusky cheeks to a rare flush. Waiting there in the soft light of a single lamp of the cluster in the ceiling, Carlotta Lancaster had never looked so splendid. And she had never felt so afraid.

Afraid of what? Ruin for her husband, misery for her daughter? Oh, dear, no! Afraid of being herself caught in a most dishonourable and traitorous act? A little, perhaps. But the fear that now made her shiver and burn was the fear lest Bullard should fail in his latest and last, as he had said it should be, plan to obtain the diamonds. Failure on his part spelled ruin for her - not just social ruin, though that were terrible enough, but financial ruin, hideous, complete.

Debts, debts, debts! The night before leaving London,

John Joy Bell

and for the first time in her life there, she had sat down with paper and pencil and made up a statement - rough, of course - of all she owed, and added it up.... Appalling! Thousands and thousands of pounds! Why, great Heavens! if she used her recent windfall to pay her debts, she would have nothing left worth mentioning. And Bullard was going to give her a hundred thousand - if - if ... Oh, but he must not fail! It was her final chance, her final hope, of averting downfall into sordid obscurity.

An hour ago another hope had glimmered, but briefly.

"Doris," she said, "you seem happy here. Will you give me a straight answer to a straight question? Suppose your father's affairs came right; suppose, also, I gave you back that money; would you - would you marry Alan Craig?"

But Doris, who had made a discovery since coming to Grey House, answered shortly yet cheerfully -

"No!"

Mrs. Lancaster did not press the matter. She was too well aware that the twenty-five thousand pounds had been the price of the remnants of her daughter's faith in her. Doris had ceased to call her "mother" except in company, and then as seldom as possible; in times of unavoidable privacy she treated her with extreme but distant courtesy.

So the glimmer had gone out, and now there was no way of salvation but Bullard's way.

The silver carriage-clock on the mantel tingled eight.

Mrs. Lancaster rose and went to the door, which she opened an inch. Awhile she listened intently, then closed it and turned the key. She had heard nothing. Twenty minutes earlier she had heard Caw moving about the study, mending the fire and putting things in order; then he had gone downstairs - to his supper, she presumed. He would not likely be up again within the next two hours - unless she summoned him. With another shudder she moved away from the door.

Presently she unlocked one of her trunks and took out a little white package with a red cross scored on it. Undoing the sealed waxed paper she uncovered several neatly cut strips of meat. She regarded them with disgust. It was by no means the first little white package she had opened since her arrival at Grey House, but none of the previous ones had been crossed with red.

She switched off the light and went towards the side window, slipped between the curtains and drew them close behind her. When her eyes were grown accustomed to the darkness, she raised the sash. Like the others in the house it worked easily, noiselessly. A bitter air from the snow-capped Argyll hills made her wish she had donned furs.

Crouching, she reached out and peered downwards. The darkness baffled her, but something had to be left to chance. She let fall a strip of meat, and closed the window - for about five minutes. Then she peered down again. A live thing was moving on the gravel. She let fall the rest of the meat, and a snuffling sound came up to her ears. Caw's Great Dane had lately been finding frequent tit-bits in that particular spot, and now he was making another tasty meal - his last.

John Joy Bell

Mrs. Lancaster closed the window and after washing her hands went back to the fire. It supplied all the light she required for the present. There was nothing that needed to be done for an hour. But she grew more and more restless, and before half the time had passed she was opening another of her trunks. From it she took that which in the doubtful light seemed a mere mass of silk, but which was later to resolve itself into a sort of ladder carefully rolled up and fitted with a steel clamp at the top. She placed the bundle behind the curtains of the side window, and returned to the trunk.

From a nest of soft materials she drew a wooden box about eight inches square. Gingerly she carried it to the couch, seated herself, and took off the lid. The removal of a quantity of cotton wool revealed a glass sphere of the size of an average orange, filled with a clear, colourless fluid. She let the sphere stay where it was, and after gazing at it awhile placed the box very cautiously on the mantel.

Feeling faintish, she got her smelling-salts and cologne and lay down on the couch. The half hour that followed was the longest she had ever spent, and yet she was not relieved when the clock tinkled nine. The fire had burned low, but she let it die....

Once more she lurked at the window - fearing one moment, hoping the next, that her message had not reached him in time, that he would not come - till another night, though she was aware that it must be now or never.... And at last, down below, a mere spark of light moved in the mirk.

Mrs. Lancaster was no weakling. The spark roused as though it had touched and scorched her. She cleared her mind for action. No useless hampering thoughts littered it now. Her intelligence reckoned nothing save the work on hand; its details she had by heart. She acted.

* * * * *

Bullard came from between the curtains white and breathing hard, but smiling. He had no head for climbing - and a loosely hung ladder of silken loops in the darkness is poor support to the nerves - but he had the will for anything that meant great gain.

"You will excuse me," he gasped, taking a sip from a tiny gold flask. "I've come out of one darkness to go into another. Is all clear? You managed the dog, I noticed. Yes, yes, very disagreeable, but necessary .... Well?"

"So far as I know," she whispered, "your way is clear, unless" - she glanced at the box on the mantel - "I fail, or that thing there does. Have you found out about the clock?"

"Not much. Nothing, in fact. The Frenchman would not take my order for a clock exactly similar to my dear old friend's, and he was not talkative. But I'm very much mistaken if Christopher's diamonds are not there."

"Tell me," she said, her hand to her heart, "how you are going to escape - detection. I must know that before we go further, for, if they catch you, they will never, with such a fortune involved, spare you for my husband's sake."

He seated himself beside her on the couch and lit a cigarette.

"There is no time for full details, dear lady. Be satisfied with these. First, I sailed this afternoon from London - by deputy, you understand. To-night I shall travel a certain distance south by car, afterwards by rail. At a certain port, a Mr. So-and-So will board and occupy his reserved cabin on a swift steamer bound for Madeira. At Madeira Mr. So-and-So and Mr. Deputy will meet - just meet and no more. Then Mr. Deputy will disappear as such, Mr. So-and-So will disappear as such, and Mr. Bullard will continue his journey to Cape Town."

"Oh, you are horribly clever! ... Your deputy is like you in appearance?"

"Very; and as I've had occasion to use him before, he knows my little ways.... But now, Mrs. Lancaster, I must ask you to get busy." He rose, took the box from the mantel and extracted the sphere. "Don't be afraid," he said, as she rose, also, with a shiver. "Only be careful." He laid it in her hand.

"Will it hurt much?" she whispered.

"No - not much. Disagreeable of course, but not deadly."

"You're sure it won't - kill?"

"I give you my word. Now, please, - at once." He went over to the door and unlocked it. "Come!"

She joined him. "Oh, yes, I know exactly what to do,"

she said, answering a question.

"Very well." He returned to the hearth. "Now I'm going to ring for Mr. Caw.... There!"

She opened the door and slipped out. At the rail directly over the foot of the stair she took her stand.

Ere long she heard a door in the distance open and shut. Then she heard Caw coming along the passage leading from the kitchen premises....

As Caw placed his foot on the first step, something bright flashed down within a yard of his eyes and burst on the stair with a slight report.

When Bullard looked over, a moment later, he nodded and said: "That's all right. He won't stir for fifteen minutes, anyway, and I hope I shan't need five."

It then appeared necessary to conduct Mrs. Lancaster back to her room and administer to her what remained in the tiny gold flask.

CHAPTER XXVIII

"Curse that green stuff!" said Bullard under his breath. "I'd sooner handle a bunch of live wires."

He was standing in front of the clock, in the glow of an overhanging lamp, the only one he had switched on on entering the firelit room.

The pendulum in its callous swing fairly blazed. There was no sound save a half-stifled, irritating ticking.

Bullard presented rather a curious, if not uncanny, spectacle then. His countenance was covered by a glass mask such as the chemist dons while preparing or studying some highly unstable and dangerous substance. Even more than death he feared pain and disfigurement. His method of dealing with Christopher's clock had been carefully thought out. In the rainproof coat which he wore was a respirator, oxygenated, as well as sundry little tools. For it was the green fluid that had engaged his wits most seriously: it must be got rid of; its powers, whatever they were, dispersed, before he dared tackle the clock itself; and the dispersal must be effected from the greatest distance possible.

Well, he had conceived a way which promised but moderate risk to his own person. Having finished his brief outward examination of the clock, he produced a disk of white paper, an inch and a half in diameter, gummed on one side. Raising the mask slightly, he moistened the disk, and applied it to the clock's case, almost at the bottom of the reservoir. Against the green background the mark showed very distinctly. For a moment or two he regarded it critically, then went to the door and turned the key. He stepped briskly up the room, halting at the heavy brown curtains drawn across the bay-window.

From inside his coat he brought a gleaming weapon with a long barrel and an unusually large butt - an air pistol of great power and reliability. In the old South African times Bullard had been a notable shot with rifle and revolver, and practice during the last few days had shown him that his hand and eye still retained a good deal of their cunning. Moreover, it was an easy mark he had before him now. The chief risk lay in an extremely violent explosion of the green fluid, but he hardly believed in such a result. Christopher was sure to have thought of something more subtle than mere widespread destruction, which might involve friends, not to mention property, no less than enemies. Something that burned, something that asphyxiated - something undoubtedly cruel and treacherous and horrible - existed in that green fluid; but when its time came, it would attack its victim with little sound, if not in absolute silence. So Bullard had imagined it, though he was prepared to find himself wrong.

The pistol was already loaded, its charge of compressed air awaiting but the touch of release. Bullard undid the safety-catch, took a glance round, and passed between the curtains, re-drawing them till they almost touched. With his left hand he grasped the

John Joy Bell

edges at a level with his chin, leaving a narrow aperture above that level through which he could aim. If an explosion did take place, he was fairly secure from flying fragments; if the atmosphere became too perilous, the window was at hand.

He raised the weapon to the aperture and protruded the barrel. An easy shot, indeed! He would soon know what ... Damn! what was that? Footsteps on the gravel beneath the window? Withdrawing the pistol, he moved to the window and listened. The fastenings of the mask encumbered his hearing; he could not be sure. But, next moment, peering through the misty pane on the right he saw a man's figure, too small for either Craig or France, move from the steps into the ruddily lighted doorway. And far away, as it seemed, an electric bell purred.

Wrath at the interruption rather than fear of discovery and capture possessed Bullard. Caw was helpless for the present, and it was not the old housekeeper's business to answer the bell. The visitor would have to wait awhile. Anyway, there was plenty of time for escape.... But was he going to flee empty-handed, leaving that cursed clock unexplored?

He turned quickly back to the curtains, and again protruded the pistol - and all but dropped it.

Between him and the clock a girl was standing - a girl in an apple-green evening frock. She had nut-brown hair and a beautiful neck, and she was inclined to plumpness. Apparently she was watching the pendulum. Soon, however, she moved and looked around her. There was a slight flush on the delicate tan of her cheeks, and she smiled faintly as at some foolish thought. Then, glancing at something in her hand, she shook her head while a tiny frown superseded the smile.

She stepped to the door and turned the handle - and gave a little gasp. Bullard saw her colour go out, saw her shoulder seek the support of the door. In that instant he might have over-awed her, stunned her with alarm, but in the next she straightened up and did an unexpected thing. She drew the key from the locked door and walked deliberately to the writing table. For a moment she seemed to require the support of its ledge, yet steadily enough she passed back to the clock.

There she wheeled about. Up went her right hand holding a little revolver. She spoke softly, not unwaveringly, but quite clearly.

"Whoever you are, I think you had better come out. They will be here immediately. I've rung for them. You can't escape!"

There was no response. Bullard was thinking hard. Ought he to overpower her or risk the long drop from the window?

"I will count three," she said, "and if you don't come out, I will shoot! One ... two ... th -"

"Do not forget," said a muffled voice, "that I can shoot also."

"You horrid pig!" she cried. "Take that!" Crack went the revolver - crash went the bulb and shade above the writing-table.

Bullard stepped forth. There was a greyish shade on his face, but his lips smiled stiffly behind the glass mask.

"Stand away from the clock, and be good enough to return the key to the door," he said.

The sight of him daunted her, yet not for long. She fired again - blindly, one may suppose. The bullet passed over his head, between the curtains, and through the window. A sound of vigorous knocking came from below.

"You little devil!" snarled Bullard, and ran at her.

Then her nerve weakened and she darted toward the door of the passage. Ere she could reach it, it flew open, and, dropping the revolver, she fell into the arms of the panting Alan.

"Good God! what's this?" he cried at the extraordinary appearance of Bullard and the smoke wreaths in the atmosphere. "Are you all right?" he whispered to the girl.

Teddy dashed in, gave a shout and made for Bullard, only to be brought up short by a shining muzzle almost in his face.

From downstairs a female voice rose in shrieks; from the stairs came a man's, shouting in a foreign tongue. Next moment there fell a frantic beating on the door.

Marjorie darted from her refuge, thrust home the key and turned it. Monsieur Guidet almost fell in, crying -

"Quick! Look after Mr. Caw! He was hurt - on the stair!"

As he spoke, Lancaster, Doris, Mr. Harvie and the doctor appeared from the passage.

"Doctor, will you go to Caw?" said Alan rapidly. "He's hurt - downstairs."

Handyside ran out, and Guidet banged the door after him. "Guard it!" he shouted to Teddy. "Let not the pig-hog escape!"

The little Frenchman was beside himself. "So I suspect you right!" he almost screamed. "You think I was greater fool than you look when you ask me to make clock the same for five hundred pounds! Bah! What idiot you was! For I think a little after you go, and I take not many chances. How to get here most quick, I ask myself. The train to Greenock, the ferry to cross the water, and the legs to run three miles. I do so! I arrive! - behold, I arrive in time!" He laughed wildly. "And so you would try to kill him - my clock!" he yelled, and with that, like a furious bantam, ignoring the pistol, he flew at Bullard, tore away the mask and tossed it against the wall.

"Monsieur Guidet!" cried Alan, running forward and catching his arm. "Leave him to us."

Guidet shook off the clasp. "Pig-hog," he went on, "behold, I pull your nose! There! Also, I flap your face! One! two! I do not waste a good clean card on you, but I will give you satisfaction when you like - after you come out of the jail!"

Alan had grabbed Bullard's right wrist. "Teddy, take the madman away," he cried, and Teddy removed Guidet, who went obediently, but blowing like a porpoise, to a seat by the wall.

Lancaster, looking ill, had sunk into an easy-chair by the fire. His daughter, pale but composed, stood beside him, her hand on his shoulder. She still feared Bullard: even now she was ready for sacrifice. Mr. Harvie, lost in amazement, had not got beyond the threshold.

As for Bullard, he had gone white to the lips at the Frenchman's affront; his expression was diabolical. Wrenching his wrist from Alan's grasp, he stepped back until he stood framed in the curtains. His black eyes stared straight in front of him, at the clock, perhaps; perhaps into the future.

Alan went back to the door, and whispered to Marjorie: "Go beside Doris, please." Then he turned to Bullard.

"I may as well tell you," he said, "that unless my servant Caw is another of your victims, like Flitch, we shall neither attempt to injure you nor give you in charge; the reason for that is our affair."

At this Teddy found it necessary to restrain Monsieur Guidet.

"But, on the other hand," Alan continued, "you are not going to walk out of this house as easily as you seem to have entered. In fact, you are not going to leave this house until many things have been settled."

Bullard gave him a glance. "Indeed!" he said quietly.

"And what does Mr. Lancaster say to that?"

"Mr. Lancaster is not going to be troubled over this matter," Alan replied calmly, "and you will have no opportunities for troubling him on any other matter. We happen to have a nice, dry cellar, and - well, in short, you are our prisoner, Mr. Bullard -"

Mr. Harvie took a step forward. This was too much for his legal mind. "My dear Mr. Craig," he began, "pray consider carefully -"

"Oh, please, for goodness' sake, keep quiet, Mr. Harvie," Marjorie impulsively interposed, and he collapsed, partly, it may have been, from astonishment.

"For how long, may I ask," sneered Bullard, "am I to have the felicity of your hospitality?"

"Till the clock stops."

A short silence was broken by Monsieur Guidet's clapping his hands and exclaiming: "How you like that, pig-hog? Bravo, Mr. Craik! That was a good bean to give him!"

Marjorie and Teddy laughed, and the others, excepting Lancaster, smiled. And just then the doctor entered supporting Caw, who looked dazed and wretched. Alan shook his limp hand and helped him to a seat beside Guidet - which was an error of judgment, for the Frenchman's eloquence was loosened afresh.

"Ah, poor Mr. Caw," he cried, patting the sufferer affectionately. "But never mind, for now you have the enemy on the toast! Cheer up, for I will tell you a good choke! Figure it to yourself, the pig-hog comes here with a glass dish over his bad face - he was so fearful of my clock that it would hurt him - he had so great terror of the green fluid - ha! ha! - I must laugh, it was so very droll." Then he flashed round on Bullard. "But listen, pig-hog, and I tell you the secret of the dreadful, fearful, terrible, awful green fluid! I know the secret, for I make it myself. It is a kind of fish - what you call a cod - understand? And I make it with the oil of castor and some nice colourings! *Voilà*! I could laugh for weeks and fortnights, and -"

"Look out!" shouted Teddy, and sprang forward - too late.

"Till the clock stops," said Bullard in a thick voice, and fired at it. Then he flung the pistol behind him and grinned.

Teddy secured Guidet just in time, and a silence fell that seemed to last for minutes.

The bullet, having made a starry hole in the glass, had pierced the face an inch below its centre, and as the company stared, the pendulum shuddered and fell with a little plash into the green liquid.

A wild cry came from the Frenchman - "Miracle!" - and he fell to hugging poor Caw.

As though the others had ceased to exist, Bullard strode forward. Now his countenance was congested, his eyes glazed. "The diamonds!" he muttered. "Where are the -"

He stopped short, as did Alan and Teddy, who had

started to intercept him, - stopped short, as did every other human movement in that room at the sound of a voice - a voice emanating from no person present.

Far and faint it sounded, but distinct enough for the hearing of all.

"Do not be alarmed," it said, and paused.

And Bullard was ghastly again, and Lancaster gasped and shivered and put his hands to his face. Marjorie caught Doris's hand, and Caw tried to rise. The others stared at the clock.

The voice slowly proceeded -

"These are my instructions to my nephew, Alan Craig, respecting the diamonds once mine, now his; and if Alan has not returned, to my servant Caw, and failing him, to my lawyer, Mr. George Harvie, who shall then open the letter marked 'last resort,' which I leave in his care. But I make this record in the full belief that my nephew lives and will hear my words." A pause.

Bullard threw himself on the couch. "'His master's voice, Caw,'" he sneered most bitterly.

No one answered save the impulsive Marjorie.

"Cad!" she said clearly.

The voice resumed:

"Alan, you will have the diamonds divided expertly and without delay into three portions of equal value, and you will hand one portion to Miss Marjorie

Handyside, the second to Miss Doris Lancaster, yourself retaining the third. I make no restrictions of any sort. I also desire you to present the pendulum intact to Monsieur Guidet, the maker of the clock, provided he has proved faithful. Finally, I ask you to present to my one-time friend, Francis Bullard, the Green Box left in the deep drawer of my writing-table, unless he has already obtained possession of the same, along with the key which Mr. Harvie will provide. And may God bless and deal gently with us all! - even with the traitor in our midst. Farewell."

There was another silence. Doris was kneeling, her arms round her father, as though to protect him, and Bullard had risen; the others had scarcely changed their positions.

Mr. Harvie cleared his throat. "Really, my dear Mr. Craig," he said, "all this is most interesting, but, I beg leave to say, extremely irregular. And - and where are the -"

"I almost forgot to say," replied the voice - and you might have fancied a repressed chuckle - "that the diamonds are deposited, in my nephew's name, with the Bank of Scotland, Glasgow. Once more, farewell."

And with that the clock, having performed its duty, though so long before its time, disintegrated, the works falling piecemeal into the green fluid, there forming a melancholy little heap of submerged wreckage.

No one seemed to know what to say, until Mr. Harvie came to the rescue. He advanced and congratulated Marjorie.

"And you, too, Miss Lancaster," he said kindly.

Doris rose and gave him her hand. "It's really true, isn't it?" she whispered. "And I can do anything I like with them?"

"Anything you like, my dear."

Alan and Teddy approached the girls, but Bullard was before them. The man refused to believe he was beaten.

"Doris," he said, almost pleasantly, "now that the clock has stopped, I feel at liberty to announce our engagement."

She looked at him bravely, but did not speak.

He lowered his voice. "Your father's debt to the Syndicate is paid, but -"

"Oh, you worm!" cried Marjorie. "Where's my revolver?"

But Alan took him by the collar and slung him halfway across the room, crying savagely: "How dare you speak to a lady?"

"Bravo, Mr. Craik!" Guidet chuckled. "Another good bean!"

"Leave him to me," said Teddy. "He has asked for it, and, by Heaven, he's going to get it! Look here, Bullard!" He held up an inch of fine gold chain with a nugget attached, and Bullard wilted. "If you aren't out of this country within three days, and if you ever defile it again, I'll use this, though I should get five years for holding it back. Now go!"

Bullard turned to the door.

"Oh, stop him!" feebly cried Caw. "He must not go without the Green Box."

Bullard made a dash, but the Frenchman was before him and held the door till Teddy brought box and key. For an instant Bullard looked as if he would send the thing crashing amongst the midst of them all. Then he took it and went.

"Mr. France," said Caw, "please take my revolver and see that he carries the box right off the premises."

"I'll see him to the gates," said Teddy.

* * * * *

And so Francis Bullard realised that he was beaten at last. Yet even in the agony of rage and hate and defeat that shook his being as he turned from the gates of Grey House, he ignored despair. Nothing was final! South Africa was before him! There was money to be made! There was revenge to be planned.... Revenge! He could think of nothing else - not even of some one who might be crazy for revenge on himself.

He came to the wood, started the car, and backed it out to the road. Then he set off for Glasgow at a more reckless pace than usual - and suddenly remembered that the Green Box was on the seat beside him. Fool that he was! - the thing must be got rid of! The water - that was the place. He prepared to slow down. No, not yet. Better get past that bit where the road ran so high above the shore. He put on speed again, and then -

A snarl behind him, a hot breath on his ear, and two hands fastened viciously about his neck.

"Stop the car!" quacked the voice of Edwin Marvel. "My turn now! I've been waiting for this, you beast, you liar, you swindler! Stop the car!" repeated the madman, and wrenched at his captive's throat so that the latter's hands were torn from the wheel.

Bullard's prayer, warning, or whatever it was, came forth in a mere gurgle. The car swerved, left the road, ran up a short, gentle, grassy slope, tilted at the summit, toppled and plunged to the rocky shore.

There was an appalling explosion.

John Joy Bell

CHAPTER XXIX

A fortnight later, Caw, in his little sitting-room, was entertaining Monsieur Guidet to afternoon tea. The Frenchman had just completed the operation of replacing Christopher's clock with one of similar aspect minus the glamour and mystery of pendulum and fluid.

"Monsoor," said Caw, "excuse my asking it again, but could you not have done what the bullet did?"

"Perhaps, Mr. Caw, only perhaps. I am not so clever as Chance. The bullet, you see, came at the exact right instant to the exact right place. It was a miracle! The pig-hog - no! I call him not so since he is dead - the poor devil might have fired a million hundred bullets without doing what that one bullet did. That is all I can say - all I wish to say, because I still am sad that my clock was not let to stop himself. But now, I will ask *you* a query, Mr. Caw. How did the young lady, so beautiful, so brave, so splendid, come to be in the room with the - the poor devil?"

"Miss Handyside, being uneasy in her mind," Caw answered, a trifle stiffly, "had come secretly to ask me to keep an eye on an unworthy person who was staying in the house. Which is as much as I care to say on the subject, Monsoor."

"But you will tell me if she and Mr. Alan Craik are now betrothered?"

At that Caw's manner relaxed; he smiled rather complacently. "As a matter of fact, Monsoor," he replied, "the event took place yesterday, at four thirty-five p.m."

"Bravo! But I am not all surprised. That night, when I see them together, I begin to smell a mouse."

"If I may say so," said Caw modestly, "it was myself who pulled the string, as it were."

Monsieur looked puzzled.

"I need not go into details, Monsoor, but I may tell you, in strictest confidence, that I had become fully fed up with the thing hanging fire. To my mind the position was absurd. Here were two pleasant young persons, worth nearly quarter of a million apiece, and as miserably in love as ever I hope to see two of my fellow creatures - and nothing doing! So, when the chance came, I felt it was my duty to take it. Accordingly, while they were going through the passage, I shut off the electric at the main switch." Caw paused to light a cigarette: he was becoming somewhat frivolous in his ways. "Later," he proceeded, "I gathered that they came out at the other end an engaged couple."

"Clever, Mr. Caw! You are a philosopher, I think."

"Oh, any idiot knows that people in that condition prefer darkness. Still, I think I have done a service to both my masters, for she was Mr. Christopher's choice for his nephew. Well" - he sighed - "I'm glad to have done one thing without bungling."

"And the other young lady - also most beautiful but too hungry - too skim - you understand?"

"Slim, if you please, Monsoor. You'll be talking about slim milk next! But to be serious, it is a case where one can only hope for the best. There was never a finer young man than Mr. France, and it is a great pity there were no diamonds for him. I understand he is none too well off, and when a lady happens to have a very large fortune - of course, I understand that is no impediment in your country -"

"Would you not shut off the electric again, Mr. Caw?" the Frenchman eagerly asked.

Caw shook his head. "I was never one for tempting Providence by trying to repeat an immense success. Likely as not, they would fall down the stair instead of into each other's arms."

"Hah! that would not be so pleasing. The broken heart can be repaired, but the broken nose - " Monsieur made an expressive gesture and rose. "But, as you have said, we must hope for the best. It is always well to take an optical view of the future - is it not? And now, Mr. Caw" - he became nervous and produced a jeweller's package - "before I go I give you a small momento. My clock has brought you dangers, for which forgive. We have been allies in the service of my benefactor, Mr. Christopher Craik, and I hope we remain good friends for ever always. Take this, mon ami, but look not at it till I have depart. The description on it I hope you will approve on. But one thing more - I trust you to let me know when the marriage - no, I say the marriages, not singular - are about to go off ... Au revoir!"

* * * * *

When Caw opened the package he was amazed to find a very fine gold hunting watch; and he was not a little touched on reading the inscription inside the case.

"To J. Caw from A. Guidet.
To Be Faithful
Is The Best Thing
We Can Do."

"Ay," he murmured ruefully, "but I've made a pretty poor show of it."

* * * * *

At the same hour, in the doctor's study, Marjorie and Alan were awaiting - without any visible impatience - the return of the others for tea. Lancaster and Teddy were still Alan's guests, but Doris was now Marjorie's. On the day following the stoppage of the clock, Mrs. Lancaster, finding it imperative that she should fulfil certain most important social engagements, had returned to London. She left Grey House in ignorance of all that had happened beyond the bare details of the division of the diamonds. Of Bullard's end she did not hear till a week later, and the particulars of his death were as vague as many of the particulars of the man's life. The "accident" had remained undiscovered for a couple of days, and the tides of the Firth had removed much. Mrs. Lancaster had departed with sullen, smouldering eyes. She honestly considered her daughter thankless and undutiful, because the latter had not promised her a share of the diamonds on the spot.

It was of her that Alan and Marjorie had been talking for the past five minutes.

"I wouldn't be too pessimistic, Alan, if I were you," the girl was saying. "Mrs. Lancaster, given her own way and plenty of money, may be quite bearable, if not charming, to live with, and Doris is evidently bent on supplying the money -"

"For her father's sake. Doris will never forgive her mother, and I don't see why she should."

Marjorie smiled. "Let's wait and see. What will the Lancasters' income be from Doris's gift?"

"If Doris spends a hundred thousand on a joint annuity, as she threatens to do, they will have about £8,000 a year."

"Goodness! what a lot to have to spend in twelve months!"

"And, of course, Lancaster, though he will have retired from business, will have quite a decent income of his own when the mines come round again."

"Well, I prophesy that they will both be fairly happy. Mrs. Lancaster ought to be able to make a pretty good display in what she calls Society. Now and then Mr. Lancaster will have a shilling left to spend on a nice book for his library, poor dear; and, with no business worries, he will probably begin to admire his wife once more as well as love her, which he has always done; and when he gets a surfeit of her friends, as I fear he will now and then, he will just take a little holiday and pay you a visit -"

"Us, please!"

"I wonder," said Miss Handyside, becoming extremely grave, "I wonder whether we ought to marry, after all."

"What?"

"We're both of us far, far too rich. You know I have always despised very rich people."

"I'm sure I'll lose my bit in no time," said Alan, hopefully.

"On the other hand, I have never admired foolish people."

"I never said you were conceited, did I?" he retorted.

"You wouldn't have said a thing like that twenty-four hours ago, Mr. Craig!"

"Twenty-four hours ago I would not have interrupted you for the world."

"What do you mean?"

"Look at the clock! Twenty-four hours ago, in that dark passage, you were whispering -"

"I wasn't!" cried Marjorie, blushing adorably. "Hold your tongue and talk about something sensible."

John Joy Bell

"Right! Do you think you could be ready to marry me next month?"

When a minute or two had passed, she said: "We're a pair of horrid, selfish things!"

"How so?"

"We're so wrapped up in happiness - at least, you are - that we have no thought for poor Doris, and poor, *poor* Teddy. Oh, what is to be done about them? ... Why don't you answer?"

"Because it's a problem, dear girl. We know it's simply want of money that's holding Teddy back, but even a fellow with plenty can't say to his friend: 'Look here, old cock, take this cheque and run away and get engaged!'"

"Certainly not! There's no need to be indelicate. Couldn't you put the cheque in his stocking at Christmas - or something?"

"While I am doubtful as to whether Teddy hangs up his sock, I know he's too sensitive and proud to accept a money gift, however delicately offered. As a matter of fact, Marjorie, I've tried - wanted him to take a quarter of the diamonds as a sort of souvenir, you know - "

"You dear, kind, generous man!" exclaimed Marjorie....

Order being restored -

"My only hope," he went on, "is that Teddy will, somehow, lose his head and take the plunge, and *then* it would be a wedding present. One can't reject a wedding present, can one?"

"No - though every one of my sisters has fervently wished one could. And I could give him a wedding present, too!"

"We!"

"No, big!"

They both laughed, then sighed, and with one accord said -

"But he'll never do it!"

*　*　*　*　*

Dusk was falling on the loch. The figures of Lancaster and Handyside walking in front were becoming invisible.

"But why," asked Doris, "are you going back to London? I thought you had decided to spend the winter at Grey House and help Alan with his book about the Eskimos."

"I'm afraid it's a blue lookout for the Eskimos. You see, Alan hopes Marjorie will agree to marry him in January. The stopping of the clock has altered a good many things," he finished, rather drearily.

"It seems to have altered you, Teddy," she said shyly.

He did not respond, and there was another of the long pauses which had been frequent during the walk.

"Father and I must be going, too, before long," she said at last.

"Your father is looking a new man, Doris," he returned, with an effort.

"Thanks to you.... Oh, I know you have told me not to speak about it, but I implore you to tell me how you did that wonderful thing about the debt to the Syndicate. Tell me, Teddy."

"You must excuse me."

"But why should you want to hide the truth from me? Do you know what you force me to think? - that you paid the debt yourself!"

"Well, I didn't."

"Not some of it?"

There was silence, then - "For heaven's sake, Doris, let the matter rest. Forget about it!"

"Forget! What do you think I'm made of? ... Oh, I'm beginning to wonder whether Christopher's diamonds have brought me any real happiness."

Controlling himself he said: "You know they have, for your father's sake alone -"

"Even so," she said, and halted.

"Doris," he whispered with passionate bitterness, "I will say it only once: it's rotten to be poor. That's all. Now let's -"

"And I think I will say it all my life," she answered almost inaudibly; "... it's rotten to be rich, and I'm afraid we shall be late for tea."

They were, - very late.

Choose from Thousands of 1stWorldLibrary Classics By

Adolphus WilliamWard
Aesop
Agatha Christie
Alexander Aaronsohn
Alexander Kielland
Alexandre Dumas
Alfred Gatty
Alfred Ollivant
Alice Duer Miller
Alice Turner Curtis
Alice Dunbar
Ambrose Bierce
Amelia E. Barr
Andrew Lang
Andrew McFarland Davis
Anna Sewell
Annie Besant
Annie Hamilton Donnell
Annie Payson Call
Anton Chekhov
Arnold Bennett
Arthur Conan Doyle
Arthur Ransome
Atticus
B. M. Bower
Basil King
Bayard Taylor
Ben Macomber
Booth Tarkington
Bram Stoker
C. Collodi
C. E. Orr
C. M. Ingleby
Carolyn Wells
Catherine Parr Traill
Charles A. Eastman
Charles Dickens
Charles Dudley Warner
Charles Farrar Browne
Charles Ives
Charles Kingsley
Charles Lathrop Pack
Charles Whibley
Charles Willing Beale
Charlotte M. Braeme
Charlotte M.Yonge
Clair W. Hayes
Clarence Day Jr.
Clarence E. Mulford

Clemence Housman
Confucius
Cornelis DeWitt Wilcox
Cyril Burleigh
D. H. Lawrence
Daniel Defoe
David Garnett
Don Carlos Janes
Donald Keyhole
Dorothy Kilner
Dougan Clark
E. Nesbit
E.P.Roe
E. Phillips Oppenheim
Edgar Allan Poe
Edgar Rice Burroughs
Edith Wharton
Edward J. O'Biren
John Cournos
Edwin L. Arnold
Eleanor Atkins
Elizabeth Cleghorn
Gaskell
Elizabeth Von Arnim
Ellem Key
Emily Dickinson
Erasmus W. Jones
Ernie Howard Pie
Ethel Turner
Ethel Watts Mumford
Eugenie Foa
Eugene Wood
Evelyn Everett-Green
Everard Cotes
F. J. Cross
Federick Austin Ogg
Ferdinand Ossendowski
Francis Bacon
Francis Darwin
Frances Hodgson Burnett
Frank Gee Patchin
Frank Harris
Frank Jewett Mather
Frank L. Packard
Frederick Trevor Hill
Frederick Winslow Taylor
Friedrich Kerst
Friedrich Nietzsche
Fyodor Dostoyevsky

Gabrielle E. Jackson
Garrett P. Serviss
Gaston Leroux
George Ade
Geroge Bernard Shaw
George Ebers
George Eliot
George MacDonald
George Orwell
George Tucker
George W. Cable
George Wharton James
Gertrude Atherton
Grace E. King
Grant Allen
Guillermo A. Sherwell
Gulielma Zollinger
Gustav Flaubert
H. A. Cody
H. B. Irving
H. G. Wells
H. H. Munro
H. Irving Hancock
H. Rider Haggard
H. W. C. Davis
Hamilton Wright Mabie
Hans Christian Andersen
Harold Avery
Harold McGrath
Harriet Beecher Stowe
Harry Houidini
Helent Hunt Jackson
Helen Nicolay
Hendy David Thoreau
Henrik Ibsen
Henry Adams
Henry Ford
Henry Frost
Henry James
Henry Jones Ford
Henry Seton Merriman
Henry Wadsworth
Longfellow
Henry W Longfellow
Herbert A. Giles
Herbert N. Casson
Herman Hesse
Homer
Honore De Balzac

Horace Walpole
Horatio Alger, Jr.
Howard Pyle
Howard R. Garis
Hugh Lofting
Hugh Walpole
Humphry Ward
Ian Maclaren
Israel Abrahams
J.G.Austin
J. Henri Fabre
J. M. Barrie
J. Macdonald Oxley
J. S. Knowles
J. Storer Clouston
Jack London
Jacob Abbott
James Allen
James Lane Allen
James Andrews
James Baldwin
James DeMille
James Joyce
James Oliver Curwood
James Oppenheim
James Otis
Jane Austen
Jens Peter Jacobsen
Jerome K. Jerome
John Burroughs
John F. Kennedy
John Gay
John Glasworthy
John Habberton
John Joy Bell
John Milton
John Philip Sousa
Jonathan Swift
Joseph Carey
Joseph Conrad
Joseph Jacobs
Julian Hawthrone
Julies Vernes
Justin Huntly McCarthy
Kakuzo Okakura
Kenneth Grahame
Kate Langley Bosher
L. A. Abbot
L. T. Meade
L. Frank Baum
Laura Lee Hope

Laurence Housman
Leo Tolstoy
Leonid Andreyev
Lewis Carroll
Lilian Bell
Lloyd Osbourne
Louis Tracy
Louisa May Alcott
Lucy Fitch Perkins
Lucy Maud Montgomery
Lydia Miller Middleton
Lyndon Orr
M. H. Adams
Margaret E. Sangster
Margaret Vandercook
Maria Edgeworth
Maria Thompson Daviess
Mariano Azuela
Marion Polk Angellotti
Mark Overton
Mark Twain
Mary Austin
Mary Cole
Mary Rowlandson
Mary Wollstonecraft
Shelley
Max Beerbohm
Myra Kelly
Nathaniel Hawthrone
O. F. Walton
Oscar Wilde
Owen Johnson
P.G.Wodehouse
Paul and Mable Thorn
Paul G. Tomlinson
Paul Severing
Peter B. Kyne
Plato
R. Derby Holmes
R. L. Stevenson
Rabindranath Tagore
Rahul Alvares
Ralph Waldo Emmerson
Rene Descartes
Rex E. Beach
Richard Harding Davis
Richard Jefferies
Robert Barr
Robert Frost
Robert Gordon Anderson
Robert L. Drake

Robert Lansing
Robert Michael Ballantyne
Robert W. Chambers
Rosa Nouchette Carey
Ross Kay
Rudyard Kipling
Samuel B. Allison
Samuel Hopkins Adams
Sarah Bernhardt
Selma Lagerlof
Sherwood Anderson
Sigmund Freud
Standish O'Grady
Stanley Weyman
Stella Benson
Stephen Crane
Stewart Edward White
Stijn Streuvels
Swami Abhedananda
Swami Parmananda
T. S. Ackland
The Princess Der Ling
Thomas A. Janvier
Thomas A Kempis
Thomas Anderton
Thomas Bailey Aldrich
Thomas Bulfinch
Thomas De Quincey
Thomas H. Huxley
Thomas Hardy
Thomas More
Thornton W. Burgess
U. S. Grant
Valentine Williams
Victor Appleton
Virginia Woolf
Walter Scott
Washington Irving
Wilbur Lawton
Wilkie Collins
Willa Cather
Willard F. Baker
William Makepeace
Thackeray
William W. Walter
Winston Churchill
Yei Theodora Ozaki
Young E. Allison
Zane Grey

www.ingramcontent.com/pod-product-compliance
Lightning Source LLC
Chambersburg PA
CBHW021320250626
47155CB00002B/555